*continued . . .*

"An unusual duke and a naive country gentlewoman sounds like a typical historical romance, but Ms. Hunter makes it so much more. These characters turn the ordinary into something special and kept me glued to the book."
—Night Owl Romance

"This is the first in what looks to be a very promising, and extremely seductive, new quartet. Most of the focus is on the main couple, Samuel and Lily. This is as it should be; however, a bit of danger and suspense makes enough surprise appearances to keep things intriguing. Few can resist a novel by Jillian Hunter!"
—Huntress Book Reviews

## MORE PRAISE FOR THE NOVELS OF JILLIAN HUNTER

"One of the funniest, most delightful romances I've had the pleasure to read."
—Teresa Medeiros

"An absolutely delightful tale that's impossible to put down."
—*Booklist*

"A sweet, romantic tale . . . full of humor, romance, and passion. Historical romance that is sure to please."
—The Romance Readers Connection

"A lovely read."
—Romance Reader at Heart

"Enchanting . . . a fabulous historical."
—*Midwest Book Review*

"[It] bespells, beguiles, and bewitches. If romance, magic, great plots, and wonderful characters add spice to your reading life, don't allow this one to escape."
—Crescent Blues

**The Bridal Pleasures Series**

*A Bride Unveiled*
*A Duke's Temptation*

# JILLIAN HUNTER

## The Duchess Diaries

### The Bridal Pleasures Series

A SIGNET SELECT BOOK

SIGNET SELECT
Published by New American Library, a division of
Penguin Group (USA) Inc., 375 Hudson Street,
New York, New York 10014, USA
Penguin Group (Canada), 90 Eglinton Avenue East, Suite 700, Toronto,
Ontario M4P 2Y3, Canada (a division of Pearson Penguin Canada Inc.)
Penguin Books Ltd., 80 Strand, London WC2R 0RL, England
Penguin Ireland, 25 St. Stephen's Green, Dublin 2,
Ireland (a division of Penguin Books Ltd.)
Penguin Group (Australia), 250 Camberwell Road, Camberwell, Victoria 3124,
Australia (a division of Pearson Australia Group Pty. Ltd.)
Penguin Books India Pvt. Ltd., 11 Community Centre, Panchsheel Park,
New Delhi - 110 017, India
Penguin Group (NZ), 67 Apollo Drive, Rosedale, Auckland 0632,
New Zealand (a division of Pearson New Zealand Ltd.)
Penguin Books (South Africa) (Pty.) Ltd., 24 Sturdee Avenue,
Rosebank, Johannesburg 2196, South Africa

Penguin Books Ltd., Registered Offices:
80 Strand, London WC2R 0RL, England

First published by Signet, an imprint of New American Library,
a division of Penguin Group (USA) Inc.

First Printing, February 2012
10  9  8  7  6  5  4  3  2  1

Copyright © Maria Hoag, 2012
Excerpt from *A Duke's Temptation* copyright © Maria Hoag, 2010
All rights reserved

ACKNOWLEDGMENTS

Accolades to the NAL Art Department for creating a cover more beautiful than I could ever have envisioned. Thank you!

# Chapter 1

*Mayfair, London*
1819

*I*t was the best of balls; it was the worst of balls. It was the annual graduation ball honoring the Scarfield Academy for Young Ladies in London. It was an evening of hope, which Miss Charlotte Boscastle had resolved would not end in disgrace. It was an evening of beginnings and farewells.

As the academy's head schoolmistress, Charlotte would receive accolades for her efforts in training another class of young ladies to enter society. She would be praised for any marriage proposals offered to her students as a result of their elite schooling.

She would also be blamed for any scandals she allowed to besmirch the academy's name. Her archenemy, Lady Clipstone, the owner of a competitive although lesser school, had predicted to the newspapers that some social misfortune was bound to occur during the event. Charlotte could take little comfort in the knowledge that she was surrounded by members of her own family—everyone in the ton knew how controversy tended to follow the Boscastles. It was said that whenever more than two Boscastles were gathered in one place, the devil came into active play.

Still, she was grateful that her cousin, the Marquess of Sedgecroft, had agreed to host the affair at his Park Lane mansion. She appreciated the fact that he had invited his battalion of friends to fill the ballroom and impress the girls.

The social futures of this group of young ladies were in Charlotte's hands for one last evening. It fell upon her to put out any flames of attraction to the opposite sex before they could blaze into an impropriety.

"Miss Boscastle, may I go out into the garden?"

"No, Amy, you may not, as I have told you a thousand and one times. Not without an approved escort."

"But it's stifling in here."

"Drink another lemonade."

"Verity drank champagne."

"Verity," Charlotte said, searching the room for the academy's recent charity-case and most trouble-prone pupil, "will be restricted to her room tomorrow. I knew I shouldn't have allowed the younger girls to attend. How will they concentrate on class tomorrow? Miss Peppertree was right. Only the graduates should be invited to the ball."

"Miss Boscastle, I broke my slipper. What should I do? May I ask the marchioness if I may borrow a pair of hers?"

Charlotte frowned. "If you can find her—without leaving the room."

"Verity is standing on the terrace, miss."

"Oh, for heaven's sake," she muttered. "Where is the Duchess of Glenmorgan? She promised she would stay close enough for me to call."

Perhaps, after tonight, Charlotte might be able to draw a breath. For good or for evil, the graduates would venture forth into the world and assume the responsibility of their reputations upon their own shoulders. If it were possible she would have drawn out a complete map of pitfalls that a young lady might encounter after she left the academy. It would depict a narrow road intersected with various pathways marked, AVENUES OF FORBIDDEN AFFAIRS, DARK FORAYS INTO DECADENCE — OR RUINED REPUTATIONS. Until dawn broke over the occasion, however, she was obligated to stand guard against any rogues who thought to take advantage of an inexperienced girl. She had her eye on one rogue in particular. He had looked at her only once. The Duke of Wynfield was without question the most elegant and hard-edged guest at the ball, and Charlotte wasn't about to let him tempt one of her graduates or distract her from her duty.

She wondered whether he even remembered the last time they had seen each other, at the emporium in the Strand. They hadn't exchanged a single word. Charlotte had been shopping for the academy that day. He had been shopping for a pair of strumpets, one draped over either elbow.

He had kissed one of the tarts on the neck — and merely smiled when Charlotte, at the opposite end of the counter, had gasped in shock.

She had returned to the academy hours later to record the incident in her diary, as was her wont, changing a detail here and there until, *en fin,* the actual event bore little resemblance to her fabricated but far more satisfying version. She had been keeping a journal ever since she could hold a pen, and she enjoyed the art of exaggerating commonplace events.

When her Boscastle cousins had first invited her to London five years ago, she had been so enthralled by their amorous exploits that she had undertaken the task of recording the family history in her diary. Soon the pages needed no enhancement. It was a challenge to follow the family's constant scandals. It seemed that everyone in the brood had led a secret life as a spy or someone's lover. She had to face a painful fact—as much as she admired her relatives, it was obvious that she led a dreary life in comparison.

It took her a month to overcome her inhibitions and let her pen wander where it would. Soon her diaries simmered with illicit truths and vicarious pleasures. In the pages of her intimate musings the duke not only adored her, but he had been pursuing her for months. In actual life he was domineering, indecent, and inexcusably taken with disgraceful women. In his fictional encounters with Charlotte he was domineering, indecent, and inexplicably taken with her. And no one else.

In Charlotte's version of the incident in the emporium, the duke had noticed her across the counter and had immediately dismissed the other women. He had walked straight up to Charlotte and, without a word, grasped her hand.

"My carriage is outside," he had said, his sinful smile mesmerizing her. "May I take you away?"

His face receded. Another voice, breathy and excited, was whispering in her ear. "That's the Duke of Wynfield you're staring at, Miss Boscastle. Do be careful. Everyone is saying that he's in the market for a mistress."

Charlotte gripped her fan and turned to regard her favorite student in dismay. "Lydia Butterfield, reassure me that he has not found one in you."

Lydia gave her a wistful grin. "Dear Miss Boscastle, I shall miss you with all my heart."

"You shall miss my guidance; that is clear."

"I won't need it any longer," Lydia said with regret. "But I will miss your history lessons."

"All the battles and beheadings?" Charlotte asked, stepping to the side to stop Lydia from staring at the duke. Or him from noticing her. "But don't be so melodramatic or I shall start to cry. Your family still lives in London. You may visit the academy whenever you wish."

"My family—well, my *betrothed's* parents live in Dorset, and he is eager to start a family—"

"Your betrothed?" Charlotte said faintly.

Lydia bit her lip, nodding toward the short gentleman standing a few feet behind her. "Sir Adam Richardson, the architect."

"Lydia, I am so—"

Envious? Yes, to her shame, she envied Lydia a little. But she was also filled with happiness for a girl whose sweetness Charlotte had feared would render her vulnerable or undesirable on the marriage mart. "I am proud," she said firmly. "He appears to be a fine gentleman."

Lydia laughed, her gaze drifting to the duke, who was *not* known to be a gentleman at all. "I was told that he is a wildly jealous lover."

"Your fiancé?"

"The duke," Lydia said, laughing again. "He has a reputation for being a possessive suitor."

"*Lydia*." Charlotte attempted to look shocked, although the same rumors had not escaped her attention.

Such gossip should have stamped the duke as an unacceptable person instead of engendering wicked daydreams about him in Charlotte's imagination. Why did it feel so pleasant to picture him tearing off his long-tailed evening coat to defend her from . . . Oh, since it was *her* flight of fancy, the other man might as well be Phillip Moreland, the cad who had broken her heart years ago.

She could picture it so clearly. The ballroom would be cleared for a duel; the duke studied sword fighting at Fenton's School of Arms. Charlotte had watched him perform at a benefit ball in this very mansion. She'd had nothing to do with him on that past night, and it was doubtful that she would capture his interest in the future.

"I don't think that either of us need worry about the duke's amorous proclivities," she assured Lydia, thus uttering the fateful words that would come back to mock her before morning came. . . .

# Chapter 2

*G*ideon doubted that he had made a good impression on Miss Charlotte Boscastle the day she had seen him in the emporium. For one thing he'd drunk too much the night before and his head had felt like Hephaestus's workshop. For another he was dressed for practice at the fencing school, and there were two whores attached to him like handcuffs, which they may or may not have used on each other the night before. He couldn't remember.

He knew he looked disreputable the day he stepped into Sir Godfrey Maitland's emporium. Godfrey, a former student at Fenton's fencing salon, had stared at him in reproach across the counter. "We have many *ladies* in the shop, Your Grace," he had said in a meaningful voice.

And that was when Gideon first noticed Charlotte, who glanced at his two companions and lifted her nose in the air as if she'd caught the scent of a noxious threat that might contaminate the young ladies huddled around her.

He inclined his head at her, to no effect. And then he

had kissed one of the harlots on her neck, hoping to elicit some reaction from the golden-haired lady in the straw bonnet. He had, too.

She had gasped and moved back to stand like a shield in front of her charges. Gideon had responded with a slow, roguish smile that brought a blush to her porcelain complexion.

"Fancy that," he murmured to the woman at his right. "I didn't know there were any ladies left in London who could still blush."

"Do not behave like a rake, Your Grace," Sir Godfrey whispered from behind the counter. "This is Miss Charlotte *Boscastle*. You know how indebted the maestro is to her family."

"Who isn't?" the duke mused.

"She is also the lead seamstress at the Scarfield Academy for Young Ladies."

"God forbid," Gideon said, straightening in alarm. "A lady with an operative brain in her head. Who's going to protect me?"

The tart clinging to one of his arms giggled. "As if anyone could threaten a man of your largesse."

He glanced down at her in amusement. "I suspect the word you just used doesn't mean what you think it does. At any rate let's not discuss my 'largesse' in public."

He had laughed off that afternoon; he had forgotten it until tonight. He had been busy practicing at Fenton's academy, and while it was true that the blushing schoolmistress had momentarily caught his eye, Gideon was in the market for a different sort of mistress. Not one who obeyed rules in bed, but one who broke them and made up a few along the way. He wouldn't object if she had a brain, though.

Therefore it surprised him that he had recognized Charlotte the moment he'd entered the ballroom. There were young women everywhere. He couldn't even recall the names of the ladybirds who had accompanied him to the emporium, and he had been far more intimate with that pair than with the frost maiden.

Charlotte Boscastle. He looked directly at her once. She returned the courtesy with a scowl that could have curdled milk. He should have known better than to attend a party given for a group of finishing-school girls. He'd be better off wandering into the conservatory and talking to the Greek statues. At least that way he was fulfilling his function as a guest at the party—all eligible young men of high lineage having been invited—and he wasn't likely to cause any trouble.

But no sooner had he made the decision to sneak off than trouble in another form appeared. Lord Devon Boscastle detached himself from his throng of friends and stepped into Gideon's path. "You can't leave yet, Wynfield. We haven't talked once. I hope you aren't avoiding me. I didn't mean to stab you at practice the other day."

"Are you trying to lure me into a dark corner?"

Devon's blue eyes brimmed with devilish intent. "Sorry, but I'm a married man. As you should be at your age."

Gideon hesitated. "I *was* married."

"I— Oh, God. Yes, I did know that. Sorry." Devon said awkwardly, "I didn't mean to—"

"It's fine, Devon. It's been almost five years. I didn't even know you then."

Devon lowered his voice. He was the playful brother in the Boscastle family, the prankster and amusing friend, who had become a devoted husband and father of a little girl. But as a reformed sinner he still liked to stir up mischief whenever he could, and Gideon, along with Devon's other friends, had come to expect the unexpected from him.

"What do you have planned for the night, Gideon?" he asked, his voice benign.

"An escape. From this party."

"Why?"

"Why? Look around you. We are outnumbered by innocents, up to our shoulders in educated virgins, who, from a bachelor's point of view, are the most dangerous entity in London."

"I was looking at it the other way around," Devon said. "A libertine could easily lead one of the innocents down the primrose path of dalliance. All he'd have to do is follow the footsteps Grayson wore through the carpets before he walked down the aisle."

"I'm not in the mood for a maiden. Anyway, you're married, a fact that renders any advice you offer null and void."

"Do me a favor, Wynfield."

Gideon's first instinct was to refuse outright. "I know what you're going to say."

"Do you?"

"Yes. You want me to stay away from Miss Boscastle. She must have told you that I paraded a pair of strumpets in front of her. It wasn't as if I did it to provoke her."

Devon arched a dark brow. "Where on earth did this happen?"

"It was at the emporium."

Devon pondered this for a moment. "She never mentioned a word of it to me. You couldn't have made much of an impression on her."

"I think I did, but it wasn't a good one," Gideon said. "If you're going to forbid me to flirt with your cousin, you needn't worry. I'm not even remotely tempted."

"That's a little insulting," Devon retorted.

Gideon laughed. "Would you rather I told you that I'm lusting after her?"

"No. I'd probably feel compelled to stay at your side. Grayson asked me to keep an eye on anyone who seemed suspicious."

"In that case he should have given you a mirror."

"The woman you have *not* been lusting after isn't married, but she does have three older brothers who are plotting to end her unhappy spinsterhood any day now."

"Are they here tonight?" Gideon inquired.

"The two older ones are traveling to London from Sussex. Jane expects them in a week. I think the plan is to find a husband for Charlotte as quickly as possible. I'll be honest with you; she won't make it easy on them. I doubt she'll ever incite anyone's lust."

Both men glanced at Charlotte, then looked away.

"And this worries you?" Gideon said, wondering what Devon's point was, or whether he even had one.

Devon nodded. "Yes."

"Well, don't look at me. I was married once and I have a daughter, too."

"Eventually you'll have to remarry if you want an heir." Devon cleared his throat. "Do me a favor, Wynfield?"

Gideon didn't respond. Here it came. Again Gideon's instincts warned him to proceed with caution, while his reason argued that Devon was mischievous but not malicious. "I'm meeting my soon-to-be mistress at Mrs. Watson's tonight."

"Then this will be your last night of freedom."

"Excuse me?"

"A mistress can be more demanding than a wife, especially if she's good at her job. The precious hours of your freedom are slipping like sand through your fingers as we speak."

"That's a good point. It makes me wonder why I'm wasting those golden moments talking to you."

"Will you do it?"

"Will I do what?" Gideon demanded.

"Ask my cousin Charlotte to dance."

A dance? Was that all? "Why would a lady with a pristine reputation want to dance with me?" he asked slowly.

"I don't know that she would," Devon replied. "But, you see, everyone else in the family would like to see her dance."

The family?

Gideon could have sworn an invisible hand tightened his neck cloth and that a candle in one of the corner girandoles writhed and died. "There are several eligible gentlemen here tonight. Why me?"

"Because you're a duke, for one thing, and my friend for another. If you could give the other guests the impression that she intrigues a man like you, a few decent gentlemen might begin to see her in a different light."

"I am *not* offering to court her. And I think you just insulted me."

Devon shook his head. "I'm not asking you to court her."

"I don't trust you, Devon. I think you're the devil looking for an instrument, and I can find my own evil without your interference."

"All I really want you to do is to pay a little attention to our lonely wallflower."

"I think the wallflower just made a face at me."

"No," Devon said. "That was at me. She knows we're standing here talking about her."

Gideon balked. "Then she might have meant it for both of us. Perhaps you should find another strategy—and by that I am suggesting another gentleman. Someone else to melt her—"

"To what?" Devon asked, one brow lifting.

"She reminds me of a frost maiden. I prefer my ladies warm and willing."

"Well, she does have a cold heart when it comes to letting gentlemen visitors into the academy. But I can't blame her for that. I think she's shy. Come and meet her for yourself."

Gideon didn't move.

"I know it doesn't make much sense—"

"That is an understatement."

"—but no other gentleman is brave enough to approach her."

"I shouldn't wonder, if you go about haranguing them for admiring her from halfway across a room."

Devon smiled. "Then you admit that you were admiring her?"

Gideon stared at him in stone-faced silence.

"Please ask her to dance."

"Why don't you?"

"I'm her cousin, and if I ask her to dance, everyone will know it's because no one else has asked her."

"Maybe she doesn't *want* to dance."

"Of course she does."

Gideon hesitated. "Why do I have the feeling that I'm about to walk into a trap? And why don't you ask any of the bachelors present to do the honors? Of all the other male guests I've undoubtedly earned the worst reputation. Present company and his kin excluded, that is."

"Exactly," Devon said, as if Gideon had just grasped the alchemical formula of the philosopher's stone. "Most of the other male guests are outstanding examples of gentlemanly conduct."

"But I'm—"

"—not. You are, however, a person who draws attention. Give in, Gideon. Chat with her until the eligible start to notice. I'll cheer you from the corner."

"Is this a sporting event?"

"In our world every time a man and woman meet it is liable to turn into a contest."

The party's hostess, Jane, the Marchioness of Sedgecroft, admired the assembly from the gallery above the ballroom. Beside her, an ominous feeling overshadowing her usual bright spirits, stood Harriet, the Duchess of Glenmorgan, a former student and once a schoolmistress at the academy. Harriet had been the first charity case to be admitted into and to graduate from the elite school. During the course of her education, which quite frankly couldn't hold a candle to what she'd learned on the streets, Harriet and Charlotte had unexpectedly formed a bond of friendship.

Charlotte had been born with the proverbial silver spoon in her mouth. She had never been caught uttering a profanity. Until the academy had rescued Harriet from the gutter, she had stolen silver for a living. The curses

that she spewed when provoked would make a Billings-
gate fishwife faint. Charlotte had taught Harriet the virtue of submitting to her betters. Harriet had taught
Charlotte the value of shocking them senseless.

Harriet knew most of Charlotte's secrets. Harriet
hadn't told Charlotte half of hers.

"Why is she always left standing alone at every ball?"
Jane lamented as she studied Charlotte in chagrin. "Could
her gown be less flattering? Was it her grandmother's
bedsheet?"

"It reminds me of the sail on Grayson's yacht."

"Well, the girls *are* about to launch. . . ." Jane sighed.
"I wish I could find a way to coax her out of her shell. Or
at least to discourage her from scraping her beautiful
hair into that knot and putting all her efforts into marrying off her students and not herself. And, my stars . . ."
Jane shuddered. "Those sandals."

"She couldn't find her evening slippers at the last moment and had to make do with those," Harriet said de-
fensively. "She has big feet, you know. No one else's
shoes would fit."

"That is no excuse for unappealing footwear. I've offered my Italian shoemaker to her innumerable times.
How does she expect to attract a suitor looking like a . . .
a—"

"—a goddess," Harriet said with a loyal smile. "She's
tall and strong limbed, and there aren't many gentlemen
who have the confidence to approach someone like her."

Jane smiled and put her hand over Harriet's. "What a
supporter she has in you. There must be one man who is
perfect. Her brothers have threatened to bring her old
beau to London if she isn't engaged before the end of the
season. No one wants to watch her slip into a lonely life."

"Charlotte won't marry her old beau."

Jane stared at Harriet's profile. "How do you know?"

Harriet shrugged a white shoulder. "Just a guess."

"Has she ever mentioned anyone else?" Jane asked thoughtfully.

"To me?"

"No, Harriet, to Napoleon Bonaparte. Do not pretend coyness."

Harriet shrugged. "Fine."

"Then—"

"If she has mentioned anyone, I don't remember who it was."

"Ah." Jane's lips curved with satisfaction. "You can trust me, Harriet. However, I do not wish you to betray a secret."

Harriet leaned over the wrought-iron railing. "Who's that handsome fellow talking to Devon down by the hall to the conservatory?"

Jane raised her brow. "Should I care?"

"You might. Or might not."

Jane peered through the glittering brightness of the chandeliers to the two darkly clad men engrossed in conversation. "I think— Oh, *dear*. That's the Duke of Wynfield. He and Devon are Kit's fencing students. Do you suppose . . . ?"

Harriet pressed her lips together. It was a good thing she hadn't taken another glass of champagne. She was dying to tell Jane about Charlotte's secret attraction to the duke. But she'd promised that she wouldn't, which was a shame. Jane was a powerful ally, and she would do anything for family.

"He's a widow," Jane mused, caressing the diamond pendant at her throat. "His wife died of cancer a year or so after she had a child. At least, I believe that's what happened."

Harriet's brow creased in thought. "His father died two years ago. The duke apparently went into a moral decline after he inherited."

Jane sighed. "I suppose that is how some men grieve."

"It's also how some men celebrate," Harriet said. "He doesn't look especially mournful tonight, does he?"

"No." Jane straightened her shoulders as if to shake off the mantle of sadness that had enshrouded them. "Still, we cannot see into his heart. No one in London has ever seen his child, either. However if he has a daughter who's been introduced at court, I haven't read about her in the papers. How long ago did his wife die?"

"Perhaps four or five years. But that's only a guess."

"His daughter would be too young for social introductions. I can only hope that— Well, it isn't my place to wonder. The duke was young to have married and lost his wife."

"Is he the rake that everyone thinks he is?"

Jane narrowed her eyes in contemplation. "I rely on Weed for all my fashion news and gossip. And he said—" Jane broke off, leaving Harriet in suspense. Weed was the senior footman in the house and the most beloved if formidable servant in the family. "I think he told me that the duke was about to enter negotiations for a mistress from Mrs. Watson's. I don't think this is mere speculation."

"I hoped it was only a rumor," Harriet said. "Who invited him?"

"Grayson, of course," Jane replied.

"Charlotte would be appalled if she knew."

Harriet felt Jane staring at her. "Yes. I'm sure she would."

"It's amazing to me, Harriet, to look at you and remember what a colorful life you lived."

"But nothing that compares to yours," Harriet said glibly.

"I'm not sure about that," Jane said. "I have always stayed inside aristocratic circles. No, that isn't true. I strayed a few times into the half-world on my husband's account. But you have moved through every segment of society."

"Yes, that's true."

Harriet glanced down at the throng of guests. She had already said far more than she meant to, and Jane was anything but dense. In fact, Jane's mind tended to devious schemes, the most wicked of which had ended with her marrying the marquess. If Harriet wasn't careful, Jane would soon charm her into confessing that Charlotte had been admiring the duke for a year now.

"I suppose as long as the duke behaves himself at the party," Jane said, "there is nothing to fear. Charlotte won't let him near the girls, and after your husband's niece was abducted last year, Grayson has retained Sir Daniel's services to patrol our residences during times when a malefactor might hope to take advan—"

Jane stopped, taking a long breath. Harriet knew from experience that she could have gone on for minutes at such an energetic pace, but not when her audience wasn't listening to a thing she'd said. Indeed, Harriet found it impossible to stop staring at Charlotte and the duke. Then at the duke and Charlotte. Devon seemed to be forgotten in the middle.

Jane turned to her unexpectedly. "I think the duke should be watched, if not investigated."

"But you just said that you felt sorry for him."

"Yes, Harriet, but what you *didn't* say told me that I

ought to feel more concerned about Charlotte than sorry for the duke. Her virtue is still a valuable commodity. A graduate accepting a marriage proposal tonight is one thing. A good thing. A baby born in nine months due to an indiscretion in an alcove is another. I won't have it. This duke must be watched. And so must Charlotte. She is so intent on guarding her girls that she seems to have forgotten that she is vulnerable herself."

"I doubt she is in any danger of being seduced while we stand here watching her every move," Harriet said. "And I don't think that as a result of carrying on a conversation with the duke that she will have his child by the end of the year."

Jane started to respond but paused as a tall, liveried manservant arrived from the other side of the balcony. "Weed! You must have read my mind. I was just remembering our conversation the other day about Wynfield."

Weed bowed, darting a wry glance toward Harriet. He would never let her forget that he'd once caught her robbing Jane's room, a crime that had ultimately led to Harriet's salvation. She had been transformed from a young monster into a civilized noblewoman.

Weed, however, remained the pompous frog that he had always been. He was not only a footman, but also Jane's confidant, fashion adviser, and partner in her matchmaking ventures.

"How can I be of service, madam?" he asked in the pinched voice that made it sound as if he were talking through his nostrils.

"I am going downstairs to mingle. Kindly remind Mrs. O'Brien to keep a closer eye on Rowan tonight. My son has still not outgrown his habit of waylaying our guests with his sword."

"Yes, madam."

"Oh, and, Weed, there is one more thing concerning our earlier conversation. Have you heard any other rumors about Wynfield?"

"He has an appointment later tonight on Bruton Street with the courtesan he appears to have chosen as his next mistress. Her name is Gabrielle Something-or-Other, and she is known to be beautiful and completely immoral. She has ruined several marriages without the least remorse."

"Thank you, Weed." She turned to Harriet as he left. "Confirmed—he is a duke. He is widowed and wealthy."

"He's a wicked devil," Harriet interjected.

Jane's green eyes glinted. "And he seems devoted to leading the sinful and shallow life of an utter scoundrel."

"And?"

"We will have to keep him in our sights. Agreed?"

"Yes, but if you let Charlotte know anything about this discussion, I will deny everything."

# Chapter 3

Devon walked Gideon around the ballroom, inundating him with so many last-minute instructions that he wasn't surprised Charlotte lacked admirers. Who would be brave enough to break the Boscastle guard to approach her? Who could remember the endless rules?

"One more word," he muttered. "One more warning, and I am going to do you a violent injury."

"You are trustworthy, Wynfield, aren't you?"

"I'm a man."

"What does that mean?"

"It means that I am human. I have failings like any other man. If you're afraid that I will do or say anything to dishonor your cousin, then come out and say it. Or do not introduce us."

"The thought never entered my mind," Devon said, then hesitated. "Did it enter yours?"

Gideon laughed.

Devon scrutinized him in silence. "On second thought,

maybe this isn't one of my brighter ideas. I'll find some-one harmless instead. There might be an earl hiding in here somewhere who isn't a walking scandal."

"Look—"

Devon held up a hand. "It's all right. I understand. You don't want to do me the only favor I have ever asked of you in all the years of our friendship."

Gideon glanced at Charlotte's willowy figure. From where he stood she looked as if she were captured in the candlelight prisms. "Oh, hell, fine. I suppose it won't kill me. But if this is one of your pranks, I promise you, I will pay you back in spades."

"Me, a model of dignity and reform? Would I play a trick on a duke who has studied under a sword master such as Fenton?"

"What do you expect me to say to her?"

"Haven't you paid court to enough women to write a book on the subject?"

"Only when I was hoping for something in return."

Devon's eyes darkened. "Can I give you one sugges-tion?"

"Damn you."

"Try not to use language like that in front of the young ladies or you're liable to be slapped witless by a dozen or so fans."


Charlotte's throat constricted. She couldn't swallow as she observed the swath the duke cut through the ball-room. She glanced about, seeking a reasonable means of escape, a group of guests to hide her, any excuse not to face the man whom her cousin had clearly sent to be-devil her.

And yet she waited. She hoped. What would she do for the chance to know him as she had imagined in her diary? What if when he reached her he announced in a masterful voice, "This ball is a waste of our time. You belong with me. Alone. In my arms. I am taking you again, and this time I will not let you elude me."

She shivered with forbidden, foolish anticipation. How wicked she could be in her thoughts. Then, suddenly, the duke stood before her. She lifted her gaze. Wickedness looked her right in the face. She forced herself to look back.

Thought ceased to matter. Reason abandoned her.

Her mind went into anarchy.

Sensation reigned, wild and undisciplined.

She'd caught only a few glimpses of him about town. His profile in a passing carriage. A stolen look at his broad-shouldered figure at an exhibition. It wouldn't have been appropriate to stare down the duke in the emporium. Heaven forbid that one of his strumpets had made a snide remark that the younger girls of the academy had overheard.

Or that Charlotte herself had broken her perfect record of propriety and given the tart a piece of her mind. One glance at him that day had been sufficient to confirm her prior beliefs. He was an insufferably attractive man who radiated the charm of an authentic rogue.

And she was only asking for trouble by allowing her infatuation to grow.

Perhaps this meeting would dampen her interest in him once and for all. Perhaps he would reveal how crude and conceited he was at heart. She would be content to prove to herself that he was handsome on the outside and hollow within.

"May I introduce myself?" he asked.

She nodded her head in the affirmative.

He said something. She had no idea what it was. He might have been speaking Portuguese.

For the life of her she could not force her mind to function.

Had he just asked her to dance?

"I'm sorry," she heard herself reply. "I can't."

Good for her. Her manners, her good sense, came to her rescue when it seemed mayhem had won.

"Are you enjoying the party, Your Grace?"

His dark saturnine smile swept her into another panic. "Not particularly."

"I'm glad to hear . . ."

What had he said?

This initial meeting was not unfolding as it had in her fantasies. She wasn't supposed to become tongue-tied in his presence. She was supposed to charm him with her wit, with the dialogue that flowed effortlessly when written. Why did words fail her now that she needed to voice them?

This was humiliation.

How awful of Devon, leaning against the wall to watch her embarrassment deepen.

The duke did not appear pleased about the situation, either.

He stood beside her as they made a few more attempts at polite conversation until finally something inside her gave up. The Duke of Wynfield might be the man of her dreams, but it was obvious he had been dragged unwillingly into her company. And that he did not share her hope for a spark between them.

Unfortunately that dismal fact did not subdue her attraction to him at all. Under different circumstances she could have stared at his beautifully sculpted face for hours. But she couldn't keep chattering on forever. He would think there was something wrong with her.

"Devon made you ask me to dance, didn't he?" she said, refusing to embarrass either of them any longer. "I understand. He's done this before."

"Not to me." His dark eyes suddenly connected with hers, and she felt her heart give a wistful flutter for what might have been. At least in her imagination.

But there wasn't a reason to keep pretending that he had any romantic motives in mind.

"I saw your handsome heads together. I know you were discussing me. And I know Devon and his antics, too."

"Nonsense," Gideon said firmly. "We were talking about political events."

"Such as?"

"Nothing I could repeat in refined company. Distressful subjects and . . . such."

"I see." What she really saw was that he wielded charm as deftly as she did her fan. "I never knew that Devon took an interest in politics."

"He might not have wanted to offend delicate ears with . . ."

"Distressful subjects and such?"

"Exactly." And then to her surprise he edged in a little closer to her instead of running off gratefully into the night, as he had every right to do. "I'm curious about something. Do you typically put other gentlemen through a grueling interrogation before you agree to a dance?"

"Only the ones I suspect are paying me court because my cousins have talked them into it."

"Don't you *want* to dance with me?" he asked with a disarming smile.

She smiled back, stealing another look at him over her lace-edged fan. "Are you trying to corrupt me?"

"No. Corruption comes after the dance, which will apparently be over before this conversation is."

She closed her fan, sighing deeply. "I think I should pay attention to the young ladies who are graduating. This is their night, not mine."

He bowed. "Then I am disappointed."

"You are not disappointed, and we both know it. It's a relief. Tell Devon you did your duty, and I released you from it. Don't let him make you feel guilty. He can be quite persuasive."

"So can I, when given the chance."

"I hope he didn't hold some dire threat over your head. If so, I apologize. He's incorrigible."

"I beg your pardon, Miss Boscastle, but I *never* do anything unless it pleases me. If you knew more about me, you would understand that."

*And if you knew more about me,* Charlotte thought, *you would understand that . . .* That what? That she was infatuated with a man who had to be threatened into talking to her? That she had never been properly courted or known a romantic love that was reciprocated? And that with each lonely month that passed, her chances of finding the perfect man—which had been him—diminished? She turned her face toward the dancers weaving like ribbons across the floor. Why did he have to be so persistent? Why didn't he leave her alone to feel sorry for herself? The diabolical man was determined to wear her down.

"Will you—"

"No, I'm dreadfully sorry. I have to keep my eye on my girls."

"It must be a difficult job."

"It is," she replied in a clipped voice, not looking at him. "Especially at times like this."

"Why are they called the 'Lionesses of London' after they graduate?" he asked, and she could feel him staring through her skin. "Do you teach them to catch gentlemen between their jaws?"

She glanced up at him again, caught unaware by the unbridled sensuality of his smile. "The reference has nothing to do with our predatory skills."

"A pity. The notion intrigued me."

"It refers to the academy's original foundress, Viscountess Lyons."

"So there's no truth at all to the nickname?" he asked in an undertone.

"If there were," she said, biting off each word, "this would certainly be the time to prove it."

"Are you—"

She swung around. "The dance is over, you— It is intermission, Your Grace," she managed in a dignified voice.

He looked up. "Well, so it is." He gave her a gallant nod. "I was so engrossed in our conversation I didn't notice. It has been . . . interesting." He smiled crookedly. "Don't you agree?"

"Yes," she said, too exhausted to argue. She could only imagine how difficult he would be to resist in a private setting. Or if he truly had his heart set on seduction. It had been more than interesting, although she could envision ways it would have been better. It could have been a romantic interlude instead of a painful reminder of her unrequited affection.

Not that she would ever have to worry about such a scandalous fate befalling her. They were complete opposites. He was a raging bonfire to her timid flame. A devil-may-care challenge to her conscientious soul. It wasn't his fault that she'd built a romance between them that had never existed. Or that he was so gorgeous she could weep on his wonderfully masculine chest.

But at least he had tried to be kind. Charlotte had to admire him for that, even if she was going to pinch Devon's head off for making her an object of pity.

"Miss Boscastle?" the duke said in a deep, irresistible voice. "Am I forgiven?"

She stirred. "For what?"

He looked at her for a long time. "I was rather obvious, wasn't I?"

"Yes," she said. "You were obvious. Painfully so."

"Well, now that the truth is out, would you give me the next dance?"

She shook her head, amused at his audacity. "No."

"Perhaps in the future?"

"Yes, yes, yes." She forced herself to turn away, hoping he would take the hint and leave her to recover her wits.

She felt him withdraw a step. And not a moment too soon. From the corner of her eye she glimpsed two of her students drifting toward the French doors. Three young gentlemen were following in their wake. She gripped her rose-scented fan, steeling herself to thwart a scandal in the making. Duke of her secret desires or not, she would not tolerate any mischief under her guard. Nor would she give Lady Clipstone any tidbits to feed the gossipmongers. For all she knew, Alice had a spy in the house. She had tried to bribe former students and servants away from the academy in the past to spill any confidences that would damage the school's prestige.

"Another time, Your Grace," she murmured, dismissing him with finality.

"I look forward to it."

He bowed again. She gave him credit for hiding his relief. She had no doubt he would forget her the moment they parted company. And she would force herself to forget him, too, until the moment she sat at her desk and poured out her thoughts in her diary.

She decided that it would be the last reference she ever made to the duke. Her imaginary affair with him had to come to an end . . . even if he were more desirable in person than she had dreamed.

One night alone in his company would ruin her reputation forever. She would not be able to defend her virtue if he was of a mind to seduce her. Charlotte well knew the passion he could show her would make every other man's company dreary in comparison. Of course no decent man would ever pursue her if she had a liasion with Wynfield. Would the memories be worth disgrace? She was afraid to admit to herself that they might be. And that was sufficient evidence that she had allowed herself to go too far with the silly fantasies about the charismatic duke. Still, any chance of a romance between them seemed as remote as the planet Venus.

# Chapter 4

$\mathscr{G}$ ideon wasn't sure that he had accomplished anything during his brief encounter with Charlotte Boscastle except to make a nuisance of himself. He doubted that the time he'd spent with her had rendered her more desirable to other men. Or that he would have felt as comfortable teasing her if she hadn't been Devon's cousin.

But she hadn't reminded him of Devon at all. There was a dreamy quality about her that set her apart from the rest of her family. She might have stepped from a watercolor painting that graced the wall of a country manor, her coolness an illusion. Her skin wasn't an innocent white. It was sinful cream with a swirl of rose petals beneath the surface. Her smile had revealed an attractive slight overbite. The gold flecks in her eyes hinted at hidden fires.

He found himself wondering what she would look like if she unknotted the thick blond hair that sat primly on her nape. He had counted twenty tightly fastened buttons on the back of her modest dress. God only knew what a fuss she'd have put up if she had any idea that he had been wondering how fast he could undo them.

And yet if he hadn't known better, he would have sworn that there was an immediate sense of intimacy between them. Which wasn't possible.

They hadn't exchanged a single word the day he had seen her at the emporium.

"There you are," a male voice called from the vicinity of the French doors. "Confess all. What did you say to chase Charlotte into the garden, and don't tell me you've made a secret assignation to meet her there, because there are more spies planted outside than trees."

Gideon snorted. "I'd prefer not to talk about it. I'm sure you will appreciate the fact that a gentleman does not discuss his dealings with a lady."

"Did you offend her?"

"Probably, and it's your fault."

"What happened?"

"Nothing," Gideon said.

Devon looked skeptical. "Nothing?"

"Nothing," he repeated, and wondered why the admission felt like a lie.

"You asked her to dance?"

"Repeatedly."

Devon shook his head. "And I thought that you were the most charming man at the ball."

Gideon laughed. "I'm sorry to let you down. I tried. I failed."

"You're determined to pursue your life of decadence?"

"I'm afraid so."

Devon nodded in grudging acceptance. "At least you gave it a go. Would you like to come upstairs to the gallery and drink a toast to your continued decline?"

"Not tonight. Other pleasures await. And I've promised to drop off a few friends on the way."

"It's just as well. Jane would probably corner you under the pretense of a friendly chat. She is unabashedly pursuing suitors for Charlotte."

Gideon resisted looking back into the room. "Good luck to the man who can get past her guard. I couldn't even convince her to lower the drawbridge."

"Her brothers have written to Grayson announcing their intent to marry her off as soon as possible."

"Thank you for the warning, after the fact. I knew I detected the scent of conspiracy in the air."

"You could do worse for a wife," Devon commented.

"I don't disagree." Gideon shook his head in amusement. "But I'm not in the market for one. I doubt I will be in the near future, either."

"That's what I thought right before I met Jocelyn," Devon said. "One minute I was on my way to a midnight assignation with another woman, and the next I was standing at the altar wondering what had happened."

Charlotte nibbled at her salad and raised her champagne flute to the woman sitting two chairs down from her. Harriet lifted her own glass high. Her feathered turban listed on her head like a dying turkey, but nobody seemed to mind. All the girls were present and accounted for. A full complement of young gentlemen had been flushed out of the gaming rooms to balance the room.

It was a rare event in Boscastle history—a party that had concluded without a scandal to make the morning news. Even Miss Peppertree, Charlotte's prudish assistant, looked pleased. Weed, always a stickler for cere-

mony, had his under footmen lined around the wall like
wooden soldiers.

"To the Scarfield Academy!" Harriet called out over
the happy chattering. And Charlotte felt an immense relief that the party was almost over. In fact, she was so
sure the night would end uneventfully that she excused
herself right after supper and went upstairs to make ar-
rangements for the girls to leave.

Jane always kept a suite of rooms available for family;
Charlotte had spent the previous night here with Harriet and the girls to familiarize them with the ballroom.

Harriet trailed her through the upper corridor. "I
need my cloak and reticule. The Duke of Wynfield is
dropping me and a crowd at another party. I don't suppose I could convince you to come?"

Charlotte smiled wistfully. She wouldn't enjoy sitting
in the duke's carriage while he was anticipating holding
another woman in his arms. It was going to be difficult
enough saying good-bye in her diary.

"Perhaps you'll be able to persuade him not to go to
Mrs. Watson's later on," Harriet teased her. "Jane and I
watched the pair of you flirting—"

"It wasn't flirting," Charlotte said in dismay, pushing
open the door to their suite. "Devon put him up to asking me to dance. What a mess in here."

"It looked like flirting. . . . Oh, Charlotte, I know that
you are drawn to him. I wish he— God above, look at
the state of my turban." Harriet confronted her reflection in the long cheval glass. "I can't believe no one told
me how hideous it looks. I don't have time to do my hair,
either. Where did I put my cloak?"

Charlotte didn't answer. Harriet turned to her. "Are
you all right?"

"No." She bit her lower lip. "I think you should leave me alone. I might cry. It's been a long, challenge-fraught evening."

"Oh, no. What— It's him, isn't it?"

She nodded ruefully. "I'm a dreamer. I had always hoped, perhaps . . . He asked me to dance because he felt sorry for me. It's over."

Harriet knelt before her. "What's over?"

"My love affair."

"Well, it wasn't real, was it?"

"Do you know what the worst part is?"

"Tell me."

"I spent so much time dreaming about that man. And it's time for that nonsense to come to an end. Except that tonight I discovered he has a conscience, and that makes him more attractive to me than ever! I'm so stupid, Harriet. Why didn't you tell me that my writing was a waste of time?"

"Because it isn't," Harriet said. "The stories you read me were beautiful."

Charlotte felt mournful. "So much of my diary is make-believe. Now I can't even dream about meeting him again. I'll have to draw pictures of butterflies to pass the time."

"Charlotte, I was a criminal. You gave me the gift of good books. There were thoughts in them that I had felt but never knew how to express."

"You express yourself more eloquently than any lady I have ever met."

"Even when I lapse into profanity?"

"Especially then." Charlotte gave an unsteady laugh. "Don't tell anyone I said that. A lady isn't allowed to show her emotions. Nor should she use bad language."

"You can trust me. Do you wish to talk about him?"

She shook her head. "Not now."

"You've been working for weeks to train the girls for this graduation. Take a well-deserved rest, my dear."

"I ought to see the girls off. I'd go with them but I have a few belongings to pack first."

"Miss Peppertree is waiting in one of the carriages. Sir Daniel is riding behind them, and there will be enough footmen during the drive to fill a cricket field."

Charlotte smiled in relief. Sir Daniel Mallory was a former Bow Street Runner who worked as a private agent for the Boscastle family. "The ball went well, didn't it?"

"More than well. The young ladies have not only survived the night due to your dedication; they have thrived. Furthermore, remember that tonight you made history. It was a Boscastle event that didn't end in scandal."

"Forgive me. I didn't —"

"Take a breath while I make myself presentable again. I could ring for some refreshment. I noticed you ate nothing at the table."

"I couldn't eat."

"Later then."

Charlotte sighed and opened the desk in which her diary was concealed inside a false drawer. Soon she forgot that Harriet was even in the room. She had time to pen only a page or two, but she *had* to purge her feelings for the duke while his impression was emblazoned in her mind.

*Tonight I kissed the duke good-bye. Well, not really, but he asked me to dance, over and over, and I was dying to accept. If I had, we'd have danced until my*

*slippers wore out and sunlight shone through the
ballroom windows.*

*"I thought you had an assignation,"* she whispered between his ardent kisses.

*"I did."*

*"What happened?"*

*"I met you."*

*"Will your mistress be angry?"*

*"Does my future wife care?"*

"Charlotte!" Jane's voice jolted her from her pleasant
fantasy. She composed her thoughts and turned to face
the elegant figure in the door.

"Is everything all right, Jane?"

"Yes. Miss Peppertree is leaving with the girls. See
them off and then take a brandy with me and Chloe before Weed calls the carriage around to take you back.
Harriet, are you joining us?"

"No," Harriet replied. "I told you we were going on a
treasure hunt. Do you have another turban I can borrow?"

Charlotte arose, closed the desk, and hurried to the
door to join Jane. "Enjoy yourself, Harriet."

Harriet smiled at her distractedly from the dressing
table, where she had settled in an attempt to tame her
hair. "I'll ask him for a kiss to bring back to you," she
said under her breath.

"Don't you dare," Charlotte whispered, her cheeks
burning. "I'd never be able to show my face again if
you do."

"You could sneak out with us," Harriet said. "Miss
Peppertree would stand vigil."

"A treasure hunt does sound like fun," she said after
a thoughtful silence. "Except that games of that nature

often end up in misadventures. I can't afford to cause a scandal."

"Take a risk," Harriet said, her eyes dancing.

"What exactly are you hunting?"

"I haven't seen the entire list. I think Devon is supposed to find a silk parasol, and Chloe is hunting for a magistrate's nightshirt."

"The pursuit of a nightshirt will definitely get her in trouble," Charlotte predicted.

"Maybe I have it the wrong way around," Harriet said, her manner blithe. "Anyway, we are dividing into teams." She dropped her voice. "Someone suggested that we pay your duke a surprise visit at his house."

"He isn't mine. And you and I both know he has other ideas for the night." Charlotte frowned. She would rather not see him again than with a woman he had chosen to be his paid companion. "Besides I have class tomorrow. The older girls may have graduated, but the younger ones still need instruction."

"You aren't the only schoolmistress at the academy," Harriet reminded her.

"I know. But that doesn't give me an excuse to gallivant about London in the middle of the night."

"Who needs an excuse?"

"An unmarried lady. It's different for the rest of you."

Harriet sighed. "Where is the turban?" she asked Jane before she closed the door.

"Go through the closet and to my room," Jane replied, backing away. "Or ask my maid. I think you've talked me if not Charlotte into the treasure hunt."

Harriet turned from the mirror, giving Charlotte a look of sympathy. "I was only joking. I would never do anything to betray you."

"Charlotte!" Jane stuck her head inside the room again. "Hurry up, dear. Everyone is waiting."

"Harriet," Charlotte said. "Shut the door after you leave. And please, please, whatever you do, don't give away my secrets tonight. This is an evening for the older girls to celebrate their success, not to be embarrassed by their self-absorbed schoolmistress."

Harriet hadn't even heard the chambermaid enter the room. "The duke's carriage is waiting, Your Grace. He has asked that you hurry. There is quite a crush in the street."

Harriet stuffed an escaped curl into the turban that she had denuded of its feathers, and glanced around the untidy room. She hadn't found another turban into which she could tuck her defiant hair. She knew she was forgetting something. What had Charlotte said?

Fans. Shoes. Her reticule. Where in the world had she put her cloak? Was it buried under the other articles of clothing that had been tossed willy-nilly on the chaise?

Gloves? She spotted her cloak neatly draped over the chair by the desk where Charlotte had been—she gasped. The desk front had fallen open, which wasn't a surprise, considering it looked as if it were at least ninety years old. Her gaze lit on the diary that Charlotte had carelessly left where anyone could read its scandalous contents.

In fact, the chambermaid's stare was riveted to it as well.

Charlotte would be humiliated if anyone read her confessions. And Harriet had promised to protect her.

"The duke is waiting, Your Grace!" Weed announced imperiously from the door.

"I'm fetching my cloak, you old frog," she called back, and she did, whisking the diary into its folds with a talent for larceny that she had perfected in her tender years. It wasn't the ideal solution, but Harriet felt better carrying the diary with her than leaving it for the chambermaid to see. There was something off about that maid's face. She looked . . . sneaky. And familiar? Harriet wasn't sure.

Charlotte returned to the room with a sigh of relief. She had fulfilled her obligation to another class of girls and to the academy. Now she could savor her success. On any other night she might have sat at her desk and written to her heart's content, pouring out secret urges she could never have revealed to anyone.

She had been in love with words since her father had allowed her into his library, and she had decided with all her gangly being that the answers to life's questions would eventually be given her by those who had taken the time to share their thoughts on the written page.

Of course, no one would ever read what Charlotte had confessed in her collection of diaries. The story of her first heartbreak might have seemed tragically poetic when she was fifteen; it had devastated her to catch the boy she adored describing her to his friends as "that giantess with big teeth" the day she had caught him with another girl.

She felt only a twinge of pain when she thought of that past humiliation. She was tall, but she no longer slouched to hide her height in the presence of gentlemen. She had an overbite which didn't stop her from smiling. She would have been miserable marrying an insensitive clod like Phillip Moreland. Furthermore, she had seen enough suffering in the world to appreciate the blessings she'd been given rather than lamenting what she lacked.

Perhaps she would tear out the pages in her diary that referred to him. The demon memory of his unkindness had been exorcised from her heart in the safest manner offered to a lady in her position.

She walked over to her desk, frowning as she noticed that Harriet had left the room a mess. And that ... the diary was gone.

It couldn't be. She must have hidden it and forgotten where. She'd done it before. She opened the desk drawer and riffled through the sheets of paper and fashion plates, to no avail. Another drawer?

*Think*. The duke. The girls. The duke. Her *diary*. Her personal confessor.

She wouldn't panic. There had been so many distractions this night. This was what happened to ladies who drank champagne like it was water.

She looked across the room. She had been writing at the desk while Harriet fussed with her hair and complained about her turban. Slippers. Discarded mantles. The dress that Jane had tactfully suggested Charlotte wear instead of her simple white satin ball gown.

Perhaps Harriet had hidden it in the room before she left. Her heart gave a hopeful thump. Where was Jane? This was Jane's house. She might have come in and recognized the diary for the dangerous article it was. Charlotte could ask the staff or, better yet, Weed. He knew all, saw all, heard all.

She ransacked the room, her anxiety increasing by the second. She wouldn't give in to panic. The diary could not have disappeared by itself.

"I've lost it," she whispered. "Somebody help me. I need to stay— I've lost it!" she wailed at the top of her voice. "I've lost it! It's gone!"

She turned as the door flew open and Jane rushed toward her, her face white, Weed at her heels. "I was on the stairs," Jane said breathlessly. "I heard you screaming, but I hope I didn't hear what I thought I did. Weed, stand at the door and make sure no one comes near. It isn't true, is it, Charlotte?"

Charlotte nodded miserably. "I've lost it, Jane. It's gone."

"Gone?"

"Gone. Taken. Stolen. I don't know. It's gone."

Jane stared at her in horror. "Your virginity?" she whispered, running back to the door and slamming it with a force that nearly extinguished the candles on the wall. "Listen to me." She clasped Charlotte's hand. "It's bad enough that it happened, but there is no need to shout it across the whole of London. I assume it was the duke."

"*What?*"

"Was it in this room?" Jane demanded, her temper rising. "When? I thought he'd left. If you tell me that he sneaked back to ravish you while—"

"It isn't the duke." Charlotte pulled her hand from Jane's. "It's my diary. I left it on the desk and it has disappeared."

"Oh, my heavens," Jane said weakly, falling back onto the chaise. "For a moment I had murder in my heart. Don't ever scare me like that again."

"Get up, Jane, please. We have to find it."

"I'm sure we will. Someone is bound to come across it—"

"*No.*"

Jane sat right up. "Pull yourself together this instant. I highly doubt that anything you have written is going to ruin you. Let us be honest. What could you recount that would do more than raise an eyebrow here or there, if even that? You have lived a circumspect life."

"That's what you think."

Jane stared at her. "Are you saying that you confessed on paper some misdeed that could taint your name?"

Charlotte gave a soft groan of despair. "The contents of that diary could bring down me and the academy. Where is Harriet? I have to talk to her."

"She left some time ago in the Duke of Wynfield's carriage with a group of friends. They were all going to Mrs. Watson's to meet up with another party. Their amusements do not begin until midnight."

"I shall send Weed to find her straightaway. No, I'll ask Sir Daniel when he returns from the academy. Who better than a former Runner to find Harriet? He apprehended her a few times in the past, didn't he? In the meantime, you must remain calm."

"How is he going to find her? She's going on a treasure hunt. And how am I supposed to stay calm? You've never read my diary."

"Then let us hope no one else does." Jane paused to look at the door to the adjoining room. "Who is there?" she asked sharply.

"Just the chambermaid," a reedy voice called out. "I wondered if Miss Boscastle wanted me to straighten the room before she retired. I couldn't 'elp overhearing that there is a crisis in the 'ouse."

Jane rose abruptly. "I don't know your name. You must be new, and perhaps unaware that there are rules of employment. You do not listen at doors. Nor enter without permission."

"Yes, milady." She curtsied, retreating to the door.

"And there is no crisis in this house.

"She must be one of the maids Mrs. Barnes hired for the party," Jane said, closing the door on the retreating figure. "Perhaps I should have asked her and the chambermaids whether they set the diary aside."

"Or whether they stole it," Charlotte said bleakly.

"Stop acting as if the world hinged on your thoughts, Charlotte. Who would go to the trouble of stealing your diary when I have a fortune in jewels in my suite?"

*Chapter 5*

$\mathscr{G}$ideon was the last person to leave his carriage. He'd dropped off Harriet and her boisterous friends at a party in Grosvenor Square, ignoring their pleas for his company.

"You don't really want to spend the rest of the night in a courtesan's bed!" Devon, the soul of discretion, shouted across the street. "You want to be with us!"

Gideon shook his head, instructing his driver to proceed to the exclusive brothel on Bruton Street. He was gathering his hat and gloves when he noticed a bulky object squashed between the seams of the squabs. He hesitated before he pulled it loose.

What looked like a dead animal turned out to be Harriet's unflattering turban and a . . . a book? Odd thing to bring to a party.

He slid across the seat to catch the light and opened to the first page of what he realized was a diary. And it didn't belong to Harriet.

*Private*
*Property of a Gentlewoman—CEB*
*Please Do Not Read.*

He grinned. Could this possibly belong to Miss Boscastle? It ought to be a thrill a minute. How exciting a day in the life of a schoolmistress must be. So many pages filled with dainty, precise script. He could only imagine what an engaging tome of propriety she had written. Something along the lines of, *Lord Higgleston used his fish fork for his steak. Oh, horrors.*

"Your Grace!" a sultry voice called out from the bordello's upper window. "Have you turned bashful all of a sudden? Or would you like me to meet you down there?"

He quickly closed the diary and stepped out of the carriage, ignoring his footman's faint smile. There was nothing subtle about Gabrielle Spencer. She sold sex for a living and considered herself worth the price she demanded. Should he take her to his house for the first night?

They had promised each other nothing, except that tonight he would make a formal offer for her exclusive services as a courtesan and companion.

A footman escorted him up a private staircase, bypassing the other visitors, and into a candlelit antechamber. Too late Gideon realized that he had the diary tucked under his arm. There was nothing to be done for it.

"Gideon," Gabrielle said in welcome, wrapping her arms around his neck before the footman was through the door. She pressed herself against him with an uninhibited enthusiasm that might have aroused him if Charlotte Boscastle's diary had not stood between them like a brick.

She laughed, looking down, her large brown eyes luminous. "Did you bring that for me?" she asked, sliding her hand down his neck. "I promise you that I can perform any act in your book."

"You absolutely could not."

She smiled wickedly. "How much would you care to wager?"

"At the price you charge I doubt I can afford to wager at all."

She shook her head. "You are wound tightly tonight. What can I do to relax you?" She reached down for the diary. "Are there secret vices inside this book that I can indulge?"

He lifted her hand from the diary. There was no denying her appeal. "Some secrets aren't meant to be shared."

"Even between lovers?"

"Yes."

"I found the house I want," she said absently. "It's close to yours and convenient for entertaining. And I have a list of my shopping needs. May I show it to you before we settle down?"

"If you like."

"Wait here," she whispered. "I have bought the most wickedly designed garments you've ever seen. There's sherry on the sideboard already poured."

He helped himself to a drink and sat down on the tufted silk chaise, flipping idly through a few more pages of the diary until he saw his name in an entry.

He sat upright, choking on his swallow of sherry. His eyes watered as disbelievingly he read:

*The duke's kisses rendered me helpless. I could not bring myself to resist him. He would not have al-*

*lowed me to escape even if I'd summoned the*
*strength to do so. I was incoherent by the time he*
*dragged me down before the fire—*

*Hell's bells,* he thought. When had this happened, and
why had it slipped his memory?

He opened a page that was marked with a long-
stemmed red rose. The rose had been preserved, but the
ink on the page appeared to be relatively fresh.

Her most recent entry?

He strained to read in the poor light.

### The Ball

*Tonight the Duke of Wynfield asked me to dance.*
*I resisted, not only out of duty, but because I knew*
*that if he held me again, I would never be able to*
*hide my passion for him.*

*There was not another man at the ball who made*
*me tremble. When he approached me I had to re-*
*strain myself from . . .*

*Dammit.* He squinted. What an inconvenient place
for an ink smudge. He'd never know what Charlotte's
unrestrained self had wanted to do with him.

He glanced at the clock in the corner. Gabrielle was
taking her sweet time.

Was she making him wait to heighten his desire? To
let him know that until he paid her price she was still
available to other men?

He didn't like to wait.

He didn't particularly like visiting a brothel to for-
malize an association, either. Nor was he proud of him-

self for reading another woman's diary. He ought to stop. But he found he couldn't.

*He asked me to dance, but I offered him more.*
    *He accepted and made me his in every way a man can claim a woman.*

"My goodness," Gideon murmured, shaking his head. "Who would have guessed it? The schoolmistress has a hankering for more than academics."

*His in every way a man can claim a woman*? Did she understand what she had written? Was there more?

He quickly turned the page.

### The Truth

*He might have expected me to fall at his knees in gratitude for the small attention he paid me. If he did, he hid it well. It was obvious Devon put him up to this embarrassment, and it was obvious that he had to force himself to converse with me. His eye wandered around the room at every woman who passed.*

Gideon frowned. That was unflattering, as well as unfair. He'd only been pretending to look around the room so that he wouldn't seem to be staring at her. Sometimes a gentleman could not win.

He read on.

*And he's rude to the footmen, condescending. He orders them about and assumes his wishes will be*

*immediately fulfilled. He does not express his thanks
and talks in a condescending tone . . .*

He snapped the book shut.

Had he forgotten to thank the footmen for his champagne? How criminal of him. He treated his own staff well. Or did he?

Well, so much for telling both sides of a story. It seemed Miss Charlotte Boscastle couldn't decide whether he was the darling or the devil of her dreams.

He set aside the diary, trying not to look as it fell open again to a random page.

*The Past*

> *Betrayal and a Broken Heart*
> *His name was Phillip Moreland and he was the
> first boy I ever loved. I thought he loved me; he drove
> his cart to our house every Saturday afternoon, to see
> me, or so I believed, pouring tea. Then I caught him
> kissing the maid in the garden. . . . Actually, they ap-
> peared to be engaged in another act, the nature of
> which I am too much a lady to describe . . . Days later
> when I confronted him, he calmly defended himself
> by calling me "a giantess with big teeth."*

Gideon burst into laugher. If she was a giantess, the boy must have been a gargoyle.

Interesting woman. Heaven help her if this diary fell into another's hands.

He'd try to put her out of his mind for the rest of the night.

And the first thing in the morning he would have his butler return it to her with a dozen red roses and his wishes for an eventful, if invented, life.

If there were other inflammatory entries in the diary, and he felt certain there were, they hadn't been meant for anyone to see. An honorable man wouldn't read a lady's secrets. A scoundrel would—and use them to his advantage.

She was infatuated with him, and he pitied her for that. What would she think if she knew he had been reading her memories in a house of Venus?

He didn't want her to know.

As a friend of her family, he was obligated to spare Charlotte any embarrassment. Not that he was to blame for her imagination or Harriet's carelessness.

"Gideon," a provocative voice said above him. "I've been standing here forever. I had no idea that you would prefer reading over me."

Neither had he.

She crossed the room to the couch, gently descending onto his lap and slipping her fingers inside his neck cloth. In her other hand she held a list of items to be bought that would probably bankrupt him. "Why do I feel that I don't have your full attention?"

"I—"

"It's that book," she said with a pout. "You haven't taken your eyes off it all night. I'm going to throw it out the window."

"No." He sat up. She reached down. "Leave the damned thing alone."

"Why don't we burn it and make love in front of the fire?"

"I'm not burning a book."

"It's the book or me." She slid out of his lap.

He smiled. "That is a very easy choice."

She waved her list under his nose. "I'm happy to hear it. I don't like being ignored."

He stood abruptly. "I don't like ultimatums." And he turned before she could find her voice, the diary under his coat once more, the attraction he felt for Gabrielle dying an unmourned death.

There was a deeper passion between the pages of Charlotte Boscastle's diary than he would find in this house.

Charlotte whirled around from the window and flew across the room to embrace Harriet. "Thank goodness you're here. I've been frantic for you to return."

"I rushed back as soon as I was given your message. What in the world is wrong?"

"Please tell me you put my diary in a safe place. Please."

"All right. I put the diary in a safe place."

"Where?" Charlotte asked, nearly collapsing in relief.

Harriet frowned as if she were reviewing the evening's events in her mind. "We were in this room when you were writing at the desk."

"Yes," Charlotte said. "And . . . ?"

Harriet looked blank.

"And what, for the love of creation?" Charlotte demanded, flinging her hand in the air. "What happened to the diary?"

The color drained from Harriet's cheeks. "Oh, God. I hid it in my cloak and took it with me. I thought you'd gone off with the girls; the front of the desk had dropped open, and I was afraid it would fall into the wrong hands."

"But it didn't," Charlotte said. "Because you put it in a safe place."

"I'll make it up to you."

"Where is it?" Charlotte asked through her teeth.

Harriet winced. "I left it in the duke's carriage."

"The duke being your husband, Griffin, I hope and pray?" Charlotte said, giving Harriet an encouraging smile.

Harriet shook her head. "My husband is in Brighton. I'm talking about the other duke. The one who's made you lose your wits."

Charlotte looked aghast. "Not Wynfield?"

"I'll lie," Harriet said quickly. "I'll swear it was my diary. I'll throw myself at the duke's mercy."

"What if he reads it before we find him?" Charlotte asked, aghast at the thought. "Do we even know where we can find him?"

Harriet hesitated. "He was going to meet his new mistress at Mrs. Watson's house the last I saw of him."

"What have I done, Harriet?" Charlotte whispered. "What demonic power overcame me that I turned tender encounters into torrid half-truths? Why was I not content to *tell* the truth? Why, you ask?"

"Well, I really don't."

"Because I am a Boscastle, after all, and passion is like a poison in my blood that, despite all efforts to the contrary, makes itself known."

"You've lost a diary, Charlotte. It's not as if you gave birth to a royal heir and forgot where you put him."

"You don't have a notion of what I've written. What if he reads it?"

"Your stories are sweet and charming."

"The diary is different."

Harriet scoffed. "What man, really, would choose reading a lovesick lady's journal over a courtesan's company?"

"I have to get it back tonight. He can't read it."

"Then I will have to help you."

"How?"

"We'll break into his house. He won't even know we were there."

## Chapter 6

*N*ick Rydell was a professional burglar and street thug who operated his business from St. Giles. His name carried weight in the underworld, and he was proud of the crimes he committed. Until tonight. He didn't know what had come over him when the lady sitting across from him in her squeaky carriage had offered him a job and he'd accepted. Spite, that was what had gotten him going. He'd been thinking like a girl.

His client looked as if she were on her way to a tea party in Bedlam, wearing a hat that reached the carriage roof and thinking herself all stylish, he was sure. He supposed her coin was as good as anyone else's. Still, he'd have turned down the lay outright if Lady Clippers, or Clipstone, or whatever the hell her name was, hadn't confessed that she knew of Nick through his previous association with his former partner. Harriet Hoity-Toity. The name poisoned his blood like bad gin. He hated how it made him feel. But that didn't stop him from craving another taste of it.

"Why didn't you ask 'arriet to do the job if you and she are such good friends?" he said, surveying her hat through one half-opened eye. The damned thing looked like a chimney with smoke pouring out of the top.

"That person and I are *not* friends. It is an insult to decency that she has ascended in society." She shook her little fist in his face. "It's an outrage that I have been re-duced to consorting with convicts as a means to justice. You promised me that I would have that diary in my possession at the end of the ball."

He glanced at the younger woman in the droopy maid's cap who sat slumped next to the miserable bat; Millie was his current lover, and he ought to have known that she wasn't quick enough on her feet to send into a fancy mansion. "I 'eard. I don't need a sermon to apprise me of the situation."

"The situation?" she said, her voice quavering. "This is much more than a situation."

"Calm down, lady. Let's go over it one more time. Millie missed a chance to collect a certain object that, for reasons that are none of my never mind, you wish to acquire."

Lady Clipstone muttered under her breath.

"My old friend the duchess appears to be in possession of this object," Nick continued. "And the duchess was last seen in the Duke of Wynfield's carriage, which was wit-nessed coming and going from a famous place of pleasure."

"It was the footman who threw me off," Millie said from out of nowhere. "And then 'arriet and that Lady Jane."

"Millie," he chided, leaning forward. "I'll take care of this."

"What do you intend to do?" Lady Clipstone inquired, shrinking into the corner as if he were an infectious agent.

"That's easy," he said. "I'm gonna track down my old business partner and dig straight to the root of this matter. What is at the root of this, by the way?"

"Revenge," Lady Clipstone said.

"Revenge? No? Between you and 'arriet?"

"Not Harriet, you . . ." She composed herself. "It is between me and Harriet's mentor."

"And this mentor wrote the diary?"

"No, no."

"Well, then, who did and what's it to you?"

Lady Clipstone's face pinched. "Why should I trust you with my reasons?"

He laughed. "Lady, you shoulda asked yourself that question before you commissioned me for this crime."

She sighed. "I have no one else to enlist. Do you want to know why?"

Nick winked at Millie. Information was always useful, and oftentimes it came in handy for a little game known as blackmail. "Tell me," he said somberly. "If you've been mistreated I might be able to avenge you.

"I don't want anyone's throat slit."

"Course you don't. That would be murder."

"And that costs a fortune," Millie said.

Lady Clipstone wavered. He waited.

"I have no husband," she said.

He shook his head in sympathy.

"That . . . that pretender of pretense stole him from me!"

"You poor thing," Millie said, actually sounding as if she understood.

Lady Clipstone gave a sniff. "You have no idea how important that diary is to me."

He nodded agreeably. The silly bat wasn't bad-looking when she closed her trap. "I do understand, madam," he lied, feeling a passing twinge of curiosity about the contents of the diary. "This is a delicate matter."

"You see," Lady Clipstone explained, twisting her hands over and over until Nick wanted to smack her. "Charlotte's cousin, Emma Boscastle, stole my one true love from me when we were in boarding school together."

Nick sat up. "Your lover was another woman?"

"No, you half— No. Viscount Lyons lived nearby at our school. I saw him first, and then he saw Emma."

"Who's Emma?" Millie asked.

"She is the lady who founded the academy," Lady Clipstone said bitterly. "She was my best friend. We planned to open a school for young ladies together. And now look how things have turned out for me."

"What did this viscount of vice 'ave that made both of you into enemies?" Nick asked, frowning as if he gave a toss.

"Manners," she snapped. "But he's dead now."

"That's good," Millie said.

Lady Clipstone glowered at her. "No. It isn't. Emma went on to marry a duke. And what do I have?"

Nick blew out a breath. "Revenge?"

"Not yet. No. All I have is a struggling academy and a useless lummox of a nephew who sprawls across my receiving couch in a food-stained shirt and wrinkled trousers, begging me to give him a few pounds, which I do to get rid of him."

"Bloodsucker," Nick said. "I know the type. But what I don't know is 'ow you came to think this diary makes a damn bit of difference, if you'll pardon the *parlez-vous*."

"I'm clever. Like you."

Nick nodded. "I got that right off."

"One of Emma's students defected. She told of the shocking liberties taken at her academy. She thought it might be recorded in Charlotte Boscastle's diary. Emma had trained Charlotte to assume the responsibility for the academy before she left. And she's always seen writing in that confounded diary."

"Liberties? Of what nature, may I be so brash as to inquire?"

"Secrets of sexual misbehavior that would paint the school in shame."

He blinked. "Secrets, eh?"

She lifted the curtain, looking nervous. "Wicked things," she whispered. "Improper. The Boscastles are worshiped like demigods. It seems the lower they stoop, the higher they rise in social estimation."

Nick nodded. He supposed he could blame them for taking Harriet from him.

"I want to bring the academy to ruin!" she cried in a quavering voice. "I'm a desperate woman. That diary is the key to it all."

"I see that."

"They steal pupils from my door every month. I don't know how much longer I can make a living. Do you understand how unfair it is that they prosper while I know their sins and must hold my tongue?"

"Let me take care of this," Nick said.

Three hours later he penned a message and had one of his boys take it to her.

*The price has gone up due to the dangerous nature of the job. I am making a reappraisal of the matter and will contact you at our leisure.*

*Fond regards,*
*N. Rydell*

# Chapter 7

Old habits died hard. The Duchess of Glenmorgan appeared to be in her element as she plotted out how she and Charlotte would break into the duke's house to retrieve the diary. To her credit Harriet had accepted full responsibility for the part she had played in the evening's debacle.

"If I weren't desperate," Charlotte said as she stared at Harriet across the swaying carriage, "I would never have agreed to this. Jane will be furious."

"We'll be home before Jane even knows we're missing."

"How do you know?"

Harriet sighed. "I've broken into more houses than you have attended teas. Charlotte?"

"What?"

"Trust me," she said, the two words now sending a chill of foreboding down Charlotte's back, when earlier they had reassured her.

"What choice do I have?"

"None."

"What if he didn't take the diary into the house? What if it isn't there or in the carriage?"

"I need to concentrate," Harriet said. "Would you please stop worrying?"

"How can I help it? It's bad enough that you instructed your coachman to drive to Mrs. Watson's house to make sure the duke was still inside. Imagine being caught, two ladies of our position, sneaking around a brothel."

"I did work there once," Harriet murmured, closing her eyes.

"I'll be mortified if anyone recognized us."

"Perhaps you should have stayed behind the curtains instead of peeking out at the place."

"The house certainly does a brisk business," Charlotte said. "I lost count of the gentlemen who arrived in the short time we circled 'round."

"One of those gentlemen is you-know-who."

"Don't remind me." She had already tortured herself with the thought. It wasn't difficult to picture him surrounded by women eager to satisfy his every disgraceful whim.

"We're in Belgravia," Harriet said, opening her eyes.

"How can you tell?"

"The sound of the wheels on the cobbles." Harriet frowned at her. "If you can't stay calm, then stay in the carriage."

"No," Charlotte said resolutely. "That isn't fair."

Twenty minutes later Charlotte wished she could change her mind. In all her secret yearnings she hadn't once imagined that she would be skulking behind the shrubbery to break into Gideon's house. A lady was never to pay a call on a gentleman unless she wished to be considered fast.

Harriet pulled her skirt free from a thorn-laden branch. "He would have to plant rosebushes right under the window."

"It seems a reasonable place to plant them," Charlotte replied, biting her thumb.

"Not when you climb through them in a gauze ball gown."

"I'm sure the duke's gardener didn't grow them there to ruin your wardrobe."

"No chattering. Someone could be listening."

Charlotte stared past the dark rows of trees in the garden. "From where?"

"From the servants' quarters. Or the house next door. There's a window looking down at us. And don't answer if someone asks who goes there. Just hoist yourself over the sill and close the window. Pass me the chisel, please."

Charlotte reached into Harriet's beaded reticule. "I don't believe this."

"What?"

" 'Pass me the chisel, please.' We were sitting at the breakfast table only this morning and you asked me to pass the sugar tongs. This is housebreaking, Harriet."

"Well, it isn't a night at the opera. Did you find it yet?"

"No. Hold my fan for a moment."

"Why on earth did you bring a fan?"

"I feel naked without it. Here." She handed Harriet the tool. "How long do you think the duke will be gone?"

"This is his first official night with his mistress. I don't think he'll come home before dawn. I saw her at a rout once. She's very beautiful. Small and dark." Harriet worked the chisel under the windowsill. "There. You go in first."

Once they had climbed into the kitchen, they waited a few more minutes before Harriet repeated the instructions she'd given Charlotte in the carriage. "We'll start upstairs first. If he came home to change, he would have done so in his bedroom. You go there. I'll search the upstairs drawing room."

"What if we're caught?"

"Make up something. Say you were sleepwalking."

"All the way from Park Lane?"

"Say that we . . . we're on the treasure hunt and that we broke up into groups after he left."

"A treasure hunt."

"Yes. He knows it was planned earlier. The beau monde is always off on one escapade or another. Haven't you ever done anything adventurous?"

"Only in my imagination."

"Well, here's your chance to be a little daring."

Charlotte didn't move.

"You're as white as chalk," Harriet whispered. "If you can't be useful, then do us both a favor and sit in a chair until I'm finished."

"Useful? I feel like I'm made of iron. I can't breathe properly, and my legs are too heavy to lift. I think I'm losing the sensation in all my limbs. I don't think I have the temperament to make a good criminal."

"There's no crime in taking back what belongs to you."

"I hope the duke sees it that way."

"I hope he doesn't see us at all."

*Chapter 8*

$\mathcal{G}$ideon had been on edge the entire evening. First there had been the challenging encounter with Miss Boscastle at the ball. Now he couldn't help wondering what would have happened between them if he'd read her diary first. He might not have teased her unmercifully if he had known she secretly desired him.

Devon would have killed him if he'd suggested anything impolite to her. Of course, Devon had not read his cousin's diary. The damned thing had ruined Gideon's chance for a gratifying night. Furthermore, he had to go about the complicated business of finding another mistress.

He felt his nerves prickle as he entered the house. The servants had been advised to retire early in case he brought Gabrielle home. The only light came from the coals glowing in the grate in his study. He walked past the open door and stood at the bottom of the stairs.

Just when he thought he was imagining things, he heard the creak of his wardrobe door.

There was a rustle of ... it might have been the rustle of bedcovers being turned down. Did he have a surprise waiting? Could Gabrielle have rushed here before him to make amends? Just in case he was wrong, he returned to the entry hall and drew his walking stick from the stand. By the time he reached his bedroom door, he realized that he would not have to subdue this intruder with a sword stick. It was Gabrielle, making herself quite at home.

A swat across the rump should get her attention.

He rested his shoulder against the doorjamb and waited for her to notice him. Her arse rose in the air at an intriguing angle, one that afforded him a view of several inches of petticoat and cotton-stockinged calves. He frowned. Plain white stockings. Unadorned white gown.

How had she had time to change her clothes and sneak into the house before he did?

In fact, she had not only changed her clothes. She had altered her entire appearance—height, hair color, her face—

*Her* face.

*Good heavens.* It was the schoolmistress, searching through his drawers, for what he could only guess: his pocket watch, cash, old love letters?

He retracted the sword blade into the walking stick. "Excuse me. Would it help if I lit a lamp behind you? I wouldn't want you to strain your"—he looked up from the lower portion of her body—"eyes."

She went still, like a small animal suddenly aware it has been marked by a predator. Carefully she lifted her hands from the drawer and straightened, her eyes wide and anxious.

His gaze traveled over her. "Miss Boscastle. What an unexpected pleasure."

"Your Grace?" she said, as if they were sitting down to tea.

He shook his head in disbelief. "What on earth are you doing in my bedchamber?"

The look of shock on her face must have mirrored his. "I'm . . . I'm"—she glanced around, studying the bed, his washstand, the chair by the window—"sleepwalking."

"*Sleepwalking?*"

She nodded slowly.

"Sleepwalking?" he said again, pushing off the doorjamb. "You mean for me to believe that you walked from the academy to my house, and climbed the stairs to my bedroom *asleep?*"

"Yes."

"You aren't sleeping now, are you?"

"I don't think so."

He swore softly. "Do I look like the type of man who believes in mesmerism or messages from the otherworld that come to us while we sleep?"

"No." She sighed. "You do not."

"It will be far easier on us both if you admit why you are really here."

She glanced at the door, as if she had the slightest hope of escaping without giving him an answer.

"You *are* in my house. When I find a woman in my bedchamber, I assume she's offering herself for pleasure."

"The truth is that . . ."

"Please. Say it."

". . . that I'm on a treasure hunt. The graduation ball went so well tonight, I thought I deserved a little fun, and so Harriet and I joined another group of friends, and here I am."

"A treasure hunt." His brow rose. "For something in my house? Why *my* house? It *had* to be my house?"

"Yes." She nodded.

"And the reason is?"

"Because . . . because the item I'm requested to collect is a duke's kiss. And since Harriet's husband is in Brighton, you were the nearest duke I know."

Gideon slowly removed his gloves and hat. He didn't know how he managed to keep a straight face. He wondered again whether he was the victim of a prank. Hadn't Devon been involved in the treasure hunt, too? But would Devon allow his cousin to be caught in a rakehell's room?

"I could give you more than a kiss," he said, throwing his gloves and hat on the bed.

She shook her head. "That isn't necessary."

He walked around her. "And you could give me the truth."

Charlotte felt the tension between them slowly rising, invisible, heated, as insidious as smoke. He studied her, his expression dark and indecipherable.

"Don't you know what happens to young women who dare to enter a duke's lair?" he asked with a shadowed smile that warned her he was well aware of the answer.

"If you knew anything about the females in my family, you wouldn't be concerned. Duke and dragon tamers, every single one of us."

His smile deepened. "If you knew what was running through my mind right now, you would realize that your family history doesn't protect you at all. At least, not while we are alone."

Her lips parted. "Are you threatening to seduce me?"

"I might be. If everyone else is on a treasure hunt to-night, why not me?"

She tried to take a breath. The air had caught fire. "You could have played if you liked, I'm sure. It was my understanding that you had other plans."

"I would have canceled them if I'd realized you'd be waiting for me in my bedroom. You should have given me a hint at the ball."

"Your bedroom," she whispered. "It was a very bad choice." Which made her wonder what had happened to his mistress. He didn't appear to be in any hurry to remove Charlotte from the house. And he didn't act like a man who was expecting a harlot to drop in at any moment.

"I think I would like to go on a treasure hunt, too," he said in a pensive voice. "One that involves only two peo-ple," he added.

"That doesn't sound like much of a party."

His dark eyes danced. "It is if both people intend to play."

Charlotte held her breath as he placed his large hand on her shoulder, moving her toward the bed. Where was Harriet? What if one of the servants had apprehended her?

"This is really accommodating of you, Charlotte." He bent his head to her neck. "How did you guess that I needed a woman in my bed tonight?"

Harriet had searched in all the obvious places—she de-cided that the diary wasn't in the house. Why would a man like Wynfield bother hiding it in the first place?

She walked down the stairs in thoughtful silence. The

duke seemed capable of being an arrogant bastard, as all gentlemen in lofty positions could be. But he was a man's man. He'd attended the ball to please the Boscastles, and then he had gone to Mrs. Watson's to please himself.

Harriet closed her eyes as she reached the bottom of the stairs. She could hear Charlotte in the bedroom, her search apparently as fruitless as Harriet's had been. She pictured the duke sitting across from her in his carriage. She'd concealed the diary inside her cloak. And then she had completely forgotten it.

That was the last time she had seen the diary.

In the carriage. Which meant that she would have to wait until he came home. Perhaps she could appeal to his higher instincts, although a man who had just come from a house of Venus wasn't liable to be in a moral mood. She could hide in the carriage house and check when he went inside. But she couldn't hide with Charlotte, who caved at the first sign of danger.

Not that this was a dangerous venture compared to Harriet's past larks. In fact, she would search the duke's study and then tell Charlotte that the best solution was to simply explain to Gideon what had happened. And hope that he hadn't disposed of the diary without realizing what it was.

Charlotte would be mortified, but she would live through it. She had a good head on her shoulders. She was stronger than she realized. It was a pity, in a way, that the duke wasn't drawn to a lady like her. In Harriet's mind they made a lovely couple.


Nick Rydell had worked the streets of Mayfair ever since he could remember, but his proudest moments of thievery had been training Harriet Gardner and her half brothers to commit larceny. He and the boys still collaborated from time to time and reminisced about their crimes and how it wasn't the same without Harriet. That girl had been born to housebreak. She could see like a cat in the dark. She could walk like a whisper through a house full of people, pinching all the silver, and no one would notice until the morning.

Millie was jealous of her, because Nick had made no secret of the fact that she would never be the born criminal that Harriet had been. "You can't blame 'er for givin' it all up, Nick. The rats, the police, the stench of the gutters, to marry a duke. You'd 'ave married 'im yourself if you'd been asked."

Tonight he fancied Harriet's company; he missed her talent for housebreaking, her rude mouth, and her blazing red hair. He had always been able to impress the other girls in St. Giles. But not Harry.

He'd taken a risk and called out a favor from a cabdriver who owed him. Then he'd waited across the street from the duke's residence for him to come home.

He waited so long that he deplored the waste of a night's work. Still, while he'd been waiting he'd taken the opportunity to burglarize the town house straight opposite the duke's.

To his delight he'd recognized Harriet's small carriage lurching to a halt at the corner of the fancy square where the duke lived.

Nick scaled the garden wall, taking out a spyglass from his jacket to watch Harriet and her fair-haired companion tiptoe through the duke's back gate.

Did Harriet have a late-night assignation with the duke? Wasn't the one she'd married enough to please her? And who was that fetching lady who'd accompanied her in Harriet's carriage?

They were up to something, and Nick sensed an interesting motive behind their mischief. Before he could investigate, the duke's carriage appeared at the corner and rolled into the gated carriage house.

Nick crossed the street and slipped through the gate. He opened the carriage door and grabbed the diary before the coachman had come back to lock up for the night.

Nick could have left it at that.

Instead, he returned to the garden wall and trained his spyglass on the upper rooms of the duke's residence. He thought he could make out one of the women flitting behind the curtains.

Anticipation surged in his blood.

God love them.

They must be looking for the diary, too.

And here it was, resting right up against Nick's black heart.

Had he beaten Harriet to the kill? There had to be more to this quarrel between two ladies. He'd be a fool to let the diary out of his tender keeping before he had estimated its worth. To hell with Lady Clipstone; if Harriet wanted it, the diary was invaluable.

What price could a man put on revenge?

# Chapter 9

The duke did not need to lure Charlotte to his bed. She would collapse across it if he kept on nuzzling her neck. His sensuality swept away reason and replaced it with irrational desire. For a year she had craved his touch. "Why don't you tell me the truth?" he whispered, his arm locking around her waist. "I might be able to help you."

"Your actions say otherwise."

"In truth." He lifted his head, his hard stare offering her no escape. "You are not here on a treasure hunt, are you?"

She drew a breath. "No. I'm not. I came here because you have my diary, and I would like it back, please. *Please.*"

His expression did not soften. She hoped he would understand. She hoped he wouldn't notice the shambles she'd made of his wardrobe drawers, or that she'd found what she thought were French letters tucked between a pack of playing cards and a pair of dove gray gloves.

But more than anything she hoped that he had her diary in his possession but hadn't read it.

His deep voice caressed her. "Come downstairs to my study, Charlotte. I find it impossible to think clearly with you so close to my bed. And, yes, I have your diary."

She was afraid to ask whether he'd read it. She felt giddy with relief that at least it wasn't lost. He led her to his darkened study. If Harriet had searched the room, she hadn't left any visible sign of her presence.

But there also weren't any signs of Harriet in the house. Where had she gone?

"Sit down on the sofa, Charlotte," the duke said. "I assume you don't mind if I use your first name." He paused, waiting for her to be seated. "Considering that we appear to know each other so well, it only seems appropriate."

"You read my diary . . . How humiliating! *How could you?*"

"It wasn't easy, believe me. It is to your credit, however, that it claimed all my attention."

"I don't think I deserve credit for what I've done."

"Or written?" He sat beside her.

She lowered her fan to her lap.

"Well?" he said, giving her an expectant look.

Charlotte raised her gaze to his. "Well, what?"

"I believe that the treasure hunt called for a duke's kiss."

"Oh, that." She twirled her fan in a bleak wave. "I made it up. I'm not really on a hunt."

"I know." He raised his hand. His fingers glided down her face, warm, knowing, in no hurry. "But I am, and I will claim my kiss."

She swallowed a gasp. His other hand curled around her nape. She felt her hair spill loose as he pulled her pins that held its heavy weight in a knot. The words that had come so easily when she wrote of him now abandoned her. Or she abandoned herself.

She knew only that when he lowered his head and kissed her, her desire for him was no playful dream. It was desperation. It was undeniable need. She closed her eyes, the better to surrender to him. His mouth coaxed a response. Her lips parted, and his kiss led her into darkness, lured her toward . . . what? She didn't know. But he did. Her head fell back against his hand. His tongue delved into her mouth and he kissed her until shivering pleasure seeped into her bones. Her pulse soared. Her blood roared. She drifted, weightless, into her first encounter with decadence.

"Is this what you wanted?" he asked, his voice harsh, his mouth a maddening breath from hers.

"I— Yes . . ."

"But I want more."

He pressed her back, her shoulder sinking between the cushions. For a moment he didn't move. His hooded eyes claimed victory, branded her with heat too intense to bear. She felt it race through her veins and to her fingertips.

He bent over her, his body hard, aroused, every inch a hot-blooded male. He brought his hand up slowly to sculpt the shape of her breasts. A sweet pain pierced her. She arched her back.

"I could carry you back upstairs to my bedroom—"

"*No.* I can't. You can't."

A merciless smile spread across his shadowed face. His hand stroked upward to the front of her gown.

"We can't do this," she whispered, lifting her hand to his chest.

"Why not?" he asked softly. "We did it in your diary, which implies consent, if not an engraved invitation. Of course, I was not consulted. But I can't imagine I would have denied you if you'd asked."

"I didn't break into your house to strike up a liaison," she said indignantly, staring up into his sardonic face.

"But you did break in, and you're in my arms. Do you know that property is nine points of the law?"

"Property?" she said, pushing herself upright.

"Would you like a brandy?"

"Yes," she said, even though brandy usually went right to her head.

"I think I could use one myself."


Harriet stood at the door to the study, unable to believe her eyes. She recognized the duke right away. But who was the long-haired lady he was leaning over and kissing with such wanton disregard that neither of them knew they had an audience?

*Oh, God. Charlotte.* It couldn't be. Yet it had to be.

She backed away.

What should she do?

She couldn't let Charlotte be ruined.

But then again, she couldn't let her lose the man she desired. And Wynfield obviously desired her, although how a harmless fancy had become a ruinous interlude the moment Harriet turned her back was a mystery to be pondered later.

Here she'd been afraid that Charlotte had accidentally locked herself in a closet, when she'd actually been locked in the duke's embrace, acting out one of the alleged entries in the diary that had started this affair.

She looked so defenseless sitting on that sofa clutching her fan that Gideon's protective instincts overpowered his basic nature. He felt like a bastard for calling her bluff. "How long have you been keeping your diary?"

"Diaries. Ever since I learned to write."

He took a swallow of brandy. "Were you always so inventive?"

"I embellished the truth in a few places. I wanted to write my life as a fairy tale. I never intended for anyone else to read it. It's not all fabricated."

"Fabricated? Embellished? My angel of mischief, not even the names were changed to protect the guilty. But *I* have to admit I'm curious—how long have we been engaged in this affair?"

"A year," she whispered, sighing over the top of her fan.

His eyebrows shot up. "All that time and you never told me? Where exactly did it start?"

"At a circulating library," she confessed with a smile.

He smiled back and pried the empty glass from her hand. "I wish I'd known. At the very least I would have sent you flowers to commemorate our anniversary."

She laughed, and so did he. He had to admit this was a unique predicament, and he was flattered that she had found him desirable.

"You didn't even know I existed until this evening, and then it took Devon to push you in my direction."

"You're wrong. I remember seeing you once at the emporium. I noticed you, and if I'd had a notion that you had such a passionate nature, I would have *insisted* we dance at the ball."

"I poured my foolish heart into that diary."

"If it's any comfort, I found what I read illuminating."

She lowered her head. "Humiliating is what you mean. Will you tell anyone?"

"Why should I?" He took a drink of his brandy. "It's our affair."

"Where did you leave the diary?"

"In my carriage."

"How much did you read?" she asked quietly.

He put their glasses on the table. "Enough that I was flattered and insulted in turns. Enough that I'm not sure I know myself whether I'm a devil or a saint."

"I'm not sure that I want to be in your company when enlightenment dawns."

"Why not? It was your observations that drew my attention to this moral dilemma."

"But you made an arrangement tonight."

"I almost made an arrangement. No papers have been signed. I'm a free man, in any event."

She looked up, her blue eyes clouded with rue. "I'm too ashamed to offer any excuses."

He reached out and traced his thumb across her cheekbone. "There's no need to be embarrassed. I can assure you that I never apologize for my imprudences."

"Imprudent," she said, sighing. "That describes my—"

He cut her off, lifting his hand from her face. "Hush a moment."

"What is it?"

"A carriage stopping outside."

She blinked. "It must be Harriet."

"How could it be Harriet?"

She rose, searching for the pins he'd pulled out of her hair. "She brought me here. I told you."

"No, you didn't," he said, staring at the row of white satin buttons on the back of her gown. "What if she'd seen us?"

"We wouldn't have heard the end of it."

He turned his head. "Harriet must have brought a few friends along. I hear voices."

Charlotte ran to the window and gasped. "Oh, no."

And Gideon didn't even bother to ask her what was wrong. He listened to the thunderous knocking at the front door; he knew that the evening held another surprise in store and it would not be as pleasant as finding Charlotte Boscastle in his bedchamber.

# Chapter 10

$\mathscr{G}$ideon didn't know at what point in the evening he'd sensed that nothing would ever be the same in his life again. Had it been at the ball? At Mrs. Watson's? Or in his bedroom with Charlotte? He had woken up alone that morning with the assumption he would end up in bed with Gabrielle.

Who could have predicted what had happened in the hours between?

The instant he recognized Lords Devon and Heath Boscastle frozen in the doorway, a small group of friends surging behind them, he realized that his life *was* about to change, but not in a particularly thrilling way. He *would* awaken every morning in the years ahead with a mistress—a schoolmistress, that was. The lady who was cowering behind him while trying to pin up her hair and making the whole situation look worse than it really was would likely become his wife. He could see no escape from the situation that had rapidly spun out of control.

He turned slowly to Charlotte and met her gaze. "Do not say a word. I will deal with this."

"We're doomed," she whispered.

His thoughts exactly.

The door flew open. Gideon looked straight at Devon, the tallest of the bunch, his friendly grin vanishing when he realized Charlotte was in the room. Pushing up behind Devon were his older brothers Heath and Drake, murder in their eyes. And there were two women, only one he knew, and another lady and gentleman close behind them.

"This is supposed to be a treasure hunt," Jane said with a strained smile. "How bad of you to start without us, Your Grace. Or have you hunted your quarry for the night?"

"Madam," he said, positioning himself between Charlotte and the marchioness, whose green eyes glittered with anger. "This isn't what it appears to be."

She lowered her voice. "Perhaps you are not entirely at fault, but my husband will not care. *This* is an insult. If I were a man, I would call you out for the damage you've done to her reputation."

Drake Boscastle deftly stepped around her. "Well, I am a man, and I don't mind murdering him. How could you bring her here without a chaperone?"

"I do have a chaperone," Charlotte said quickly. "Harriet drove me here, in fact."

Drake stared around the room. "Then where is she? I don't see her."

"I have no idea," Charlotte said. "We were in the duke's bedroom and we separated."

"In his bedroom?" Drake's hand shot out to grab

Gideon's neck cloth, but Charlotte jumped between them to intercept the attack.

"I did ask you not to say anything," Gideon said softly.

"Aren't you the generous protector?" Jane said. "Weren't you supposed to meet your new mistress at Audrey's tonight?"

Devon shoved forward and pulled Charlotte out of his way. "How could you do this to me?" he demanded of Gideon.

"I was wondering the same thing about you," he replied.

Devon snorted, pulling off his cloak. "Did you plan this before I spoke to you?"

"Plan what? My self-destruction at a graduation ball?"

"Where is Harriet?" Jane asked, staring at the two empty brandy glasses on the table. "Charlotte, why didn't you come to me before committing this folly?"

Gideon restrained the urge to throw everyone except Charlotte into the street and let them argue all night long. His butler, Shelby, was trying to squeeze through the room, his passage blocked, his voice rising in woeful apology.

"I swear I tried to stop them, Your Grace. I swear I did. But they insisted it was a game, and that you wouldn't mind."

"Well, I do mind," Gideon said, looking disgruntled.

Devon looked as if he wanted to kill him, and Gideon would have been glad for the chance to do the same to him. He knew he looked as guilty as hell. What was done was done. All the excuses in the world wouldn't change the outcome.

"I didn't invite Miss Boscastle here."

"Did you invite Harriet?" Jane inquired archly.

He ignored her.

Devon shook his head in disappointment. "I asked you to flatter her with your attention for a few moments, not the entire night. And I didn't mean this sort of flattery, as you damn well know."

"I didn't start this," Gideon said tersely, trying to use the truth as his defense. There were only two feasible solutions to satisfy honor. He'd either kill or be killed in a duel. Or . . . A second possibility loomed off again in the distance, which was death of a different order: He could propose marriage rather than be bullied into it. Marriage.

To a schoolmistress. Granted, she defied the prim reserve that one associated with her profession. Granted, her hidden fire was a fascinating element he had not expected to arouse. But he hadn't intended to enter another marriage at this point in his life.

He cut Charlotte a concerned glance. She looked like a watercolor lady again. It didn't matter that her appearance was deceptive. He couldn't expose her in front of all these people by explaining the truth.

What would her family and friends think if he announced that he'd found her exploring a drawer that held his French letters? The gossips wouldn't care that she was looking for what was hers. Or that he was particular about where he put his rod.

Devon's wife, Jocelyn, had waddled into the room to put a restraining hand on his arm. The glare she sent Gideon made him feel like a great villain.

Then he heard Devon mutter, "I shall never forgive myself for this."

Charlotte raised her voice, not shy or reserved at all. "That makes two of us, Devon Boscastle. It wasn't enough for you to disgrace yourself as the Kissing Bandit *and* force poor Jocelyn to marry you. You had to poke your nose in my business and ruin *my* life as well."

The duke turned to Devon with a dark expression. "I did ask you to be quiet, Charlotte. Let me take care of this."

"No," Devon said, handing his cloak to his wife. "We've fought each other plenty of times at the fencing salon. Why don't we settle our differences with another match?"

There was time only to nudge Charlotte back toward the sofa before he swung around to defend himself. Gideon understood why Devon was enraged; given a chance he could explain this predicament when the young hothead was ready to listen to reason.

But for now a pair of great fists were flying at him, right and left. He ducked, dancing around a chair until it was obvious he was either going to knock Devon out or take a hit himself.

"Stop it!" Colonel Lord Heath Boscastle inserted his lean frame between the two hard-breathing opponents, his brother Drake pushing over his shoulder. "If you do end up fighting you will do it at the proper time and place, and *not* with ladies present. For all we know, there is no reason to quarrel."

Gideon turned, inadvertently meeting Charlotte's gaze. The regret in her eyes looked too genuine for him to believe this had been an elaborate scheme.

He pulled his neck cloth loose, then looked around again to discover Devon glowering at him.

"I thought you were too interested in her at the ball."

Gideon's eyes flashed in warning. "It was your idea for me to ask her to dance."

Colonel Lord Heath Boscastle intervened again. "The rest of this conversation will be conducted at Grayson's house in private tomorrow. I think it is safe to say that this hunt is over and it's time for everyone to go home."

*Chapter 11*

*H*arriet had just returned to the front steps after searching the mews behind the garden when the subdued group emerged from the duke's town house. She came immediately to Charlotte's side and took her hand.

"Did you find it?" Charlotte whispered.

"No."

"Where were you?"

"In the carriage house and the rear," Harriet whispered back. "And then I caught a glimpse of you and him in the study. Just weep buckets when anyone questions you. Pretend to faint."

"I wish you'd found that wretched diary."

"Look on the bright side. At least after tonight you have some genuine experience to write about."

Charlotte looked around.

Devon was scowling at her as if she were a Hydra-headed monster. Her cousins-in-law, Jane and Jocelyn, gave her supportive looks. At least Jane seemed to have sympathy for the situation. The other members of the party hurried toward their carriage. As she passed Charlotte she whispered, "Chin up. Lips sealed."

Her dark-haired cousin Drake strode toward her, inclining his head to murmur, "Let those blue eyes talk for you."

But Heath, the Sphinx and master of the intimidating silence—he whose gaze could penetrate stone and the human soul, the man who had served as her guardian when she first came to London—sat back and stared at her in unblinking absorption during the entire drive home, his finger propped beneath his chin. Was he upset? Was he disgusted? Amused? Disinterested? No one could know for certain. It was best for her to hold her tongue until she knew how her explanation would be received.

Nevertheless it was clear she had fulfilled the family legacy. She had brought disgrace upon herself and proved that her blood ran with all the passion of her predecessors.


Gideon went upstairs with a bottle of brandy and drank half of it before he fell back on the bed. His "guests" had departed.

He was too tired and conflicted tonight to solve anyone's problems. He had gone out earlier in the evening certain he would make an arrangement with a courtesan. Instead, he'd ended up mired in scandal.

If there was an exit from the situation that would not damage Charlotte's name, he could not see it.

God, he wished he did not despise cowardice.

He would be forced to choose between dishonor or marriage, which was quite an accomplishment on Charlotte's part, considering the string of women who had schemed to become his wife.

He had faced numerous opponents on the dueling field without qualms. Was this any different? A man could not call himself brave if he fought only the battles he chose.

As he contemplated his future he heard the door open and the approach of footsteps across the floor. It could only be his butler, perhaps checking to see whether he was still alive.

He didn't bother to open his eyes. He hoped to fall asleep and awaken the next day to discover that tonight had been only a dream. "Leave everything as it is, Shelby. You can tidy to your heart's content in the morning."

A spume of cold water struck his face. He jolted upright, managing to dodge the ceramic pitcher that hit the headboard of his bed. In that moment of surprise he decided that Gabrielle did not have the makings of a courtesan at all.

A Gorgon, perhaps. But not a woman with whom a sane man would feel comfortable confiding in or sharing his bed. He rolled to his side and onto the floor, holding the bed curtains to his chest as a buffer.

The washstand bowl hit the bedpost. Gabrielle glanced around, presumably looking for another weapon to hurl. He dropped the curtains and made a dash for the door before she launched her shoes at his back.

"You liar! You schoolboy! I can't believe that you left my company for that . . . I don't even know what she is!"

Gideon reached the top of the stairs. His entire staff had assembled below in their nightclothes.

"All these women in one night," his housekeeper said, and obviously didn't mind that he could hear her. "It isn't natural. It's unhealthful. I can't be party to this much longer. What a sorrow if young Lady Sarah had witnessed this."

Gabrielle ran sobbing around him to fly down the stairs. "He's a swine!" she said to the servants who parted to allow her passage. "The man ruined my reputation! I'll never command a top price again."

"Good riddance," Shelby muttered, shuffling to close the door after her. "That's another one who won't be coming back in a hurry."

Harriet arrived at the academy early the next morning to take breakfast with Charlotte. They sat alone sipping tea until it turned too cold to enjoy.

Harriet put down her cup. "I don't know what to say. It was my fault. All of it."

Charlotte sighed. "It wasn't. And I admit I wanted to see what his house looked like inside."

"For a man alleged to live a decadent life he had nice furnishings. I didn't see any evidence of the riotous orgies he's said to hold."

"I don't know whether that means he's been maligned or has an attentive staff who tidy up the damage as he goes about it."

"It could mean he isn't as bad as he's supposed to be."

"Well, he had French letters in his drawers," Charlotte said in an inaudible voice.

Harriet stared across the table. "What did you say?"

"French letters. You know, the articles that a man wears when he's about to indulge in a carnal act."

Harriet frowned at her. "In the first place, you're not talking to the vicar's wife, Charlotte. I know what they are. Condoms."

"Lower your voice."

"I'm whispering. Besides, all that means is that he's a more conscientious lover than most men."

"The fact that he had them in his drawer suggests to me that he is loose with his affections."

Harriet choked back a laugh.

Charlotte regarded her in irritation. "Scoundrels amuse you?"

"No. You do. The possession of those 'articles' could mean any number of things."

"Really?" Charlotte looked past Harriet with feigned indifference.

"Really. It could mean he's practical and particular about where he puts his—"

"Harriet!"

"Or it could mean he likes to be well prepared in the event, you know . . . in the event he finds a certain lady hiding in his bedchamber when he comes home."

"Don't remind me."

"Or perhaps he's hopeful that the right woman, and we're talking about you again, is waiting for him to come home."

"Don't. I won't delude myself anymore."

"Some men carry articles everywhere they go," Harriet continued, warming to the subject. "To church in case fortune smiles on them after the sermon. To the club in case a lady is waiting in the coach to rendezvous. I've known gents who bring them along when they attend a ball. Did you notice whether he had any when he asked you to dance?"

"I'm not talking to you anymore," Charlotte said with a reluctant laugh.

"You're too much fun to tease. I'm sorry. But I think in the end that what he has hidden away in his drawers says more good about him than bad."

"You're beginning to sound as if you find him attractive yourself."

"Oh, no," Harriet said, her eyes glittering. "One duke is more than enough to keep me occupied, thank you. In fact, if Griffin were in town I wouldn't have had the time to get you in all this trouble."

"My life is a mess," Charlotte said morosely.

Charlotte knew she had committed an unpardonable sin in society's eyes. She had confessed, not once, but innumerable times, not in a whisper, but on the written page, to experiencing a surfeit of emotion.

A lady was not allowed to emote. A gentlewoman would bite off her tongue before admitting that she felt such longings. And the feelings she had expressed for the duke . . .

She hadn't merely indulged in a flight of fancy. She had soared on waxen wings straight into the sun, like Icarus of Greek legend.

She sighed. Perhaps it was overdramatic to compare herself to a Grecian youth who had dropped into the sea after his hopes had melted midflight. But Charlotte had always maintained that mankind would be better off if it took a few moral lessons from mythology. Why should womankind be any different?

"Charlotte? Are you dreaming again?"

"I still have to face my family."

"And the duke," Harriet reminded her.

"He was furious last night," Charlotte said, drawing a

slow breath. "Maybe he will leave London before he's called to the family trial."

"He won't run," Harriet said. "A duke is not like other men."

"I gathered that," Charlotte said softly. "That's the appeal." After a deep sigh, she continued. "I wouldn't have chosen to force him into marriage like this, no matter how much I desired him from afar. I'll admit marriage does sound more exciting than teaching manners for the rest of my life. But even that option will be gone."

"You couldn't have worked at the academy forever. Your brothers have sworn to have you married off before autumn."

"I guarantee there won't be a better match in the candidates they choose for me. But I do want a family," Charlotte confessed.

"Then wait until you meet the right man."

"I did," Charlotte said, smiling wistfully. "I'm just not the right woman."

"We'll see what the afternoon brings."

# Chapter 12

Charlotte considered it ironic that her first lesson of the day for the undergraduates centered on the three Fates, the goddesses who randomly decided an individual's destiny. Birth, life, death. It was theirs to enhance or to destroy. The Fates made few concessions to those who appealed for mercy.

"Is there a lesson that we as ladies of a refined culture can draw from this? Do any of you think it is possible to change one's fate?"

One of the younger girls stood up. "Lady Dalrymple is coming with her sketching club to give her weekly painting class. I just wanted to remind you."

Charlotte's mouth tightened. The last thing she needed was to supervise a group of naughty-minded matrons who delighted in painting nude gentlemen for their Greek deity collection. Charlotte did not believe for an instant that these silver-haired artists created their controversial works of art for the sake of charity alone—

although it was true that their rendition of Emma's husband as Hercules fighting the Nemean lion had sold at auction for an ungodly sum to benefit a hospital.

Another girl slipped out of her chair. "One cannot change fate and it is arrogant to try. Only the elite class, for example, should rule society."

Charlotte glanced at the pale girl fidgeting at the back of the room. She was the most recent charity case rescued from the slums, and she appeared to resent all attempts to educate her. Charlotte had to keep reminding herself that Harriet had been more belligerent when she had been a pupil. And that secretly she had doubted many times that Harriet could ever be civilized.

"What do you think, Verity?"

Verity shrugged. "About what?"

"About the Fates."

"I think I'd rather watch old Lady Dalrymple paint rude pictures than listen to this load of rubbish. It's a waste of me time."

"It's a waste of time to try to teach *you* anything," one of the girls murmured.

Charlotte took a breath. "Why were the Fates sometimes called cruel?"

Verity stood up and made a mocking curtsy. "They made girls go to school when they could've been outside chasing boys."

Charlotte stared at her. "What did you say to me?"

"Girls like boys and not books."

"Not necessarily," Charlotte said, her voice rising. "A decently bred girl seeks the company of young gentlemen only with a chaperone. She does not chase them."

"Then why did you get caught last night in the dark with that duke if you weren't chasing after 'im?"

Charlotte closed her book, her face flushed with guilt. "Do we believe every word of gossip that we hear?" She held up her hand, forestalling any answers. She was dying to ask *how* they had heard about last night.

She glanced past the girls. She thought she detected hoofbeats from outside on the street, the cry of a coachman warning all pedestrians to step aside. Such a dramatic arrival could mean only one thing—the Marquess of Sedgecroft had sent his coach and six to collect her for an official meeting at his house.

The Fates had not put off deciding her future.

Would she be banished to the country? Sent back to her family home and three brothers?

The girls broke into spirited chatter. She listened for the inevitable knock at the door. She stood in benumbed silence until Miss Peppertree, Charlotte's assistant, flapped into the room like a bird of prey with another schoolmistress trying to follow her.

"Miss Ames, take the girls upstairs for a few minutes," she said with the authority of a French general assuming command of an army base.

"Very well." Charlotte rapped her knuckles against her book. "Girls! Compose yourselves. I shall say this only once, and the wise will listen: Tomorrow we will continue our studies in Greek mythology. The new subject will be Arachne."

"Our what?" Verity interrupted with an impertinent grin.

Charlotte ground her teeth. "Arachne was the legendary weaver whose tapestry enraged the goddess Pallas Athena." She stopped, wallowing in a moment of self-pity. "You will be asked to relate Arachne's fate in your own words. That is all."

She fled from the room. Miss Peppertree ran after her, leaving the class in an eruption of feminine giggles and whispering gossip.

"Miss Boscastle!" Daphne cried. "Miss— Oh, gracious, Charlotte. You will not escape me! I never dreamed you were capable of such . . . mischief."

Mischief. She shivered as Gideon's dark image flitted through her mind. "How do you know? How did the girls find out? I haven't even spoken with my family." Although she knew that it was Grayson's coach she had heard outside the academy.

Miss Peppertree herded her into the formal dining room.

"The girls know."

"Yes. I know they know, but I don't know how they found out so quickly."

Miss Peppertree closed the door, set the lock, and darted to the windows to draw the curtains.

"What on earth are you doing?" Charlotte asked, certain she detected the footsteps of doom in the street.

"Sssh." Miss Peppertree put her finger to her lips and then proceeded to the fireplace, motioning repeatedly to the vase that sat upon the mantel.

"Have you suddenly become a spy or are we playing a pantomime? Because I—"

She broke off as Miss Peppertree swung around and grabbed her by the hand, whispering, "I put the pieces in there."

"Pieces of what? In where?"

"In the vase that resembles a Grecian urn. You will recall we moved it to this room when one of the girls found a book in the library that mentioned the practice of cremation in ancient Greece."

She tugged her hand loose from Daphne's talonlike grasp. "As I doubt you've had occasion to put anyone to rest in the vase, I insist you stop this nonsense."

"The broadsheets. I burned them the moment they arrived. Of course, there will be others, and you will have to help me dispose of those as fast as they come."

Charlotte put her hand to her temple. "Why don't I ring for some tea while you have a nice sit-down? Because to be frank, you're beginning to frighten me."

"You should be frightened!" Miss Peppertree exclaimed, and they both glanced around at the imperious pounding against the front door. "Oh, bother. There's no hiding it. Your scandal was in the papers." She pulled a footstool to the hearth, hiked up her blue muslin skirt, and reached precariously for the vase.

Charlotte sprang forward instinctively to wrest it from her hands. Miss Peppertree dropped like a spiderling to the floor. "Do you understand now? I left a snippet intact for you to see."

Charlotte swallowed, braced herself for a shock, and peered into the dust-coated depths of the vase. She wrinkled her nose.

"All this ado about—"

"—the duke." Daphne slipped her hand into the vase and withdrew a slip of paper that looked as if it had been meticulously snipped with a pair of scissors. "Read this. And to yourself, please."

Charlotte watched in growing exasperation as Miss Peppertree laid out several pieces across the whatnot table. She refrained from pointing out that it would have been easier to have merely saved the entire clipping, but Miss Peppertree did like her drama. The poor woman might lead an uneventful life on the surface. But the vicarious pleasure she took from poking her nose into everyone else's affairs was altogether different.

Not that Charlotte was in any position to talk.

In fact, Charlotte's imagination put Daphne's to shame. They did make a pair.

"There," Miss Peppertree whispered with a victorious air, stepping away from the table.

Charlotte heard noises drifting from the entry hall. "Daphne. I know you tend to exaggerate. And so do I. But tell me. Is it really dreadful?"

"Yes. On this table are the ashes of your reputation."

Charlotte looked down at the shreds of paper pieced back together. The boldfaced print blared at her like a coachman's bugle. It appeared to be a caption from one of George Cruikshank's caricatures.

### HEAD OF ACADEMY CAUGHT IN THE ACT WITH AMOROUS DUKE! ONE OF THE TON'S MOST DEDICATED BACHELORS TAKES TWO MISTRESSES IN ONE NIGHT!

"Oh," Charlotte said, and fell back into a chair, feeling sick. "I think I'm glad I didn't see the cartoon. No wonder the girls were so agitated this morning."

"It will be a wonder if we have any girls left to worry about once their parents catch wind of this."

Charlotte looked up anxiously. "Most people know not to believe these despicable scandal sheets."

Miss Peppertree swept the pieces back into one hand, clutching the vase in the other, and returned to the hearth to toss the incriminating remnants onto the coals. "Most people," she whispered, "sense whether there is any truth to a rumor or not."

"Perhaps people will lose interest if a betrothal is announced." At least she was hoping for such a resolution. Gideon might certainly have another opinion.

Miss Peppertree climbed atop the stool again to return the vase to its proper place. "I highly doubt that. In fact, I think you will find the opposite is true. A duke ranks just below a prince, as you're aware. The excitement of his engagement and subsequent marriage would create a stir in society that might mitigate your disgrace until it dies a quiet death."

The excitement Gideon would stir in Charlotte's heart if he married her would live forever.

"There's nothing to do for it, Daphne. I have made my bed and now I must lie in it."

Miss Peppertree put her hands on her hips. "I hope you realize that you're not going to be lying in that bed alone."

"No," Charlotte mused. "I suppose I won't. That is a sacrifice I shall have to make."

"Miss Boscastle," Ogden the butler said from behind the locked door. "The marquess has sent his carriage to collect you."

"If I didn't know you better, I would suspect that you schemed to bring this scandal about."

"I didn't," Charlotte insisted.

But she had dreamed of it.

And sooner or later, Miss Peppertree, if not the entire world, would know exactly how scandalous her daydreams had been.

"What will happen to the academy?" Miss Peppertree asked, trailing her to the door and then into the hall, where the butler waited in impassive silence. "I won't be able to find another position—Lady Clipstone won't hire me to wash her floors if there is any truth to this scandal."

"It is *not* time to abandon ship yet."

"Maybe not." Miss Peppertree's eyes glittered with tears behind her spectacles. "But it might be time to lash ourselves to the wheel and ride out the storm."

# Chapter 13

$\mathcal{G}$ideon arrived at Grayson's Park Lane mansion three minutes before noon the day after his ignominy. Throughout the previous night he had thought up several speeches to plead his case, but as it turned out, he arrived in the middle of a family argument. Grayson stood in the corner, as elegantly dressed as ever. Heath sat in a winged armchair as Drake and Devon engaged in verbal combat.

Gideon settled back in the chair he was offered and glanced up to study the plaster Jupiter on the ceiling.

"We will wait until the toddlers can behave," Heath said with a sigh.

"I admit it," Devon said from the window where he stood. "I encouraged Gideon to talk to Charlotte at the ball. She looked lonely and wistful. It was my fault that—"

"It usually is," Drake said from the sofa, where he was sprawled out lengthwise with his eyes closed.

Devon tunneled his hand through his hair. "I didn't think that simple kindness would lead to this."

"That's the trouble," Drake murmured, and steepled his fingers on his chest as if sending up a prayer. "You never think. I can't remember a time from childhood when you did."

Devon snorted. "This criticism from a man who for years drank so much he couldn't remember his own name in the morning?"

"Past imperfect," Drake admitted with a smile. "We are older now, aren't we?"

"You are," Devon said. "Not me. I'm still an infant."

"My point exactly."

The broad-shouldered man slumped against the wall straightened. His voice broke through the argument like a thunderbolt. "Cease, the pair of you."

Drake smiled at Devon. "The marquess has spoken. Let there be silence."

Gideon glanced up in expectation. He was only casually acquainted with Grayson, a situation that he assumed would soon change. As the story went, the marquess had reluctantly become the patriarch to the London branch of his scandal-prone family when his father, Royden Boscastle, died. Grayson was said to be honorable, fair-minded, and good-natured.

But then, Gideon had never been caught in an indiscretion with one of Grayson's relatives before. The marquess appeared to be anything but of a good nature this morning. In fact, unsmiling and heavy eyed, he looked as irascible and disgruntled as Gideon felt.

Heath, however, sounded cordial when he ventured his opinion. "Squabbling like schoolboys will not help anyone. Why don't we give Gideon a chance to explain what happened?"

"Devon asked me to approach Charlotte at the ball as a favor. And I did."

"Was it a favor to invite her to your house?" Grayson asked with a deep scowl.

Gideon hesitated. Should he lie to protect her, taking on the role of a Lothario? Not if she had already admitted the truth. Yes. The truth was preferable, no matter how much pain it might cause. "She came to my house." He concealed a smile as he remembered discovering her on his bedroom floor. "She *broke* in, I should say, in an apparent search for her diary. She made quite a muddle of my drawers."

"Your—"

"*Wardrobe* drawers."

"Why did you take her diary in the first place?" Devon inquired. "It's an odd thing for a man to do, especially one who is meeting his mistress."

*What mistress?* he wondered. By now Gabrielle would have let the world know she was back on the market and that he was a heartless swine. His housekeeper shared the same opinion, as she had so eloquently demonstrated by serving him stone-cold coffee and a plate of stale tarts for breakfast.

"I found the diary in my carriage last night after the ball," he said. "I thought I was protecting your cousin's privacy by keeping it out of another's hands."

"That's all well and good," Grayson said. "But why were the pair of you caught in a compromising position in the dark?"

Gideon smiled thinly. "I wish I knew myself how to explain what happened. I can't really give you an answer. One thing led to another. Does the reason matter at this point?"

Heath shook his head. "Not if the outcome is a wedding. Is that a possibility?"

Gideon let a moment pass. "I enjoy a good duel now and then. But a match isn't going to solve anything in this instance."

"I was hoping that you would say that, Your Grace," Heath said in palpable relief. "I have no desire to kill you."

"Nor I you," Gideon admitted.

Devon cleared his throat. "Well, I'd like to kill him."

"Nobody asked you, genius," Drake said with mild scorn.

"Girls, do stop quarreling," Heath said.

Grayson heaved a sigh. "The damn wedding will have to take place as soon as possible. Gossip grows like a fungus in this city."

"I'll need a special license."

"I disagree with you, Grayson," Heath said, leaning back in his chair. "There should be a short if concentrated period of courtship before the ceremony. A public courtship would help avert some of the scandal. Two weeks or so should do."

Grayson considered the suggestion and nodded slowly in accord. "I concede there is an art to wooing a young lady whom one does not love while convincing the world that one does."

"In a fortnight?" Gideon asked, not hiding his skepticism.

"Yes," Grayson said. "I shouldn't need to explain how to go about it to a man of your experience. But as one scoundrel to another it is an intense but rewarding bit of work."

Gideon glanced away. "And what do you suggest I do within this intense period of courtship?"

"You were caught in the dark with her, Wynfield," Drake said without a trace of pity. "I'd guess you are capable of taking it from it there."

"If I pursued her as ruthlessly as I have other women," Gideon said, "she would go into hiding."

Grayson shrugged. "Then you will have to smoke her out. Make her burn for you. If you go about it the right way, it might prove to be very rewarding. I think it would be appropriate for you to at least pretend you are in love."

Gideon shifted in his chair. "Love? You will have to be more explicit in your advice."

"Don't tempt him," Drake said with a grin.

Grayson looked at Gideon. "If you're going to be married, you might as well make the most of the situation."

"In public or in private?"

"That's up to you, as long as you are altar-bound. A discreet announcement will immediately be placed in the papers. A formal celebration can wait."

Drake started to laugh at Gideon. "You're damned fortunate her brothers didn't discover the two of you together."

"It's all water under the damn bridge now," Grayson said magnanimously. "Wynfield is behaving with honor and honesty." He frowned at Gideon. "And if I may be honest, you have my sympathy for landing in this mess, and my admiration for accepting your responsibility."

"Well, the damage is done. I did not lure Charlotte to my house to debauch her. For what it is worth I swear I was astonished when she confessed that she had broken in to find the missing diary. What followed afterward is impossible to explain."

Heath stared at him. "The unsettling thing is that I believe every word you've said. But I must add in Charlotte's defense that until this imbroglio she has never caused her family a spot of worry."

"It was only a matter of time," Drake said with a shrug. "She couldn't stay innocent forever."

Gideon frowned. "I believe that she is still innocent. It's her diary that isn't. What I read was . . . incendiary. We should take care that it doesn't fall into the wrong hands."

"It has to be found," Heath agreed. "Are you sure, Gideon, that you left it in your carriage?"

"Yes. My coachman and staff have searched high and low for it, with no success."

Devon leaned against the windowsill. "What could Charlotte have written that anyone would go to the trouble of stealing?"

Heath picked up a pen from Grayson's desk. "I have the sense that we should find the diary first and ask questions later. I will instruct Sir Daniel Mallory to begin an investigation." He rose from his chair and extended his hand to Gideon. "In the meantime let me be the first to welcome you to the family. And may God have mercy on your courageous soul."

Gideon laughed.

With this agreement, an ancient machine ground into motion. Grayson would be accepted into Gideon's circle, and vice versa. The two houses that could have ended up enemies had merged. A link had been forged without even a single person raising his voice.

# Chapter 14

The ladies of the family had gathered around Charlotte in Jane's spacious bedchamber suite. The marchioness presided over the meeting that included Julia, Heath's wife; Jocelyn, who belonged to Devon; and Eloise, a governess until Drake had swept her off her feet. Last, but perhaps the most lively, was Chloe, a Boscastle by birth, which was why no one in the family had been shocked to learn that she had hidden the man she loved in her closet while he hunted a murderer.

"Who is missing?" Jane demanded, standing in a circle of mismatched shoes, a champagne bottle in hand.

Julia picked a path through Jane's elegant footwear, holding up her glass for a refill. "Eleanor and Sebastian are in the Highlands. Alethea and Gabriel never leave the country or each other's company. Emma and Adrian will be on the way as soon as they hear the latest. And I know there's someone else I'm forgetting—"

"Where is Harriet?" Jane asked, filling Julia's flute without a drop spilled.

Chloe turned briefly from the looking glass, where she stood fluffing her cropped black curls. "She told Weed that she would find Charlotte's diary no matter what she had to do."

"I don't like the sound of that," Jane remarked.

Chloe smiled. "I do. I wish she'd ask me to join the adventure."

"Adventure," Jane said with a frown. "That's one way to look at it."

"How did I allow this to happen?" Charlotte whispered. She was slumped in a blue velvet chair at Jane's escritoire. Her head was buried in the crook of her arm. She presented a picture of classical misery, although the only earnest understanding she had provoked was from Jocelyn, who was expecting her second child and therefore was prone to universal empathy.

"There is no point in crying over spilled ink," Jane said practically. "We must view this for the blessing in disguise it is. Grayson will persuade Gideon what a delightful wife you'll make, and that is that."

Charlotte lifted her head, studying the marchioness with skepticism. "Blessing? Either you have had too much Cliquot or I haven't had enough. The duke will resent me for the rest of his life. He was my dream. I am his nightmare."

"But if you had to be caught with anyone, at least it was a duke," Julia said as she bent to prop a pillow beneath Jocelyn's feet. "Besides, you would have to leave the academy sooner or later."

"Why?" Charlotte asked bleakly, dropping her head

back on her arm. "Why did I ever write a single word? Why did I not take my own advice? How often have I warned the girls to never put their incriminating thoughts on paper?"

"Dominic read my diary when he was trapped in my bedroom," Chloe mused. "He was quite nasty about it, too, as I recall. He mocked me. And then he seduced me, or I seduced him. It's irrelevant now, I suppose. We are married and our past sins with each other were swept under the veil."

"But at least you had an element of choice," Julia said, walking in front of the window like a barrister in court.

"No, we didn't," Chloe retorted. "Dominic threatened every manner of vile misfortune on me if I gave him away. He was a dead man and a very desperate one, if you'll recall. The beast bullied me around until I took charge."

"But he adores you," Jane said, frowning at Jocelyn in concern. "Are you comfortable, Jocelyn? You look like a hedgehog, the way you are sitting. All I can see of you is your nose and an enormous ball of brown taffeta."

Chloe nodded in agreement. "Devon was uncommonly large when he was born, too."

"He still is," Jocelyn said, uncrossing her ankles with an incriminating smile that stopped the conversation for a full half minute.

"I appreciate what all of you are trying to do," Charlotte said. "I even appreciate Harriet's efforts on my behalf, despite the fact that it was her neglect, coupled with my romantic self-indulgence, that caused this misfortune. And—"

She broke off, distracted by the sight of Jane staring down the neck of her empty champagne bottle. "And what?" Jane prompted, gesturing with an equally empty glass.

"And— Oh. None of you understand. I am not waiting for a well-intentioned scoundrel to reform or for the viscount I've concealed in my closet to ask for my hand."

Jocelyn's arms and legs flailed for several moments before she abandoned her efforts to sit up properly. "If it's any consolation, Charlotte, Devon didn't marry me of his own free will."

"I understand that," Charlotte said, "but can anyone in this room claim to have waited for a man to decide whether he'd rather fight a duel than marry you? Think of it. He has to choose death or me."

The group subsided into a guilty silence until finally all eyes turned to the only one in the room who had not ventured an opinion: Eloise, who, as a former governess, understood the value of keeping her opinions to herself. "Do *you* want this marriage to take place, Charlotte?" she inquired softly.

Charlotte sighed. "I can't lie. I—"

She looked up—everyone did—at the imperious rapping against the door. She crossed her fingers. She held her breath and hoped. . . .

Jane weaved a path across the room to answer the door. Her husband, Grayson, stood in the hall, his eyes gleaming with triumph. "He has agreed to our terms— What is that empty bottle doing in your hand at this hour of the day?"

Charlotte felt like a snowflake melting in the sun. *He has agreed.*

"Agreed to our terms?" Jane said with a sniff. "You make it sound as if they are two warring nations." She handed Grayson the bottle and glanced over her shoulder with a smile at Charlotte. "Let us all go downstairs and toast the happy couple."

The Fates had decided in Charlotte's favor. She would marry the man she had wanted from the moment she saw him. Charlotte forced herself not to rush down the stairs to greet him, even though she had watched his arrival from Jane's window with the same rapt fascination as the domestic staff below.

She'd already shown herself to be smitten with the man. If she was to be the cause of ruining his carefree life and thwarting his aimless existence, she would have to make the most of the situation and carry herself with confidence.

Unfortunately all her resolve went to pot as she took the stairs one step at a time, pretending polite indifference, and he turned to look at her.

It didn't take any effort on his part to affect her composure. Not a word. Not an overt gesture. The promise of retribution in his eyes, the twist of his lips, undid her. But she would *not* dissolve with half the house watching. She would—

"Is anything wrong?"

The deep voice laced with mockery roused her from her musings. At that moment she knew everything in her life would change. For a time she had fooled herself into thinking she could manipulate this man with her quill. Now the duke's imposing presence hovered over her like a dark angel who had been waiting for a moment of weakness to descend and take advantage. Except that *she*, in truth, had ensnared him.

She shook her head. His thoughtful gaze locked with hers. "I'm fine," she said, willing herself not to wilt from the heat in his eyes. "And you—"

"I have faced the inquisition."

"It will be my turn next."

"I trust you will survive."

"How good of you to wish your captor well."

"I have many wishes," he said, and offered her his arm with a dark smile that reminded her that while he'd agreed to marriage, she could trust he had no intention of being good at all.

Roman statues lined the walls of the chamber where the small party met for a subdued celebration. Gideon decided that Charlotte could be mistaken for a goddess herself at first glance. Fortunately, after last night, he knew he could bring her to life. There could be joys to discover in this marriage. He watched her raise her champagne flute to her mouth. A kissable mouth, indeed. Then she caught his gaze and smiled.

His blood flared with familiar instincts before he turned away to gather himself. Conquer, caress, overpower. Possess. But somewhere, mingled in the midst of urges that didn't need an explanation, another emotion arose. For a moment he tried to identify what it was.

Was it excitement at a challenge? Gideon felt a stab of surprise as he turned back toward Charlotte. "I can't guarantee that you will find love or happiness as my wife, because I don't know whether I'm capable of providing either."

"I can't expect you to love me. . . ." Her voice trailed off.

"Meaning I shouldn't expect the same of you?"

"I didn't say that, Your Grace."

He hesitated. He and Charlotte stood apart from the

others, a ploy on her family's part that he assumed was meant to force them together.

"I want to warn you, that is all," he said to her. "I might not live up to your expectations. Some ladies seek my company. Others swear I am the devil's spawn."

"Yes," she said. "I can understand their concerns. I hope to find a compromise in your character."

He inclined his head to hers. "I hope to sleep with you soon. In my experience sex is an excellent prelude to an association."

"How profound of you," she said.

He drew away, delighted at her show of fire. This was more like the uninhibited lady who wrote delicious lies about him. "For the moment I am forced to behave."

Her eyes glinted. "That is wise—especially if you are going to be part of the family."

"And you're to become part of mine."

They broke apart as the marquess approached them.

At least, Gideon reflected, he had acted with honor today, if not last night. Charlotte seemed relieved that he had come up to scratch. He could give her his name. He could offer her pleasure. If she expected more, well, it was time she learned the past had stolen his capacity for hope. He saw no point in making plans that he'd learned from painful experience might never be fulfilled.

Charlotte sighed when Gideon excused himself from the party and took his leave. He might have agreed to marry her, but she had to face facts. He wasn't brimming over with enthusiasm about their engagement. He had made his decision for honor's sake, not romance. She wandered across the room and found herself suddenly standing in front of Jane.

"Charlotte," Jane said. "He will be back."

"What if he runs away?"

"We'll run after him."

She saw no pity on Jane's face, but only the strong will of a woman who had tamed her beast and made him worship her.

"He is yours," Jane said. "You do want him, don't you? It is obvious to me."

"Yes. But I want him to . . . to burn for me as I do for him."

Jane's smile said she understood. "Then you need to be fire with fire."

"That's from Shakespeare." Charlotte felt oddly consoled. "Of course. I will bear those words in mind."

"Put them to work," Jane whispered, then glanced up as Weed approached her with a bow.

"The master would like Miss Boscastle to meet him in his study for a confidential talk," he said in a hushed voice.

"A lecture," Jane said. "It was inevitable. Bear up, Charlotte. Grayson is more growl than bite."

# Chapter 15

*C*harlotte braced herself for a long, well-meaning lecture. Grayson had his hands full protecting a family known for its passionate scandals. But she had never been called into his presence before.

"Sit down, Charlotte," he said, motioning her to an armchair. "First of all, congratulations on your upcoming marriage."

"Grayson, I'm ashamed—"

"It came about in standard Boscastle style," he said, brushing aside her apology. "Are you content to marry Wynfield?"

*Content?* "More than I can say."

He frowned. "He is a man of the world."

"Yes."

"And you"—he shook his head—"are not as sophisticated. Do you understand what I'm trying to say?"

She nodded. He was warning her that she had fallen

into an unfathomable well—at the bottom of which she hoped to see Gideon waiting to catch her.

He looked at her closely. "I have to admit you're remarkably composed about the whole thing. But then, what else can you do? Our next problem is to find that diary of yours. Knowing you, I doubt there is anything in it to concern us."

She slid down in her chair. "I'm afraid there is."

"Such as?"

"Personal reflections."

He raised his brow. "Could you give me one example?"

"No."

He rose from his chair, frowning in concern. "I thought I'd heard you were writing the family history."

"I was. And then I . . . I . . . I never meant to expose myself in any way."

"What do you mean by 'expose' yourself?" he asked in alarm.

"I—I am afraid I revealed my secret desires in the pages of that diary."

"Oh, God."

He strode across the room to the bell cord. "Thank you for giving me the truth. I shall deal with this as I must. I am not the expert in these matters that Jane is, but I suggest you spend your spare hours shopping for a wedding trousseau instead of spilling the soup. Chronicles are all well and good, but there are some secrets that should stay buried."

"Grayson—"

"Charlotte, remember that you are about to take a place in the peerage. Do not acknowledge your mistakes with an apology but with your actions."

"Thank you, Grayson."

"In a short time Gideon will be one of us. The betrothal will be announced in the evening papers with mention that a formal supper party will be held here at a later date to celebrate the event."

She hid a smile. Few people would have seen this union from Grayson's lofty view. The Boscastle men were simply too accustomed to ruling supreme to ever change.

"One more thing, Charlotte. Sir Daniel Mallory is waiting in the antechamber to ask you a few questions about the diary. He is in my employ. I would advise you to be more . . . well, I hesitate to use the word, but I think you should be more revealing with him than you were with me. Details could prove useful in his pursuit of your missing diary."

Sir Daniel Mallory expelled a sigh. This was an embarrassing interview for both him and Miss Boscastle. Perhaps he was handling it badly. Perhaps he was too brusque for a gentlewoman of her delicate sensibilities.

"You can describe this book, Miss Boscastle?" he asked again, pen ready to jot down the normal fare.

"Of course."

Then silence.

He gestured with his pen. "And the contents?"

She swallowed, turning her comely face to the window. "I should think that its nature would be obvious or else there would not be this fuss."

"Miss Boscastle, the world is full of innumerable books, and if I am to help locate this diary, it would behoove you to give me an honest description. . . ."

He paused. She appeared to be fascinated by a boy rolling a hoop behind a cart in the street. Then she turned back to him, her eyes evading his.

"There is some erotic material in my writings," she whispered in a small voice that he had to strain to hear. Or perhaps he hadn't heard her at all. He couldn't have.

"Excuse me?"

Not erotic. She must have said *exotic*. Or *erratic*. Or possibly even *quixotic*. "You will have to forgive me. I was not listening as closely as I should have. You said—"

"*Erotic*." She turned her head and looked him in the eye. "Yes. That was what I said. I'm sure I do not have to explain the meaning of the word to a man in your profession."

He looked deeply into her blue eyes. He thought he was a good judge of character. She seemed so demure and reserved. "It is true," he said in the most detached voice he could manage, "that I have investigated many aspects of vice—I mean *life*. However, that does not make me an expert on the erotic arts."

"It doesn't make me one, either," she burst out. "It is my imagination and indiscreet desires that have gotten me in this trouble, sir. Not my practical experience."

"I see." But he didn't. He frowned. "I'm trying to understand. You have kept a diary in which you have written sexual content?"

"You will have to describe exactly what you mean by that if I'm to be able to answer you."

The deuce he would. Not to a young schoolmistress who seemingly never raised her voice and wrote ... erotic something or other in her diary. "With all due respect, Miss Boscastle, I do not completely understand what you're telling me."

"Oh, does it *really* matter?"

"If I may speak honestly—"

"I expect nothing less from you. Besides, we are bound to be truthful and trust each other."

"Yes. Quite right. But is there anything in the diary that would incriminate any living persons?"

"There would be a prison built if one could be tried for amorous exploits."

"One can, in certain cases. I daresay, and I intend no discourtesy, but your family has probably been accused of even greater misdeeds than you could have devised."

"Perhaps." She folded her hands in her lap, her eyes full of remorse. "But never have my fictional ones been so vividly described."

He blew out a breath. "Unless you have libeled the Duchess of Wellington, for instance, or—"

"The Duke of Wynfield," she said, nodding morosely.

"Did you?" He chuckled. "Well, I'm sure he is used to being the topic of controversy."

She was silent.

"Fine, then. Now for a physical description of the diary itself . . ."

Charlotte reached behind the chair and produced a handsome brown vellum book, beautifully bound with gilt pages.

"This is empty, I assume? For now, at least?"

"Forever," she said with a sigh.

He left the Park Lane house with an empty journal and an enormous wrapped ham that the marchioness said he must give to his housekeeper. "She'll make some tasty sandwiches for you and the children. You look a little peaked, Sir Daniel."

"Madam, I apologize."

The Marchioness of Sedgecroft lowered her voice. "Do you think you'll be able to find this diary?"

"Eventually, madam. The problem will be locating it before the public is aware of its loss."

Charlotte returned to the academy and drifted through the rest of the day. It was evident by their sly smiles that the news of her betrothal had reached the girls and that Miss Peppertree had warned them it was not a subject to be discussed.

But anarchy erupted at teatime, when Charlotte received a message from Grayson informing her that he, Jane, and Gideon would accompany her to the theater tonight.

"The theater?" she said aloud, the note in one hand, a teacup in the other. "This will be my first public appearance as His Grace's intended, and I have nothing suitable to wear. I'll have to refuse."

"You cannot refuse," Miss Peppertree said. "It would be rude."

"But it's so sudden," Charlotte said.

Miss Peppertree's mouth thinned. "So was your engagement."

"Well, I am not attending the theater dressed like a—"

"—a schoolmistress?" Miss Peppertree said.

"Wear the dress you wore to the ball, Miss Boscastle," one of the girls suggested.

"But I can't be seen in it twice in the same week."

"The duke isn't going to notice," the girl said with a confidence that Charlotte wished she could share.

She put down her cup, her lips pursed. The duke would notice. He would definitely remember the dress.

Lucy Martout spoke up. "I have a gown that is too long for my height and rather risqué in the bodice."

Charlotte bit her lip. "Isn't that the gown that I forbade you to wear outside your room?"

"Yes," Lucy said, rising from the table. "We'll make you look a queen, Miss Boscastle."

"A duchess will do well enough," Miss Peppertree announced from her table.

"She is quite right, girls," Charlotte said. "I should not aspire to look tawdry."

Miss Peppertree's next pronouncement startled Charlotte but delighted everyone else in the room. "On the other hand, a lady does not need to appear underdressed and unconcerned about the latest fashion. A future duchess should look stylish."

Charlotte sent her a grateful look. How could she leave this gentle harbor of refinement? "Miss—"

"You need to wear a better corset," Verity said, separated from the others by her background of coarse abuse. "Gentlemen like nothing more than a big pair of kettledrums."

Charlotte turned to her in despair. "Verity Cresswell, you should have your mouth rinsed out with vinegar for that."

Miss Peppertree sniffed and drew a handkerchief from her pocket. "Why? It is the woeful truth and has been since time began. There is no need for an engaged woman to hide either her bosoms or her light under a bushel."

Her light? In the three hours it took for Gideon's carriage to arrive, the entire academy conspired to ignite an inner flame of confidence inside Charlotte. They brushed and fussed and pinned her blond hair into loose curls upon her shoulders. They draped her curves in shimmery pink silk. She felt elegant as Rankin, the footman, proudly escorted her from the house.

Gideon was waiting outside his carriage, his back toward her, his arm resting on the door. How arresting he looked in his black top hat and long-tailed woolen evening coat. But how different they were from each other. And—they were virtually strangers who would soon be forced into intimacy.

He turned, his face set in an impatient frown until she moved under the lamplight. His dark eyes swept over every detail of her appearance. She couldn't decide whether he was amused, displeased, or something else. But his brooding stare riveted her to the spot. She wondered, in fact, if they would stand there forever, suspended in hesitation, until Miss Peppertree and the girls made an unsubtle appearance at the window to watch them.

"Charlotte," he said, holding out his hand, both of them ignoring their audience in the window above.

*Be fire to fire.*

"Charlotte!" Jane's cheerful voice called from inside the carriage, and the spellbinding moment snapped like a thread. "You are stunning tonight! Isn't she, Gideon?"

"Yes," he said, his grasp on her hand tightening. And as he drew her to the carriage he added, "I have an opera cloak inside here." He reached back across the seat. "Maybe you should borrow it for the night."

"Is that your way of telling me you don't approve of my dress?"

"Not at all. It's my way of telling you that I don't wish to share with London what I have acquired at such a steep personal cost."

She held still as he draped the cloak around her bare shoulders. "I do have my own shawl with me," she murmured in amusement. "Your cloak does not match my dress, Your Grace."

"We do not match, either," he said, reclaiming her hand. "But we will still make a marriage. And in case I have not made myself clear, I agree with Jane: You look beautiful this evening."

heard a peep from the players. I think the management might have asked some young men in the audience to stop tossing about an orange, and, well, I don't think you missed anything."

Jane turned to her with an angelic smile. "I wasn't talking about the stage, dearest."

"Oh."

After that Charlotte could not even pretend to concentrate on the performance. The actors might have been trained monkeys, for all she noticed. She wanted the evening to go on forever. But at last the curtain fell on the final act. Gideon rose, enveloping her briefly in the disconcerting warmth of his shadow.

There was a small crowd waiting outside their box, friends calling out greetings to Gideon and Grayson; others were sweeping Jane off toward the stairs. Charlotte felt a hand descend heavily upon her shoulder. She heard a masculine voice repeating her name.

She turned into the press of bodies, the scent of tallow, sawdust, and perfume overpowering. Engaged or not, she would have to advise Gideon that his affectionate gestures should be saved for when they were alone.

Actually, he was pulling at her with such dogged determination that she was tempted to give him a solid thump of her fan. Except that as she looked up she saw Gideon was standing in a corner of the lobby, engaged in conversation with Grayson and three other gentlemen. Alarmed, she realized that it wasn't Gideon's gray-gloved hand that had so rudely claimed her. She glanced around slowly into a grinning face she had done her best to forget.

"Charlotte, I almost didn't recognize you," Phillip Moreland said, his eyes bright with excitement. "We've been in London only a few hours and I was dying to see you. I know I should have waited until the play was over. But I couldn't. I wouldn't. Caleb and I traveled together."

She backed up against another theatergoer, resisting Phillip's painful grasp. Caleb, her eldest brother. Where was he? Where had Gideon gone? She glanced around the lobby in search of him, of anyone, to rescue her.

"Charlotte?" Phillip laughed. "Why don't you say something? I hoped to surprise you, not give you a shock. What is this nonsense that spinster at your school was spouting about your marrying a duke?"

"It's true."

"It isn't."

"It is. Let go of my hand."

"Not likely. I lost you once. It's not going to happen again."

"Well, I'm warning you again. Let me go."

He didn't. He gripped her harder.

She lifted her free hand in the air. He glanced up. And her fan came down.

"Jesus!" he exclaimed, reaching up to either protect himself from another blow or to feel whether a lump was coming out on his forehead. "I'll have a bruise there in the morning. How will I explain it?"

"Perhaps you should have thought of that before you attacked me."

"Attacked?" He narrowed his eyes. "London has changed you, Charlotte, and not for the better. I will be glad to take you back where you belong."

She leaned away from him. Where she belonged? She knew where she belonged. It was here, with Gideon, and not with this embarrassing pretender from her past. Perhaps when she'd first arrived in London she had been homesick for her family and their country home. But she hadn't missed Phillip. And she most certainly had no intention of allowing him to take her away from the duke.

Sir Daniel Mallory often walked alone at night, usually with no destination in mind. Tonight he was on his way to London's most exclusive brothel. For business. A clash with the proprietress was certain. They had engaged in a secret liaison last year during one of his investigations. These days they met infrequently and clashed like thunderclouds when they did.

He expelled a sigh, reviewing his conversation with Miss Charlotte Boscastle. She had caught him off guard with her confession.

Working for the Boscastles paid well; it gave him time to spend with the niece and nephew he had taken into his home after his sister had been murdered.

Finding a lady's diary wasn't exactly the pinnacle of his profession, even though he understood why it caused the family distress. Even though it meant he would have to question a witness who harbored an intense hatred for him in her heart.

Gideon straightened. He could not have seen what he thought he saw—a man accosting Charlotte in the corner of the theater lobby. Who did this joker think he was? Who dared to lay his hands on a lady in public? Well, Gideon did, but that was entirely different. He had yet to meet a woman who shunned his attention when he set his mind on seduction.

"Excuse me, gentlemen," he said, cutting off an acquaintance midsentence. "There is trouble afoot, and I intend to stop it."

He plowed unceremoniously through the crowd, ignoring the whispers he left in his wake, until he reached the man Charlotte had just crowned on the pate with her fan.

*Chapter 17*

*A*udrey Watson sat alone in the upstairs parlor where she occasionally entertained select guests.

She maintained an elegant but well-guarded seraglio. Secret traps from the roof to the cellar caught the curious intruder who hoped for a glimpse of the house's celebrated decadence. But privacy was guaranteed to a paying guest.

Many university students thought the risk of capture was worth the chance to meet the infamous Mrs. Watson. On occasion she had even invited a brave invader or two to enjoy her company.

Naturally she had her favorite guests. The Boscastles had the right of entrée on any given evening, and her attachment to the family had nothing to do with sexual favors and everything to do with friendship.

Therefore it was unfortunate that the family had hired Sir Daniel Mallory as their private agent and bodyguard.

It was well after midnight, the time during which the house came to life. She had already been informed that Sir Daniel had arrived to speak with her. She waited for a servant to bring her uninvited caller into her presence. Her nemesis, as she tauntingly referred to him. Sir Daniel challenged every aspect of her unconventional life whenever he had the chance. Ever since they had engaged in their short affair, he seemed to have assumed the unsolicited role as her personal policeman.

Her heart seemed to beat in time with his footfalls on the carpet. She could feel the disdain in his eyes as he waited for her to acknowledge him. With a provocative smile she looked up past him to her bodyguard. "You may go. I don't think our hero of the metropolis means me any harm. Do you, Sir Daniel?"

He smiled without humor. "No more than you mean yourself." He gestured to the chair across from her. "May I?"

"Please." And at length, because she was a person who indulged herself in any random pleasure, she looked him in the face. Fascinating countenance, his. Not at all handsome, with that obstinate chin and those craggy cheeks that might have been creased from the tears he shed for the sinful world he could not save.

Then she felt the judgment in his eyes that he had once masked, and her hackles went up in self-defense. "What do you want of me?"

"A decent life, but we both know that will never happen."

"As long as there exist men like you to shift the blame. Why don't you remove your cloak? Or are you afraid you will be tempted again?"

His lips tightened. He turned his hat over in his hands. "I didn't come here to fight."

"Or to find pleasure?"

"The family we both respect has asked my help in finding a personal diary that disappeared in the night. It was last in the Duke of Wynfield's possession."

Audrey stared at him. "The only rule that I faithfully observe is that all secrets remain safe in this house." And for that reason she maintained a faithful clientele that consisted of politicians, dignitaries, impoverished poets, and affluent lords alike.

He cursed through his teeth. "I know Wynfield was here. I would like to speak to the woman he met. Her name is Gabrielle, as I understand it."

She came to her feet. "In that case, Sir Daniel, you will have to make an appointment. However, I assure you that the diary is not in this house."

He rose and stepped forward to obstruct her way. "Damn it to hell, I will break you, Audrey."

"For a price I cater to all manner of improper desires— but these affairs are conducted in private. I'm sure you recall that I employ many bodyguards. At the slightest indication from me you will be escorted outside."

She dismissed him with a smile as the door opened to admit one of her guards. "I will do everything in my power to help find the diary."

"All the bodyguards in the world aren't going to protect you from yourself."

"You are not going to save me," Audrey said with a pitying smile. "Save yourself instead."

"From what?"

"From your overbearing righteousness."

"What makes you think that I have unselfish motives?"

"If this is a business proposition, I doubt that you could afford me."

He stared at her for a delicious moment of uncertainty before he exited the room. She followed him into the hall but went in the opposite direction without once turning around.

"What a prick," she said in a loud enough voice for him to hear her, and even then she caught a low drift of his laugh.

Just like that he had ruined her night.

Reform her, would he?

She could sleep with him or ignore his existence at will. But she would never allow herself to want him again.

Gideon turned in annoyance to the gentleman who was trying to get his attention. He had yet to deal with the lout who was rubbing the sizable lump that had risen on his perspiring forehead. "And who might you be? Another court jester to join the one I'm about to throw down the stairs?"

Charlotte gave him a gentle poke with her fan. "Your Grace—"

He wasn't listening to her. He had just noticed that yet another gentleman had forged through the thinning crowd to reach Charlotte. He conceded that she looked beautiful tonight, but three persistent admirers at once?

"Give me your names," he said arrogantly to the tallest of the trio. "I will personally knock all your heads together if any of you offend this lady again."

The tallest man, whose face had begun to look familiar, flashed him an impudent grin. "And who do you think you are to act as her protector?"

He snorted. "I think I'm the Duke of Wynfield."

"And he is," Charlotte murmured, looking quite pleased with the fact.

"Is he?" the tall fellow asked Charlotte, with a familiarity that made Gideon wonder what other secrets she had to hide. "Imagine. Heath said that you were engaged to a duke, and we laughed ourselves back into the street. As if you would marry a peer of the realm we had never met."

The lout with the lump gave an uneasy laugh. "As if she would marry *anyone* without asking her family for permission."

The quietest member of this circus glanced thoughtfully from Gideon to Charlotte. It occurred to Gideon that except for the difference in hair color, this reflective gent resembled . . . well, hellfire, he could have been her brother. Gideon glanced appraisingly at the taller man. Those blue eyes betrayed a similar ancestry.

He looked down at her. "These are your—"

"—brothers," she said. "Unbelievable, isn't it, that we sprang from the same source? Oh. And this is Mr. Phillip Moreland, my old . . . friend."

Phillip. An indefinable memory rose in the back of his mind.

Where had he heard that name before? Surely not from Charlotte's lips. But her diary—oh, yes. He stiffened. Phillip was the object of her past infatuation. Charlotte's heart had been broken by this clod. And why should Gideon care? Because if Phillip had returned her affection, Gideon would not be standing on the edge of that cliff called matrimony.

Still, no man could interfere in his affairs with impunity, even if Gideon himself had lost control of his own destiny. He felt foolish enough for having landed in this situation. He did not need anyone's help to make him look worse.

He took a menacing step forward. As if sensing trouble abrew, a group of passing theatergoers paused to stare.

The duke in the company of an unknown lady was reason enough to stir interest.

But Wynfield's challenging a man in the theater was far more enthralling than the predictable play they had just sat through.

"What gives you the right to approach this gentlewoman?"

The lout straightened, managing to come to the level of Gideon's chin. "You're obviously unaware of my identity or you wouldn't dare to ask."

Gideon scoffed. "You're obviously unaware that I'll dare to do whatever I want. And keep your grubby hands to yourself."

"Grubby? *Grubby?*"

Gideon nodded enthusiastically. "That's right. A grub is one of those little maggoty creatures that leaves a residue of slime wherever it crawls."

"Oh, my goodness." Charlotte snapped open her fan and applied it with a vigor that was presumably intended to dampen his rising temper. "Gentlemen, please, this has gone far enough."

Gideon leaned away from her reach, conceding that she was more dangerous with that lone accessory than her delicate appearance suggested. In fact, everything about Charlotte was misleading. How else could he explain why he was standing in a theater lobby with smoke billowing from his nostrils, willing to defend her to the death?

Then Charlotte gave him a smile, and it didn't matter whether she had deceived him or not. In some unsullied remnant of his heart he recognized that her intentions were pure and passionate, and that he needed to guard her for his sake as well as hers.

"Move away from her," he added. "Or I shall move you myself."

Phillip's face reflected a slow-dawning realization that Gideon was serious. "You wouldn't."

"I think he would," a voice cheered from the growing crowd. "Do it, Your Grace!"

Before Gideon could take further action to thwart this pest, Grayson and Jane made an ill-timed appearance and everyone started talking at once. In the midst of the mayhem Charlotte's two brothers managed to introduce themselves to Gideon, and vice versa. But her former love remained silent, his eyes straying to Charlotte with a wistfulness that tempted Gideon to finish with his fists what Charlotte had started with her fan.

Unfortunately Grayson dispelled that satisfying possibility by suggesting that all seven of them pile into one carriage and go out for chops. "I'm half-starved," he announced, oblivious to the tension in the air.

"I'm not eating chops in my new Devine evening gown," Jane said indignantly. "Your chefs can make chops at home if you have a hankering for them. Come, gentlemen. Charlotte. In case none of you has noticed, there is a nasty-looking man on the stairs making a sketch of us that will probably appear in the morning papers. I for one do not intend to dignify his existence by posing for him."

# *Chapter 18*

*C*harlotte was relieved that her brothers had trundled off with Phillip in a separate carriage. It had started to rain, and she could only imagine how intense the ride back to the academy would prove with Gideon in his mood. She had thought the rumors of his pride to be exaggerated. She could not fault his behavior tonight, however. He had clearly taken his role as her betrothed to heart.

She *could* fault him as he followed her through the front door of the academy into the hall. The residence was quiet, but Charlotte instantly detected the whisper of curious girls at the top of the staircase.

"Your Grace, I cannot thank you enough—"

"Yes, you can," he said, and pulled her into his arms. Evidently he intended to further explore the passion he had shown her at the theater.

"Miss Boscastle!" a shocked voice said in the mounting silence. "Your Grace! There are ladies present!"

Gideon released Charlotte with a deep sigh and

glanced at the bespectacled woman lurking in the shadows. "Good evening, Miss Boscastle," he said, his gaze smoldering as he backed toward the door. "And to you, Miss Peppertree—" He blew her a kiss. "Proper dreams."

Gideon felt a presence a few moments after he returned home and as he entered his drawing room for a brandy. He reacted before his uninvited visitor had time to rise from the high-backed wing chair that faced the fireplace. Swallowing an oath, he reached back for the walking stick he had propped against the door.

The blade flashed in the dark. The other man turned, looking down his nose disdainfully at the weapon. "Do not move," Gideon said, wondering whether the planets were in misalignment tonight. "I have trained at Fenton's School of Arms—"

"Well, so have I. In fact, we have trained together for many an hour."

"Dear God, Sir Daniel," Gideon said, retracting the sword in vexation. "I almost bobbed your apple. What do you mean by breaking into my house? And don't tell me you are on a treasure hunt. I do not find you desirable in the least."

Sir Daniel waited for Gideon to set down his stick. "To begin with I did not break into this house. Your butler admitted me."

"Nice of him to inform me. Where is he, anyway?"

"In the kitchen consoling the housekeeper."

Gideon pulled off his gloves. "She is never awake at this hour. I assume your appearance frightened her."

"No, Your Grace. But the man lurking around the kitchen earlier tonight did."

"What man is this?"

"I have no idea. It is not unusual for a thief to return for more goods once he has successfully burglarized a house."

"Sit back down, Sir Daniel, please. And tell me how you have arrived at the conclusion that the diary was stolen from my carriage."

"It is rather an unwieldy item for you to have dropped without noticing."

Gideon frowned. "Yes. But then, Harriet dropped it and didn't notice in all the rush." Gideon, however, had not been in any hurry to be admitted to Mrs. Watson's house. It seemed as if the minute he'd touched the diary it had begun to unsettle his affairs.

Sir Daniel cleared his throat. "Excuse me. I should not have referred to the duchess by her first name. Now to return to this diary. I gather there is concern about its contents."

Gideon schooled his face into an impassive stare. Far be it from him to betray Charlotte's secrets, especially when he happened to be the best-kept one until now. "I'm not sure what you mean."

Sir Daniel shook his head. "I thought perhaps you might enlighten me."

"No. I'm in the dark, too. However, I will assist you in any way I can."

"Do you have any enemies?"

"The only one who comes to mind is Gabrielle Spencer. She works at—"

"Mrs. Watson's. Yes, I shall have to interview her personally. And perhaps you should, too."

Gideon's brow lifted. "Haven't you heard the news? I am an engaged man. It would be rather indelicate of me to visit a mistress when my wedding day is hurtling down at me like a meteor."

And his wedding night. Why did that seem to be approaching at a crawl? More importantly, why did *he* seem to be warming to the idea of marrying Charlotte? Because he had strong physical desires that he needed to satisfy? Because at vulnerable moments he found himself charmed by her and anticipating their future together more than he dreaded the idea of a marriage?

"It would be more than indelicate if someone used that diary to ruin your nuptials," Sir Daniel said, breaking Gideon's concentration.

"Do you have any idea who would resort to such behavior?" he asked.

"Not yet."

It couldn't be Phillip Moreland, as much as Gideon would like another excuse to dislike him. The man had only just arrived in London. Clearly he hoped to regain his place in Charlotte's affections. Judging by her response tonight, she did not return the sentiment.

Gideon put himself in the man's shoes. If he were Moreland he would not easily give up the woman he desired. In fact, he might be at Charlotte's door this very moment.

The thought provoked Gideon. Any man fatheaded enough to accost a lady in a crowded theater surely wouldn't hesitate to visit her alone this late at night.

Gideon reminded himself that he didn't care. His courtship was an act to satisfy Charlotte's notorious relatives. Yet her brothers were her *immediate* family. And they had brought Phillip Moreland to London, presumably to make a match.

A match that Charlotte had made clear tonight she no longer wanted.

"Is anything wrong, Your Grace?" Sir Daniel inquired, apparently sensing that he had lost Gideon's attention.

"I'm not sure," Gideon said, annoyed that his inability to concentrate on their discussion was obvious. "All I know is that I was living a straightforward if shallow life. And then, somehow, through no machinations of my own, it has become a twisted knot I cannot begin to untie."

Sir Daniel smiled. "I suppose those unpredictable turns are what make life interesting."

"And what make men insane."

"I've a feeling you have more control over your affairs than you realize, Your Grace."

Gideon gave a negligent shrug of agreement. Of course Sir Daniel was right. Gideon was still in charge of his life. Which did not explain why he planned to pay Charlotte an inappropriate call at the academy the moment the other man took his leave.

Charlotte watched the piece of paper curl and blacken in the small fire that burned in the grate. No one would ever read what she had written tonight. *When I am with Gideon, I can think of nothing else but him. Away from him, I—*

She glanced up. Sprinkles of rain had been pattering against the window. But that hard rapping was not rain. She rose from the hearth and went to the window to investigate. She pushed apart the curtains and swallowed a scream to see a face grinning at her from the other side of the glass.

"Gideon!"

He drew his coat up over his head, mouthing, *Let me in. I'm getting wet.*

She hurried from the room and into the front hall to open the front door. He smelled of fine brandy and damp wool.

"Gideon, what on earth are you doing in the rain at this time of night?"

"I saw the light in the window."

"And?" she asked, clearly suspicious of his motives.

"And I thought I ought to make sure that you were well."

"Did I appear to be unwell when we parted?"

"No," he admitted. "You appeared to be the very picture of health."

"Come into the drawing room and be quiet, please. Why are you here?" she whispered as they went down the hall. "My heart jumped into my throat when I saw you."

Once inside the room, he peeled off his coat and then his jacket. The damp air must have penetrated to his shirt. The crisp linen molded lightly to his well-muscled chest and shoulders. She sighed as he closed the door. "I wanted to make sure that you did not have any uninvited company."

She lifted the coat from his hands, compressing her lips. "And you consider yourself to be invited at any hour?"

"Yes, I do." He glanced at the flames leaping in the grate and drew off his gloves. "You took the liberty of visiting me unexpectedly, as I recall. And that was before we were engaged."

"That was an emergency."

A beguiling smile ghosted his face. "So is this."

She took his gloves, giving a start of alarm. "Your hands are cold."

"Thaw them for me," he said, his eyes issuing an illicit challenge.

"Come closer to the fire."

"That isn't what I meant."

She laid his coat and gloves over the back of the sofa, feeling his sultry gaze follow her. "I know exactly what you meant. I chose to let the insinuation pass."

"You chose to bring me into the house," he said. "And I notice that you locked the door after we entered."

She was torn. Should she insist he leave or encourage him to stay? She knew what she wanted to do. She had a fairly good notion of what he wanted, too. He was anything but hesitant about letting his needs be known. And it would soon fall on her to satisfy those needs.

He caught her elbow and drew her against his hard, damp torso. "Why are you up this late, may I ask?"

"I stay up late sometimes to think."

"About?" he asked, cupping her chin in his hand. "What do you think about?"

"Well, the diary, the consequences to the school, the younger Miss Martout's cough, our wedding, my brothers. I have to interview applicants for my position. . . ."

"And Phillip? Did his appearance at the theater make you restless at all?"

"Not as restless as it seemed to make you. What a fuss the pair of you made." And over her, she thought.

"I am still discomposed," he said, his thumb sketching the curve of her cheek. "Do you know of a way to soothe me?"

Anticipation tingled in her veins. Her heart pounded in want, in warning. He touched her as if he already owned her, and her body answered in swift agreement. She had never dreamed that she would have to fight her own urgings. The fanciful seductions that she'd written in her diary seemed to be on the verge of coming true.

"Charlotte," he said softly, "what are you wearing underneath your robe?"

"My night rail."

"And beneath that?"

She hesitated, her pulse quickening. "Nothing."

"That is what I thought."

He wrapped his arm around her waist and drew her down to the circle of firelight on the carpet. "Gideon," she whispered, her eyes widening. "You are behaving very impolitely."

"I am, aren't I?"

She vented a sigh. "I am surprised that you admit it."

He frowned in feigned concern. "I didn't mean to forget my manners. Let me go about this the proper way."

She stared at him in suspicion. "The proper way?"

"*Excuse* me while I untie your robe," he said, tugging the sash apart.

She went still. "You demon, I don't believe your audacity."

"And *pardon* me for loosening the drawstrings of your night rail." Which he did with ease.

She gasped, and the sound drew his attention to her mouth. "You are utterly—"

"And do *forgive* me while I gaze upon your hidden charms in the firelight."

Her eyes grew wider until he skimmed his hand down her throat, and she squeezed them tightly shut. "That," she whispered in a warm voice, "is not at all what I meant about manners."

"Then . . ."

Gideon lost the focus of his thought, too entranced by the soft flesh he had unveiled to find his voice. She lifted her head, only to moan softly as he bent to kiss the tip of the breast that peeked temptingly through her loosened garments. His tongue lashed back and forth in a flagrant act of enticement. Lightly he lifted both robe and night rail to expose her lower body to his view.

"Gideon," she groaned, reaching her hand down in an attempt to cover herself. "I'm indecent."

"No, darling." He caught her wrist, his gaze riveted to the inviting hollow between her upper thighs. "You are perfection."

"But you—"

"I like to look," he said. "I could reach a climax if I looked at you long enough."

"I feel immodest," she said, shivering as he stroked his other hand over her knee and then higher.

"And do you know what I like even better than looking?"

She opened her eyes and stared up at him, another helpless shiver betraying her. "No."

"This," he said as he gently parted the folds of her cleft and pressed his fingers into her beckoning softness. "I like touching better." In fact, he liked touching her intimately better than any other act he could remember from his recent history. Perhaps from his entire life. Her response to him was so natural and unstudied that she might have been the one well-versed in seduction.

She turned her head, a cry breaking in her throat as he tested, teased, and stretched her to the boundaries of what either of them could take, and he knew he couldn't trust his control another minute. He knew his body had reached the limit, and all he could do was give her blessed release and draw pleasure from that.

Dark temptation swam in his mind. If he coaxed her a little more, he could take her maidenhood and soothe his own passions in her beautiful body. He could unravel the rest of her restraint with his mouth, his hands, his throbbing cock. He could fill her tight heat with the length of him. Oh, God, he would move within her so hard and fast and high, that she would probably pass out in a delirium of sensation.

His body ached as she broke, pulsing against his knuckles, bathing him in the sweet dampness of desire. He grasped her soft white arse in his free hand and savored every quiver that she couldn't suppress.

He drew a breath that he hoped would still the temptation that urged him to slake his hunger inside her. But all he could do was watch her come back slowly to her senses. And with a sigh of regret, he drew her night rail and robe over the flesh that he could not wait to possess. "There," he said, lifting his hand away. "I hope you are satisfied that I have not breached the rules of proper behavior."

She smiled, her blues eyes sultry. "Did you get what you came for tonight?" she queried softly. "Are you always on the prowl this late at night?"

"Are you complaining about the pleasure you just experienced, my dear?"

"Not at all. But is that really all you wanted?"

He glanced away, his jaw set in a hard answer.

"Gideon?" she whispered, her voice concerned. "Was it only passion that brought you here?"

Even now she unsettled him with the sweet concern that she didn't try to hide. It made him ache with lust and guilt and other insidious emotions that he wasn't ready to confront. He wouldn't grow weak and open himself to pain again. This was enough. Charlotte was happy to share his name and his bed; she hadn't made any other claims on him that he didn't intend to give.

"To answer you previous question," he said without looking at her. "Yes. I prowl at night, but never alone."

"Well, isn't that a comfort?"

He smiled wryly. "All right. I'll be honest. I was afraid your old sweetheart might make the grave error of visiting you tonight."

"I doubt that my brothers would allow that."

"But I'm here," he pointed out. "And I didn't see a guard at the door."

He felt her hand alight on his arm. He ached for her touch. "Perhaps," she whispered, "after what they witnessed tonight at the theater they were convinced you had assumed that position."

# Chapter 19

Charlotte listened to the light rain tapping against the window. She could feel the throbbing pleasure he had given her recede and fade to a faint ache. She would have burrowed against Gideon's strong body if he had not drawn away from her.

And if he had not looked so pleased with himself. "You are undeniably the most arrogant man I have ever met."

"Thank you." He rose to his feet and smiled down at her as if she had praised him. "Anything else?" he asked, extending his hand to lift her from the scene of her undignified surrender.

"Yes. You are entirely too wonderful, and we are fortunate no one saw you enter the academy. I doubt you would be wearing that smile if Miss Peppertree had listened in on our mischief."

"Miss Peppertree needs a good—"

"Gideon."

He reached to the sofa for his coat and jacket. "My respect for Miss Peppertree does not extend beyond blowing her a kiss."

"A memory I'm sure will stay with her forever."

He slid one arm into his jacket. "How long have you known the lout?"

"The who?"

"You know who I mean. Moreland. Your first love."

She knotted her sash. "Exactly how much of my diary did you read?"

"Not as much as I should have."

"I've known Phillip all my life. Now it's your turn to reply."

"I read a few recent entries that regarded me. And the part about the lout who is nursing the egg you laid on his noggin."

"Is that all?" she asked skeptically.

"Considering the short time it was in my possession and the distractions that competed for my attention, I think I did quite well."

She stilled, her mind sensing an omission. "I thought you left the diary in your carriage and did not take it in that house."

He shook his head. "I was . . . Well, I read some of it in my carriage."

"And you took it—you didn't! You did *not* take it into that place of ill repute?"

He turned away to slip his arm into the dangling sleeve of his jacket. Charlotte narrowed her eyes at him in chagrin. "Don't tell me you engaged in any lascivious acts with my diary sitting there as an unwilling witness?"

"Of course I didn't," he said hastily. "Do I look like a complete rogue?"

"Yes. *Yes, you do.*"

He captured her face between his large hands. "What just happened between us is the closest I have come to a lascivious act in a long time."

"It's the closest I have ever come," she whispered.

"Which is as it should be."

He lifted her face and kissed her lightly on the mouth. She shivered instinctively. "You shouldn't be here."

"How else are we to learn anything about each other during our all-too-brief courtship?"

"I suggest long walks together in the park."

"Not private enough for a—"

"Neither is this house, Your Grace," she said, collecting her wits again. "You *have* to leave."

He released her with a deep sigh. Before he could disconcert her with another charming ploy, she reached around him for his coat. He took it and turned to the door. "Don't walk me out," he said, glancing back at her with a look that made her start shivering all over again. "And stay away from the windows. There are dangerous men about this time of night."

He escaped quietly from the house and hurried out into the gaslit drizzle. He wasn't sure what was happening to him, but his thoughts seemed to be as twisted into knots as his body was.

He glanced back to catch her peering through the curtains at him. He shook his head in warning. She disappeared. Any passerby could see her if he hid in the greenery under the window. The thought unsettled him. Indeed, when he turned around he saw a man in a long cape hurrying across the street.

He stared at him through the misty haze. "Sir Daniel! You again?"

"Good God, Your Grace. I did not recognize you at first. I was about to show *you* the sharp end of my walking stick. I thought the academy might have a Peeping Tom at the window."

Gideon hesitated. It was a damn good thing Sir Daniel hadn't looked through the window a few minutes earlier. "Do you ever sleep?" he asked, gesturing to his coachman to draw up the parked carriage.

"I sleep off and on through the day."

"Shall I drive you home?"

"No, thank you. It isn't raining hard, and I was supposed to meet a contact on the corner."

Gideon stared down the street. "I don't see anyone. What manner of person is he?"

"An unreliable one," Sir Daniel said in a disgruntled voice. "I should have known he wouldn't show up on time."

"This meeting doesn't concern Charlotte, does it?"

Sir Daniel shook his head. "I doubt it, but I would like to know whether word of this dilemma has reached the streets. It is more likely that instead of sharing any helpful information this person would hope to profit from the situation."

"I assume it isn't a woman. Do you know his name or whereabouts?"

"His name is Nick Rydell, and a more unprincipled character I've yet to encounter. As to his whereabouts, all I can say is that when you want to find him, it is nigh on impossible. Yet he seems to be everywhere you do not wish him to be at other times."

"Why did you choose this location for an encounter?"

"I didn't, Your Grace. He did. And now if I may be so bold, I would like to ask you to leave in case he has spotted you and will not come forward until I am alone."

There wasn't much Gideon could do under the circumstances but to respect this request. Clearly he could not stand vigil outside a school for young ladies without causing another scandal. But that did not justify sitting useless while a diary that had been in his possession was perhaps being passed from one stranger's hand to another's. His future wife's reputation was at stake.

He had to launch his own investigation, and whether it was to prove his honor to himself or to the Boscastles seemed to matter less by the minute.

Nick ambled about the street, oblivious to the bustle of another London morning. He calculated that there would be several bidders for the diary, which he had first stowed in a place of honor under his pillow beside his pistol and then, reappraising its worth, had hidden under a loose floorboard. He had been up half the night reading select passages from the lusty tome. He was shocked, titillated, and impressed. He might stumble over an occasional word he didn't recognize, but he got the gist of the entries that described Miss Boscastle's encounters with the duke. Naughty, naughty. She used words as well as he used a knife. Quite the wicked girl. He thought he was in love.

Still, business was business. Who wanted the diary the most? The bat who had commissioned its theft? The publisher on Fleet Street who'd had the displeasure of conducting business with Nick before? The fancy courtesan whom the duke had thrown over for the lady with the red-hot pen?

Trickier to predict was whether the duke would let himself be blackmailed or would go off his head and throttle Nick. He'd seen Wynfield fencing at Fenton's School of Arms. The duke was a natural fighter; he had to be good if Fenton had trained him, and Nick had to respect that, if nothing else. Then there was the lady herself.

It was no wonder the duke was marrying her. Nick had been curious to find out what she looked like and had finally caught a glimpse of her this afternoon when she and her pupils set out for shopping in the Strand. Fair hair, a sweet face, and white muslin.

"Who'd have thought it?" he mused to the costermonger, who'd moved out of the street to let the lady's carriage pass. "It's the quiet ones you got to watch."

"Do you want to buy any or not?" the vendor asked in a testy voice, pulling the apple away from Nick's nimble fingers. "I ain't pushin' this cart for charity."

"No, old man. I'm not purchasing your wares today. In a day or so, I reckon. I've recently come across a mint. After a few negotiations I'll return with a fat purse."

"Fat chance of that is what I predict."

But Nick took no notice.

He had a fortune under the floorboard.


Gideon was surprised when Audrey Watson agreed to see him the next morning. He had sent her a note asking whether they could meet away from her house, and she had returned his message by suggesting she pick him up outside a bookseller's on Bond Street.

Her carriage was nondescript and not likely to attract notice on the congested streets. Nor was she, dressed in a leghorn bonnet and high-buttoned sage green morning gown that made her look more like a matron going about her domestic errands than the abbess of a thriving bordello.

"Your Grace," she said with a genuine warmth that he also did not expect. "Is the gossip true? Must I mourn the loss of another rogue?"

He couldn't help laughing at her candor. But then, Audrey was a popular half-world hostess, and she boasted a network of influential friends. She was accomplished in the social as well as the amorous arts.

"It is true," he confessed.

"Then I must congratulate you, although I hope this sudden engagement is the result of romance and not anything that happened in my house."

He shook his head. "I don't think I can explain it."

"I see," she murmured, and he guessed she already knew more than she wanted to reveal. "Innocence often holds a stronger appeal than sophistication. I could have offered you another courtesan, but I doubt I could have found one with your fiancée's heritage."

He hesitated. Could he trust her? He decided that he had to take that chance.

"I wanted to make a personal appeal for your help. I brought my betrothed's diary into your house. If Gabrielle thought to avenge herself by stealing it when she visited me later on, well, I will offer a generous sum for its return and leave it at that."

"I doubt Gabrielle has the wits for anything that

elaborate. She is already looking for another protector. But if you would like to see her, I'll have to warn you that she is very put out and upset with you."

"I gathered that," he said with a wry laugh. "I shall be in trouble with not only Charlotte's cousins but the two brothers who have just arrived in town."

"Brothers?" Her eyes lit up. "Are they married?"

"You probably know the family better than I do." He laughed again. "I don't believe in romance."

"But you do believe in honor?"

He nodded. "What else does a gentleman have to go by?"

The carriage had returned to Bond Street. He had made his case and had to leave it at that.

"We'll meet again, Your Grace," she said with confidence. "If not here, at a party or another soirée."

He leaned forward to the door. The slight rustling of paper unfolding in her hands stopped him.

He turned his head reluctantly, hoping it was not a random page from Charlotte's confessions. She appeared to have drawn from her reticule one of the satirical broadsheets that littered the gutters of London.

"I don't know whether you saw this," she said. "But in case you haven't you should be prepared for the days ahead."

He took the paper from her hand and stared down blankly at a caricature that took moments for him to interpret; it was a rude depiction of himself as a fire-breathing dragon in the theater last night and a cowering Moreland in a dented steel helmet, with Charlotte holding her open fan between the two men like a medieval shield.

Jane, too, had warned him that the scurrilous press

had scented a scandal in the theater lobby. He had been too infuriated to listen.

"These filthy rumors come and go," Audrey said with a reassuring smile. "It won't touch you."

"No."

"Still, the sooner you are married the better."

*Chapter 20*

A note arrived for Charlotte shortly after she returned from shopping with the girls. The duke would like to take her to the park with her brothers; the Marchioness of Sedgecroft would act as chaperone. Charlotte immediately sent the duke's messenger off with her acceptance. Their rushed courtship might not deceive anyone, but that didn't mean she couldn't enjoy it.

The sky was overcast when he came to call, but Gideon against the gloomy backdrop seemed larger than life, a magnificent creature who could master his milieu. Evidently she was not the only woman of that persuasion. She noticed that every housemaid the academy employed had found an excuse to swarm the hall.

The added bonus of her brothers Caleb and Jack chatting against the duke's coach had drawn even the under footmen to the door. It seemed to her that the entire world wished to experience every aspect of this romance almost as much as she did.

They reached the park at the fashionable hour, Gideon's carriage halting in the parade of stylish phaetons, gigs, and curricles whose owners had come to see and be seen. It was apparent to Charlotte that Gideon belonged to the former group, and that the arrival in London of her eligible-bachelor brothers had already caused quite a stir.

Grayson and Jane, of course, drew their own circle of admirers, as did Grayson's sister Chloe. But the majority of females abroad at this time of day, from governesses to gentlewomen to ladybirds looking for a lovely duke to land on, aimed covetous glances like Cupid's arrows his way. Charlotte kept a good grip on his hand until another tall, attractive gentleman, who was giving a fencing demonstration by the water, called out a challenge to Gideon across the green.

It was Sir Christopher Fenton, Charlotte realized, the dashing sword master whom Grayson and Jane had retained to instruct their young son, Rowan. Fenton was said to be Gideon's closest friend.

"Sorry, I'm courting today," Gideon called back with a sly grin.

"That was a subtle announcement," Grayson said wryly.

Gideon glanced down at Charlotte. "Do you mind if I take him up?"

"Not at all."

It was a brief but impressive show of swordplay. The two men started with the five positions of the salute and launched immediately into a heated contest.

"Why don't they wear protection?" Jane wondered aloud.

Chloe's lip curled in a knowing smile. "It's considered

unmanly when one is fencing an opponent of equal skill."

Charlotte watched Gideon and his friend in admiring silence. She might have never been able to look away had a strain of conversation not disturbed her.

"I wouldn't want to meet those two in a dark alley," a gentleman standing next to Grayson remarked.

"I would," the lady in front of him announced to the shocked laughter of her friends. "I could happily become the hostage of either or both of them."

Charlotte reminded herself that it was rude to eavesdrop, although it wasn't until the lady dropped another disconcerting statement that Charlotte realized *she* was the topic of this unfortunate discussion.

"I would choose the duke over the master, despite the fact that we were about to conclude negotiations for an arrangement when he became involved in a scandal with some milksop schoolmistress."

"Really?" said one of her companions, her eyes lifting to Charlotte in uncertain recognition. "Well, I'm sure she is a lovely person."

"I'm sure she is a spoiled chit who will lose his interest a week after the wedding. I'd like to tell her to her face."

"Gabrielle," the other woman whispered, gesturing with her head to Charlotte. "I think you already have."

Jane turned around, her elegant nose in the air. "Kindly pick your sour grapes in another vineyard, if you please. His Grace's betrothed is trying to enjoy the match. And so am I."

At that moment Caleb strolled up to join them, Jack at his heels. "Ah. I see we have a contest under way. Who is winning?"

Jane smiled. "Charlotte is."

"Charlotte?" Grayson turned his head in confusion and stopped his gaze on Gabrielle. "I know you," he said. "I met you at a rout last week. Aren't you the woman whom Wynfield—"

"—doesn't know," Jane finished for him. "Is that what you meant to say, dearest?"

He tipped back his top hat and stared over the heads of the audience to the fencing match. "If you say it was, Jane, then it was."

By the time the match ended, having been called a draw, Gabrielle had fluttered off to the other end of the park with her trio of subdued companions in tow.

"Well," Charlotte said quietly when Gideon returned in a casual stride to her side. "Would you like me to leave you alone? I know that she is the one you hoped to be with now."

Not to mention that he could still take Gabrielle as his mistress after the wedding, and they both knew it was not only a possibility but a standard practice in the ton.

But he glanced only once toward the woman in question before giving a decisive shake of his head. "I want to be alone with you," he stated. "Shall we go for a walk so that the upper ton has another reason to stare?"

"I don't know whether that's a good idea," she said, and glanced around to see Jane nodding in consent, if not encouraging her to comply.

So Charlotte took his arm and let him lead her to a well-worn path, the world of mistresses and fencing matches receding like a wave. It was another first, she thought, to walk with Gideon in comfortable silence.

Perhaps she felt at ease because there were no more

secrets between them. She had met Gabrielle. He had thwarted Phillip in the theater lobby.

How good it felt to have confronted the truth. The only secrets that need concern her were those they would share, both in daily life and in their marriage bed. She felt her heart sing with the anticipation of it all.

And then he turned to her with a gravity of purpose. His face bore no trace of the wonder she felt. Instead, it reflected a discontent that made her afraid of what he was about to say.

"Charlotte, I have to tell you something," he said, his eyes searching hers. "I should have told you before, but everything has happened so fast."

She braced herself. *I don't really know him,* she realized with dismay. *I have made him up the way I wanted him to be.*

"If you have changed your mind about this marriage, Gideon, I will try to convince my family to release you. I will deal with the aftermath. I'm responsible for this tangle."

"You don't understand. What I'm about to say, and should have said before, might make *you* reconsider. Come. We can walk a little farther and still be seen."

A dark foreboding filled her.

"I cannot change who I am," she said, feeling defensive. "I know what sort of beauty a man seeks in a lover."

"How would you know?" he said. "There is no one standard of beauty. Your beauty is—"

"Quiet."

He frowned. "I disagree. May I finish?"

"Yes. Of course."

"I need to be honest with you," he said. "I never

planned to marry again after my wife died. But we were both young. I am expected to produce a male heir."

"I am sorry for her death, Gideon. What was her name?"

"Emily," he said, still holding Charlotte's hand. "She died of cancer four years ago." They paused beneath a canopy of tangled branches. "When she died everything in my life dissolved. Our marriage was arranged, and both of us were shy of each other. Neither of us was even twenty. But then she fell ill and there was nothing I could do. She was sweet. She would have liked you."

"Oh, Gideon."

"I couldn't do anything except watch her go. And then I lost the courage to care. Everyone urged me to marry again. But it seemed like too much effort to look for anyone else. After all, I didn't look for her. And so I was drunk and belligerent for two years following her death."

Charlotte felt an aching sadness that she was afraid to express. She didn't want to embarrass him with an excess of sympathy. Yet she wished him to know that she cared.

And then he said, "My daughter doesn't remember her at all. She may remember me even less. In effect she lost both of us at the same time."

Charlotte pulled her hand from his to stare up at him in disbelief. "Daughter? I wasn't sure whether her existence was a rumor. You have a daughter and have never mentioned her to me?"

He nodded. "Yes, a five-year-old girl."

"I don't understand," she said, her voice dropping in distress. "Why is she not here with you in London? Where have you put her? It is one thing to keep a mistress in secret, but your own flesh and blood? Has someone threatened to kill her?"

"She's a bit of a handful," he admitted. "She never holds still and . . . well, you would probably be horrified the first time you saw her climb a tree."

"No. I wouldn't."

"And spit. She likes to spit on unsuspecting people as they pass."

"She sounds unsupervised." And rather happy, Charlotte thought, recalling her own youth. She had never complained when her brothers engaged her in their adventures, or equipped her with a bow and arrow to play Robin Hood. But then, the four of them had been blessed with two doting parents and the gift of one another's company.

Gideon glanced down at her. For the first time since Charlotte had known him he seemed unsure of himself. "I wondered whether we could wait a few more days for her to arrive before the wedding."

She melted. "Oh, Gideon, I've been afraid this whole time that you would yearn for that other rude female whose name shall not be mentioned. I had no idea that you missed your daughter."

"I would like you to think of her as our daughter."

Her throat tightened. "I do love girls."

"I warn you that she's a little outspoken for her age."

"You should meet some of the girls who have gone through the academy. Think of Harriet. I don't mean to boast, but I have trained a formidable armada of young ladies."

"From my perspective you also have a talent for bringing gentlemen in line."

"That remains to be seen. There are temptations everywhere you turn."

"For you or for me?"

"I meant you, of course."

"Isn't Phillip a temptation?"

"Not in the least."

"Come here a moment," he said, his dark eyes kindling. "Slip behind the tree where we can't be seen."

"What is her name, Gideon?"

"It's Sarah," he replied, and drew her slowly toward him.

"Sarah." She sighed, not resisting as he dipped his head to cover her mouth with his. "She must be lonely."

"Not for long," he murmured against her lips.

"Yes. I so want to meet her. Oh, Gideon, I'm quite annoyed with you."

"Everyone is," he said idly.

"You don't seem to care."

"What can I do?"

"Accept some responsibility as a father, I suppose."

"Yes," he said, taking her criticism on the chin. "But the fact is that her grandmother made me promise before *her* death that I would not expose the child to the life I lead in London. She said I had to either change my ways or place Sarah in the custody of responsible guardians."

"Well, I can understand that," she said. "I might have felt the same way."

He leaned back against the tree, staring up through the branches in a short, brooding silence. "I thought it was better to place her in the care of trustworthy servants and let her live in the country atmosphere that she has always known."

Charlotte frowned. "When was the last time you saw her?"

"I don't recall," he said. "Nine or ten months ago, I think. I spent last Christmas with her. The entire day. We played puppets and gorged ourselves on pudding."

"That is ages ago." Charlotte shook her head in chagrin. "I don't know what to make of you."

"A good husband and a better father, I expect. Don't count on it, though. I have trained myself to live for pleasure, as you have trained others to live in the polite world. I've no intention of being improved."

# Chapter 21

*J*ane and Chloe strolled off together toward the path that Gideon and Charlotte had taken. "Where have they gone?" Jane asked.

Chloe shrugged, not at all concerned. "Maybe he's taking her to his carriage. I know another girl who was banished to the country for kissing a man in the park."

"And I know who she was," Jane said.

"But what was his name?"

Chloe fought back a smile. "I don't remember."

Jane shook her head. "Do you think that he will— No, not in the park, where anyone could interrupt. Charlotte would never allow it."

"Did you see the way she was looking at him?" Chloe asked. "Her face was radiant. She's in love, and nothing we could say would make a bit of difference."

"Yes." Jane sighed in resignation. "But Charlotte is not an expert at the games he plays so well. His would-be mistress didn't look happy about the engagement."

Chloe's eyes clouded over. "Speaking of . . ."

They fell silent as Gabrielle Spencer flounced their way, an older gentleman doing his best to keep up with her pace. "Don't trip on a wet patch of grass and sprain your back, Gabrielle!" Chloe called after her. "It would be a shame to see you lying about for a good reason."

Gabrielle's mouth dropped. "If it isn't the lady who had to keep a man in her closet to force a wedding proposal from him."

"You'll make a fool out of yourself if you pursue Gideon after he's married," Jane said crisply.

"Maybe he'll pursue me," Gabrielle said with a careless shrug. "He knows where to find me."

"So do I," said Chloe.

Gabrielle tossed back her hair. "He needs an heir, and once that bun is in the oven, he'll be done with his duty."

"I doubt it," Jane said, her voice clipped.

"I've known him longer than you," Gabrielle retorted. "He isn't a man who deprives himself of pleasure."

Chloe smiled. "The fault with that line of thinking is that the pleasure you give can be bought on any street corner."

"No." Gabrielle smiled back at her. "He has expensive tastes. The schoolmistress is in over her head."

"And so is he," Jane said, giving Gabrielle her shoulder. "He hasn't looked at you once all afternoon. In fact, I doubt he'd notice if you walked into the lake."

Early that evening, as Charlotte was mulling over Gideon's confession, her brothers paid her a call. Ogden, the academy's butler, deigned to smile as he ushered the two rogues into the drawing room.

Jack took one look at Charlotte's face and the hand-kerchief in her lap and sighed.

"I thought you were happy about this engagement — even if from what I gather it did not come about in a typical manner. Lord above, Charlotte, how did you land in this place?"

"What are you weeping about?" Caleb said, dropping down on the couch beside her. "Aren't you supposed to save that for the wedding?"

Jack settled down on the other side of the couch. "You could still marry Phil—"

"No," she said forcefully. "I couldn't."

"He claims that he's turned over a new leaf," Caleb said.

"I'd rather turn over a stone and marry what hides beneath than him," she said.

Jack coughed. "Didn't Wynfield refer to Phillip as a grub in the theater?"

She caught them exchanging glances over her head.

Caleb let a few moments elapse before asking, "Did Wynfield do something to make you cry?"

She didn't want to break Gideon's confidence by explaining that she would soon become a mother to an outspoken girl who spit at people and had been left to her own devices. Her heart clenched at the thought of the young girl being brought up without any parents. Her brothers wouldn't understand that Charlotte hadn't shed tears for herself but for Gideon and Sarah and the young woman who had been taken from them too soon. No one could take a mother's place. Was it any wonder that the child misbehaved?

She sat forward in annoyance. "Stop crowding me."

"I suppose we should prepare ourselves," Caleb said.

"For what?" she whispered.

"Everything started with a diary that may never be found. If it isn't we will have to bear up and endure."

"That's easy for you to say," she muttered.

"The deed is done," Jack said unhelpfully. "Our house has endured the slings and arrows of outrageous scandal since the first Boscastle was born. No doubt we shall cause, and live through, a multitude more."

"That's the longest speech I've heard from you since . . . forever."

He gave her a taut smile. "Then let it be the last, at least regarding your guilt. You are a lady. Any scandal you're anticipating will not come to fruition. You couldn't have written anything in your diary that would cause you more embarrassment than we've brought on ourselves."

"I wouldn't bet on that," she whispered.

Jack removed a clean linen handkerchief from his long jacket and offered it as a replacement. "Charlotte, look at me. Has Heath been ruined because his wife drew a risqué picture of his male parts that was printed and distributed at random throughout London?"

She pressed his handkerchief to her face.

"Well?" he asked, waiting for her to react.

She bit her lip hard to no avail and burst into laughter. "I don't mean to be disrespectful to Heath, but . . . but . . . it's different for a man."

He nodded. "Good. I have made you forget yourself for a moment. Now, as to your impending marriage, I take it that you are still not opposed?"

"No," she said, her unseemly giggles subsiding.

Caleb arched his brow. "Then all is not lost. And one more thing, Charlotte."

"Yes?"

"Let these be the last tears you shed for a very long time."

She saw the nuisances to the door and returned to the drawing room to pour a small glass of sherry and extinguish the lamp. It was past time to check on the girls and retire for the night. The visit had buoyed her spirits, and she knew that paying distress calls was not typical of the male nature.

Nothing had been solved. But still she felt better. Gideon would protect her from scandal, and for all she knew the diary had been tossed into the Thames by an itinerant peddler. But then, not knowing its whereabouts would follow her forever like a storm cloud.

For all—

A noise at the window penetrated her thoughts. It was a noise reminiscent of Gideon's light tapping at the pane. She turned, vacillating briefly before she hurried to draw back the curtains at the window where he stood. She could just make out a portion of the hand that pressed against the glass. He faced the street and then, as if he sensed her watching, he turned his head. It struck her that he was acting rather strangely. Had he been waiting for her brothers to leave? She couldn't quite make out his face in the darkness. Or had one of them forgotten to tell her something that couldn't wait until the next day?

Sir Christopher Fenton, master at arms of a popular fencing salon, ordered his assistant to crack open a bottle of porter when he entered the school and saw Gideon practicing his lunges in the gallery. "What's the matter?" he called out jovially. "Couldn't think of another excuse to visit Miss Boscastle tonight?"

Gideon shot a wry look at his friend. "Let's not use foils tonight. That way I can hurt you and pretend it's an accident."

"I was thinking the same thing," Kit said. "Except I was going to hurt you so that you'd have a genuine reason for Charlotte's sympathy. Women love to take care of reckless men like us."

"I don't think we need to go that far."

Kit grinned. "You've missed several practices. I would have been worried about you if we hadn't met at the park. Some of the lads thought you'd given up the sword."

"What are you grinning about?" Gideon straightened from a lunge. "I'll be giving up more than fencing practice after I'm married."

"I don't see anyone holding a pistol to your head," Kit retorted.

"And the fact that you work for my betrothed's cousin does not influence your opinion?"

"Well—"

"And," Gideon continued, "the fact that Grayson used *his* influence so that a commoner like you is now *Sir* Christopher and not ordinary 'Kit' has not swayed your point of view?"

Kit rested back against the wall. "If this is how you behave when you're away from the lady, I don't think I want to see the pair of you together."

Gideon ignored that. He wasn't about to admit he would have given in to the temptation of visiting Charlotte again if he could think of an excuse.

Kit Fenton was a hard man to fool. He'd been orphaned at birth and brought up in a workhouse, where he'd lived on his wits and brawn until he had been adopted by a retired cavalry captain. It was Captain Fenton who had taken advantage of Kit's skill with the sword to reform his ways.

Gideon suspected that there wasn't much Kit hadn't seen in his time. He'd turned around the lives of many young men attracted to ruinous adventures. He demanded that his pupils train hard and follow a code of honor.

Gideon was sure that he wouldn't be the man he was now if not for Kit's influence.

Even now his friend saw through him. "Your mind is not on your blade, Gideon. If you can't pay attention, go for a walk."

"I'm afraid of where I'll end up again."

"Then for God's sake, go to her."

"No." Gideon shook his head in refusal. "I can't do it again. I'll appear to be desperate." Which they both knew he was. "Did I tell you about my incident at the theater?"

"I saw the broadsheet."

"The other man was her first love. He didn't return her desire at the time."

"And he does now?"

"To his misfortune, yes."

"It's only been what? One day? Three?"

"What can he do?" Gideon asked with the aristocratic negligence that seemed to define his nature.

"Challenge you?"

"Good. I'd enjoy that."

Kit frowned, drawing up his shirtsleeves. "It would be unpleasant to duel right before your wedding. Bloodshed and brides do not mix."

"If my memory serves me well, you fought a match *on* your wedding day."

Kit grimaced. "I didn't have a choice, did I? And don't be modest. I doubt I could have concentrated if you hadn't been watching over my bride."

"What else was I supposed to do?" Gideon shrugged. "I know you would stand as my second in a duel."

"Every pupil in the salon would. But that doesn't mean I'm encouraging you to challenge anyone."

Gideon shook his head, listening to the laughter of students and the clatter of their foils from the lower rooms. "There are times when honor is an unpalatable brew to swallow."

"Love is far worse, Gideon. At least with honor one has warnings along the way."

Gideon made a mocking bow. "Thank you, O wise king, for the belated advice that doesn't do me a damned bit of good."

He straightened with a grin that quickly faded when he recognized Devon Boscastle pounding up the stairs toward him. "And here comes my fairy godmother. I think he's waiting for me to thank him for giving up the rest of my life."

Devon reached the top of the stairs. "Is that any way to greet a member of the family?"

"Excuse me. I should have referred to you as the 'evil fairy.'"

Devon was impossible to offend. "Anyone care to practice?"

"Yes," Gideon said. "Stand right where you are and let me find the darts."

Devon regarded him with approval. "You look well these days, Gideon. Stopped drinking, did you?"

"I look the same as I did two nights ago. What do you want with me now, you wretch?"

"First off, I want to apologize for calling you a hopeless philanderer."

"I didn't know you had," Gideon said. "But now I really would like those darts. Or a set of Gypsy knives."

Kit walked between them, shaking his head. "Gentlemen, either air your differences outside or desist. If it is action you crave, then I suggest you put your stubborn heads together and concentrate on finding a certain lady's lost epistles instead of creating new fodder for another scandal."

"Pax?" Devon said uncertainly to Gideon.

"Why the hell not?" Gideon said, throwing up his free hand.

"What are you waiting for?" Kit asked Gideon as he led the descent down the gallery stairs into the main area of the salon. "Why don't you go to her? You're damned useless as you are. I've fenced with seamstresses who ply a needle with more threat than you do your sword."

Gideon glanced at Devon, who shrugged, shook his head, and said, "Well, don't look at me. You have the wedding license. I know that *I* would not be kept from the lady I desired."

"Go," Kit said. "It's inevitable."

"Idiots," Gideon muttered, and strode out into the street, where his carriage waited.

He wouldn't dare visit the academy at this time of night. Then again, he wasn't comfortable calling in the middle of the day, either. A compromise, perhaps? Yes. He would drive past the house and not call.

If he was fortunate he would catch a glimpse of Char-

lotte in the window, and that would have to hold him
until the next phase of their courtship began.

The lady's full-bodied screech rattled every bone in Nick's
body. It froze the blood in his veins. Lord God help the
neighborhood, but she had a pair of lungs. He wouldn't be
surprised if she shattered the windowpane with her hys-
terical shrieking. He stumbled back in the flower bed,
grateful he hadn't been tippling or he'd have wet himself
from the fright. He hopped over the wall and darted into
the street, waving off a dog that ran after him.

"Hey, you, move out the way!" a coachman bellowed,
or something to the effect. Nick hadn't heard a single
hoofbeat or carriage wheel approach. He swore his ear-
drums had sustained lasting damage.

As had his heart, pounding through his body like a
military parade.

Who'd have guessed that his beautiful lady of the
lustful page could make that ungodly blast from hell?
He hadn't decided who would offer him the most coin
for the diary, or if he would sell it at all. All he'd wanted
was a peek at her, to see the face and form that matched
her earthly confessions. And him thinking she was on the
quiet side. He couldn't imagine what he'd do if he had
her under the blanket and she went to that voice.

He stopped, hands on his knees, drawing in draughts
of air to still his pulse. Had she gotten a look at his face?
He doubted it. He hadn't but glimpsed hers before she
lost her senses.

He hawked in the gutter and resumed walking, con-
templating his future. The next thing he knew a gang of
thugs had fallen in line behind him, asking what he had

planned for the night, and how they could be of help. He looked at them and slowly the lady's voice receded. Nick could never concentrate on any one thought for long. It was about time he got in a good knife fight and impressed the band of homeless street boys who considered him a hero.

# *Chapter 22*

"*M*iss Boscastle! Miss Boscastle!" Daphne Pepper-tree was beside herself with concern. "Charlotte, speak to me! What has happened? Did that duke break in here and take advantage of—"

"Do *not* utter another word," Charlotte said from the depths of the tufted couch to which Ogden and the footmen had borne her after bursting into the room. "There was a face at the window."

"The duke's face?" Miss Peppertree demanded in a smug tone.

"No, it was not," Charlotte replied, struggling to sit up. "It was a leering face, a face with . . ."

Miss Peppertree sniffed at her in suspicion. "Do I smell spirits on you?"

"You certainly . . ." Charlotte stared down at her ruffled silk overskirt in dismay. In her panic she must have spilled her glass of sherry on herself. To make the situation worse, two or three of the girls stood listening at the door.

"Where is he?" Miss Peppertree whispered, backing up a step. "Is he hiding in this room?"

Charlotte sank back against the cushions, scowling at the preposterous question. "Do you *see* him hiding anywhere, Daphne? Is there one piece of furniture behind which a grown man could hide?"

Miss Peppertree's eyes narrowed. She couldn't see two inches in front of her without her spectacles, let alone distinguish Gideon from a gargoyle. "A man?" She gasped, drawing her hand to the bosom beneath which it could be assumed that her heart was racing in maidenly consternation. "There was a *strange* man staring at you through the window?"

Charlotte nodded weakly, the explanation nearly as exhausting as the ordeal.

"A genuine prowler? Charlotte, are you sure?"

"Yes," she said grimly. "His face was— Oh, Daphne. The expression . . . I can't think of how to describe it. You'd have had the shock of your life if you had seen him."

"I had enough of a shock when I heard you scream."

Charlotte shuttered. "I feel violated."

"That makes two of us," the other woman said. "Violated by a man I've never met."

Miss Peppertree continued to stare at her in myopic sympathy. "Rankin has gone to fetch Sir Daniel. It's his night to patrol. He's probably down at the pub. And speaking of which . . ." She edged closer to Charlotte and sniffed the air again. "Is that sherry I smell? Is that odor of spirits coming from *you*?"

Charlotte glanced down at the dark brown stain glistening in the fold of her skirt. "I'm afraid that it is."

The infamy.

She had lost her diary, snagged a duke, and now appeared to have given herself to drinking and going into hysterics over a stranger at the window.

"Trenton," Miss Peppertree said to the footman standing helplessly behind the tea table. "Go and have a look about the house, and take a cudgel."

"I feel sick," Charlotte said.

"I would, too, if I were drinking this late at night. I never knew you liked to imbibe."

"Well, I've had a lot on my mind."

"As everyone is aware." Miss Peppertree glanced up. "There's a carriage pulling up now. It must be Sir Daniel."

"That was fast," Charlotte said, sitting up again. "Daphne, find the glass I dropped, and please don't bring up my drinking. I didn't even have time to take a sip."

"Here." Miss Peppertree gave her a cushion. "Hide the stain with this so that Sir Daniel doesn't see it. We don't want him thinking you've taken to the bottle."

"I haven't—"

The girls huddled in the doorway retreated suddenly into the hall to make way for the arrival. Charlotte's heart lifted as Gideon cut across the room to the couch, moving with power and purpose. She didn't know how or why he had appeared, but she had never been so glad to see anyone in her life.

"I saw the lights on and noticed Trenton running down the street," he said, the pitch of his voice gruff and oddly soothing. "What is wrong?"

"A prowler, Your Grace," Miss Peppertree answered before Charlotte could reply. "How fortuitous that you happened by at the same time."

"Oh, Gideon!" Charlotte whispered, staring up at his worried face. "I'm all right."

He went straight to the couch and knelt at her feet. "What is all this frenzy about?"

"A man . . . There was a man at the window watching me."

"Is he gone?" he asked, already rising, the thought apparently so infuriating that his first impulse was to fight.

"Yes. I gave a cry when I saw him."

"A cry?" Miss Peppertree said. "It was more like a banshee's wail. It went through the walls of every house on the street and may even have reached the corridors of Whitehall."

"What did he look like?" Gideon said.

Charlotte closed her eyes briefly. "Horrible, vile, nasty, leering."

"I meant the details of his face, Charlotte."

"It was pressed to the window, Gideon."

"Try to describe him. What color was his hair?"

"He was wearing a cap."

"What kind of cap?"

"I don't know. Dark. Woolen."

"And his eyes?"

"He had two."

There was a commotion at the door, and Sir Daniel came in, bowing hastily to Gideon. "What did she say?"

"There was a horrible, vile, nasty, and leering man in a dark woolen cap watching her through the window. Other than that, she has not been very helpful."

"Oh, Gideon. I'm sorry. It gave me quite a start."

He rose and sat down beside her on the couch, Miss Peppertree compressing her lips in disapproval. "It's all right, Charlotte. I am here."

He pulled her into his arms. It was a breach of protocol, and she didn't care.

"Gideon," she said against the warm support of his shoulder. "I thought it was you again. I went straight up to the window and pushed back the curtains like a ninnyhammer. And there you weren't, and he was. I don't know how long he'd been watching me."

"What had you been doing?" he asked quietly.

"I was going to put out the lamp."

"Did he say anything?" Sir Daniel inquired, moving to the window and testing its integrity.

"He might have said, 'Hell's bloody bells,' but it was hard to hear." She frowned. "He was tapping at the window, I think, to get my attention."

"And then?" Sir Daniel asked.

"I lost my wits."

Gideon glanced up at Sir Daniel.

"I'm glad you're here, Gideon." She lifted her face from his shoulder. "I feel better now. I shouldn't have screamed. I should have remained calm and sneaked away to get help. But he scared me."

"There was nothing unusual about him, Miss Boscastle?"

"Nothing. Except—"

"Yes?"

She shook her head. "I only got a glimpse of him."

Sir Daniel glanced up from his notebook. "Young or old?"

"Oh. Young, I think."

"Tall or short?"

Charlotte swallowed. "Tall. But he could have been standing on a brick in the flower bed. The gardener will be furious."

"Think again. Take your time. What did he look like?"

She covered her face with her hands. "Horrible, vile, nasty, leering."

Gideon nodded patiently, pulling the cushion from her lap. She pulled it right back. "I think we've covered that. But as to his features—"

"Snarling."

"Snarling? Did he have big teeth? No teeth? Yellow ones?"

"I didn't think to examine his teeth, Gideon. He took me off guard, as you did last night, and I wouldn't have gone to look if I'd known it wasn't you."

"But I wasn't snarling at you."

"That's true. And you didn't show your teeth, either. Now that I think about it, he wasn't snarling."

"Well, then," Gideon said in a quiet voice, "what *did* he show?"

"Nothing that you seem to be implying."

"I know this is a provocative question," Sir Daniel said, "but it is important: Were you undressing in here, by any chance?"

"This is the drawing room, Sir Daniel."

Gideon smiled.

Charlotte felt her cheeks flush. "I don't undress in the drawing room, sir. I review accounts. I read and I write."

Sir Daniel shook his head in frustration. "My assistant is outside interviewing people who may have been passing by when this happened. If you think of anything that might be helpful, please send for me."

"What if he's dangerous?" Charlotte wondered aloud. "We had a girl kidnapped from here last year, as you well know. It was a terrifying experience."

"I can testify to that," Miss Peppertree said with a shiver. "The men who enter this house nowadays are ones who have been willfully admitted." She looked pointedly at Gideon. "Perhaps we should place a footman on guard here with a pistol."

Charlotte paled at the suggestion. "We cannot chance an accidental shooting with so many girls in the house."

Gideon rose, his brow furrowed. "The fellows of my fencing salon often volunteer to stand guard at the charity school. We should alert the watchman and have a nightly patrol going until this peeper is found."

"Peeper?" Charlotte said, aghast. "Why would anyone peep at me?"

Miss Peppertree pursed her lips. "I should think the answer to that is obvious. You have drawn some attention to yourself in the last few days."

"He could as well have been looking at you," Charlotte said indignantly.

"I doubt that," Miss Peppertree retorted, and Charlotte heard Gideon mutter something under his breath that sounded like, "So do I."

"You could stay with one of your cousins," Gideon said, falling silent as he lifted the curtain and stared.

"What is it?" Charlotte asked, her voice rising. "Is he back?"

"No. It's only Sir Daniel's man. Perhaps I should go out to talk to him."

Charlotte rose. Now that the initial shock of seeing that face had begun to wear off, she was starting to put her thoughts together. "He might have been anyone passing by," she conceded. "It's just that . . ."

Gideon closed the curtains. "We could move the cabinet here for a temporary measure. What were you saying, Charlotte?"

"The look on his face—I sensed a familiarity."

He turned sharply. "Are you sure it wasn't the man from your past?"

"Certainly not."

"What man?" Miss Peppertree asked. "Do you mean to say there's another?"

"I would never have screamed if it were Phillip," Charlotte insisted.

"No?" Gideon said. "What would you have done?"

"I would have waited until the morning to notify my brothers."

"And?"

"And you."

He appeared to be unsatisfied with her answer. She decided it was fortunate that Sir Daniel returned to the drawing room before Gideon could work himself into a state.

"Miss Boscastle, other than a few trampled roses, I can find nothing out there of help in identifying the man."

"There was something else," she said, "but it sounds silly."

"Perhaps you'll think more clearly after a good night's sleep," Gideon said.

"I know it doesn't make sense," she said, hugging the cushion in her arms. "But he was looking at me as if he knew me."

"We'll find him, Charlotte. Until then I do not want you alone in this room again."

# Chapter 23

The formal courtship between the Duke of Wynfield and Miss Charlotte Boscastle successfully captivated society. They became the couple to invite to one's party, to read about in the papers, to gawk at and gossip about when they were spotted by the observant eye.

A wedding between two houses of the nobility did not take place every day. The aristocracy commanded attention. Somewhere around the globe a kingdom toppled. An investment scheme collapsed. A war raged in a remote land.

One could forget these distressing events for a few hours at an elegant wedding.

Jane had volunteered to plot out an itinerary that would have worn out the Prussian army. As their appearances grew more demanding, Charlotte and Gideon actually began to think their engagement might be the death of them.

Between her duties at the academy, the strain of hir-

ing another lead schoolmistress, the wedding preparations and appointments with the dressmaker, and the
picking out of linens and monogrammed sheets, there
were moments when Charlotte wished Gideon would
cancel an event or two so that she could drop into a
chair and sleep.

And one night when his carriage arrived to pick her
up for a supper party, she found him slumped against the
seat in such a deep slumber that she not only was
tempted to let him sleep but to join him for a nap herself. Jane's presence deterred her.

"Bear up, both of you," Jane said. "You cannot enact
a courtship looking half-dead."

Gideon stirred, his heavy-lidded gaze meeting Charlotte's across the carriage. All of a sudden she felt wide-
awake. "Where are we going again?" he asked, stretching
his arms.

"To the Earl of Stanwood's supper party," Jane replied, shaking her head.

"I hope it doesn't go on for hours," he said. "I'll sleep
until noon tomorrow."

"No, you won't," Jane said. "We are attending an auction for charity bright and early in the morning. And afterward there is an open-air concert and dinner at the
Pulteney."

In her spare moments Charlotte gave her attention to
the academy and to interviewing and reviewing character references for another schoolmistress to take her
place.

The image of the stranger's face in the window began
to fade. She felt embarrassed by the fuss she'd made. It
became easier to believe he had been only a happen-
stance passerby, a pedestrian who had indulged his curi-

osity, rather than to accept that a stranger meant her harm—a stranger whose eyes had hinted of . . . well, the only word she could think of was *intimacy*.

But that was impossible.

There was no reason to think they had ever met. Charlotte had been sheltered all of her life. What on earth had given her the impression of a prior association? Unless—no. A man like that could not possibly have found and read her diary. Gideon had been bad enough. The thought of a stranger invading her secret world was too upsetting to consider.

Charlotte could almost pity the man. If he should disturb the house again, a veritable army of servants would go on the attack. Miss Peppertree had taken to checking the windows herself every night.

As Gideon so tactfully said to Charlotte the day he escorted her, Miss Peppertree, and two young ladies of the academy to the emporium, "He's the one who'll start shrieking if he's expecting you and sees her face instead."

"That is rude."

"She doesn't like me," he said, examining a silver filigree chest set on display.

"Nonsense. She doesn't like men in general."

"What about you?"

"I have to like men, don't I? I have three brothers and innumerable male cousins."

She feigned an interest in an ivory hunting horn displayed in a glass case. "Isn't this an interesting piece?"

"Interesting, yes. Necessary, no." He propped his elbow on the counter. "It seems to me that you, my huntress, have already cornered your quarry."

"People are staring, Gideon."

"I don't care."

"What about the girls?"

"They are pretending not to notice the youngbloods who are flirting with them."

"Where?" She craned her neck to see around him.

"The girls are fine. Miss Peppertree is aware of the situation."

"She's aware of you."

"Do you like me as much as you did when you wrote about me in your diary?"

"No."

"No?"

"I like you more. Is that what you wanted me to say?"

"Yes. Now pick out anything your heart desires."

The emporium's owner, Sir Godfrey Maitland, suddenly recognized the duke and approached him with a solicitous smile. "Miss Boscastle. Your Grace. How good to see you without a sword pointing in my direction."

Charlotte blinked. "Excuse me?"

"Didn't your betrothed tell you? He and I used to practice at the same school. Business is so brisk that I no longer have time for the sport."

"What a shame," Gideon said, knowing full well that Kit had stripped the pompous merchant of his subscription to the salon over a personal matter.

"Yes, well, I hear you have been active yourself," Sir Godfrey said with glee. "Congratulations to both of you on your engagement. I hope you will keep the emporium in mind as you plan your nuptials. We carry a silver bridal service, linens, and clocks. Wedgwood china and camphor-wood chests equipped with brass locks."

"My fiancée is interested in that hunting horn," Gideon said.

Charlotte shot him a look. "No, I am not."

"It's a nice piece," Sir Godfrey said. "But it is rather heavy for such a delicate hand. Perhaps the lady would be interested in our collection of Welsh love spoons."

Gideon smiled. "Darling?"

"Not today, thank you. I was looking for a fan."

"Why?" Gideon asked. "You have more fans than I've ever seen in my life."

"A lady needs more than one fan if she is to have a complete wardrobe," Charlotte said.

"Aren't they all the same?" Gideon asked blankly.

Sir Godfrey hastened to enlighten him. "Goodness, Your Grace, they are not."

"I am teaching a class at the end of the week on the language of fans," Charlotte said. "Perhaps you would like to observe, Gideon."

He made a face. "I don't think so."

"It is an art," Sir Godfrey said. "It never hurts to understand what a lady is saying with her fan, if you take my meaning."

Gideon looked unconvinced. "An art?"

"Nothing turns a gentleman's head like a lady versed in the language of the fan," Sir Godfrey said.

"I don't know about turning a man's head with her fan," Gideon said. "But she can certainly hit one on the head with it and make herself understood."

Charlotte gave him a strained smile. "That evening was the occasion of an unprecedented emergency."

"Plying the fan is a learned skill much like fencing," Sir Gideon said. "The fan speaks volumes when wielded by the educated female."

Gideon subjected Charlotte to a long, considering stare.

Sir Godfrey moved to another counter and brought out two different fans. "This," he said, snapping open a black fan, one hand on his hip like a toreador's, "is for mourning." He drew it up to his eyes. "I can hide my tears and still express my grief."

"And this one," Charlotte said as she took the fan made of lace with mother-of-pearl sticks, "is a wedding fan."

Sir Godfrey waved his fan in agreement. "Do you see the Cupid painted beside the bride and groom, Your Grace?"

"Hmm. It isn't a before-the-wedding baby?"

"I have to have this one," Charlotte said.

"It's indispensable," Sir Godfrey agreed.

"It looks exactly like your other fan," Gideon remarked.

"I use a different fan every day and every night. Haven't you noticed?"

"It isn't the first thing about a woman that catches my eye."

Charlotte and Sir Godfrey glanced at each other, neither of them daring enough to ask Gideon to elaborate.

"A lady could hardly teach etiquette without an assortment at her disposal," Sir Godfrey said at length. "There is a secret code that must be learned to move in society."

"A code?" Gideon grinned. "Do you expect me to believe that ladies tap their fans at one another to send signals like drumbeats?"

"A lady would not *tap* unless it was absolutely necessary," Charlotte said. "Considering Your Grace's vast experience, I surmise that you have been the subject of many clandestine conversations."

He shrugged. "Maybe I have. How would I know?"

Sir Godfrey glanced at Charlotte. "Shall we give him a demonstration?"

"Oh, by all means."

Sir Godfrey swished open the black fan with a flick of his wrist. "Let us spell the word 'love,'" he said, and proceeded to lay the fan upon his chest, smiling coyly. "That is L."

"O," Charlotte said, placing her fan in a similar movement to her breast.

Sir Godfrey lifted the fan to his forehead. "V."

"And for E one moves the fan in the left hand to the opposite arm," Charlotte said. "Then, to indicate that the conversation has ended, the fan is fully opened."

Gideon stood between the two suspended fans, not uttering a word until Charlotte broke the silence. "Your Grace," she whispered. "It's rude not to make a comment."

He shook his head. "Forgive me. I was stunned speechless. To think these secret parleys have been conducted all my adult life, and I hadn't a clue. I might have been mocked while dancing a minuet and been none the wiser."

Charlotte pursed her lips and carefully placed the fan on the counter. "I would like the bridal fan, Sir Godfrey. And I shall need at least six church fans. His Grace and I will be attending services together every Sunday."

"We will?" Gideon asked.

"And a dozen brisé fans decorated with pastoral scenes."

Gideon smiled at her. "A dozen? Darling, you have only two hands and I have a hundred ideas on how better to use them."

Charlotte smiled at Sir Godfrey. "The other fans are for the academy."

"Oh, silly me," Gideon said.

Charlotte pretended not to hear him. "Now that I think about it, a dozen isn't enough. The sticks are often broken during practice. I should have twenty, just in case. Oh, and Lady Sarah—I want an assortment of appropriate fans for a little girl."

Sir Godfrey flushed in pleasure. "A wise investment, Miss Boscastle. His Grace is fortunate to have found a lady of your discernment. By the way, I've received a new shipment of vellum journals."

"For what?" Gideon demanded.

"A person of Your Grace's lineage must appreciate the importance of recording the daily minutiae of the elegant life in a collection of well-kept diaries."

"A collection?"

Sir Godfrey's voice rose. "History should be recorded for posterity. Imagine the thrill of your descendants when a hundred years hence they read the musings of ancestors who might otherwise be nothing more than portraits collecting dust on the wall."

Gideon stared at Charlotte. If posterity read her musings, a hundred years would not give them enough time to recover from the shock. "What a fascinating thought," Gideon said. "Kindly put the fans on my account. The diaries can wait for another day."

Sir Godfrey beamed. "One trembles in anticipation at the prospect of a ducal wedding."

"Doesn't one?" Gideon said, clasping Charlotte by the hand to drag her away from the counter. From the corner of his eye he noticed Miss Peppertree and two young ladies listening avidly to this exchange. "Good day, Sir Godfrey—"

"I don't suppose I could interest you in a tric-trac table for your honeymoon?"

"I have other games in mind for my bride, but thank you for the thought."

Sir Godfrey bowed. "The very best to you both. It will be an honor to serve you in the future."


When Charlotte came downstairs the next morning, she discovered that a package had been delivered to her by a private courier. For a wonderful moment her hopes soared that some goodhearted stranger had found and discreetly returned her lost diary.

Indeed, when she sat alone at her desk to unwrap it, the contents proved to be far more scandalous than those she had so unwisely "confessed" in the pages of her diary. For secured in a red silk ribbon was a portfolio of detailed sketches that depicted a variety of erotic acts.

And tucked under the ribbon was a brief note that read:

### A GUIDE FOR THE WELL-INFORMED WIFE
by
Audrey Watson
Fondly,
Jane

"Oh." She put her hand to her mouth as she came upon a picture that resembled...a rocket? Going where? *"Oh."* This was worse than anything she had written. Or was it? Odd, but there was comfort in the knowledge that she was not the only woman on earth who fought forbidden desires.

Still, she would not leave these drawings about for anyone to find them. Daphne would go off like a whippet if she realized what they revealed.

She intended to return them to Jane that same evening. Grayson was giving a soirée at his house to officially celebrate Gideon and Charlotte's engagement.

That gave Charlotte several hours to study the prints alone upstairs. Until then she dared not let them out of her sight.

She had learned her lesson, even though it appeared from Mrs. Watson's portfolio that she had a few others still to grasp.

# Chapter 24

Charlotte admired the gilt-edged Greek frescoes that decorated the walls of Grayson's mansion. An array of mirrors added glittering dimensions to the entrance hall. One could reside in this house for a lifetime and miss a myriad of details, such as the tales of Odysseus that were inscribed on the Corinthian columns, or the rubies embedded in the three-tiered chandeliers.

The engagement party dined at a black oak table with plush Persian carpets under their feet.

Grayson's French chefs had prepared a supper of spring pea soup, herbed quail, and grilled trout, with truffles and buttered French beans. A bevy of underbutlers served a dessert of pineapple jelly and strawberries soaked in brandy and smothered in cream.

Devon remarked that the gold-plated service reminded him of head platters.

"I'll have you know that these settings came out of

the vault in the duke's honor," Jane retorted. "It took two days to lay this table."

"Why?" Devon asked. "How hard is it to throw down a few knives and forks?"

Charlotte looked dismayed. "Can't you tell that the place settings have been precisely arranged to the exact proportions? Every plate and goblet has been measured with a ruler to match the others around the table."

"And," Jane added, "that the beverage you are quaffing is vintage wine and not cheap ale?"

Gideon was of a mind to agree with Devon. He wasn't interested in what he was eating or how it was served. He waited through supper to be with Charlotte.

He stared at her across the table.

He studied the choker that encircled her delicate throat. It seemed a safe place to stop, between her face and tempting décolletage. No. Not safe. He could almost feel the silent beat of her pulse. And when her gaze met his, he hoped he would never do anything to dim the dreamy glow in her eyes.

He waited through the playlet performed in the amphitheater by a cast of Drury Lane actors. He waited for the guests to go to gaming rooms or to gather in the summerhouse for champagne and conversation that centered on the dwindling value of the pound and the influence of foreign markets on England's prosperity. The war might be over but its debt had deflated the economy. Families had lost their homes, their incomes, their last hope. Unemployed soldiers roamed the streets. Factories were closing up, leaving scars on the discouraged land.

Soon no voices could be heard around them.

It became apparent that he and Charlotte were not missed by the crowd.

"It's a conspiracy to leave us alone."

"Was it something we said?" he asked her as they walked unhurriedly through the house and came to the spiral staircase. "What's up there?" he said.

"The Italian gallery."

"I've heard of it. Shall we explore?"

"Yes." She took the first few steps, trailing her fingers up the railing, and of course he followed; a gentleman must ascend behind a lady lest she slip and he had to catch her.

But the moment they entered the candlelit gallery he dropped all pretense and pulled her to him. His lips sought hers. His hands stroked down from her shoulders to her hips, fusing her body to his. "Charlotte," he whispered against her lips, "I haven't been able to think of anything but you all night."


She was consumed more and more by thoughts of what would happen when he took her virtue. All she understood was that this was a prelude to the passionate acts illustrated in Mrs. Watson's portfolio, which Charlotte had examined until returning it to Jane's for safekeeping. Every picture had told an explicit story.

She twined her fingers in his hair. *Be fire to fire.* She had sought to follow the advice, but what would happen when the flames erupted into a conflagration? When he ravished her mouth as she fell into an inferno of her own need? His kisses whetted her desire for other pleasures and left her trembling and begging silently for the darker knowledge of his touch.

"You are in a wicked mood tonight," he whispered into her hair. "I wish I had known earlier so that I might have planned accordingly."

"You're making my legs go weak," she whispered back. "And I think you already know this, but we've become part of a grander plan."

She felt the heavy warmth of his hands, their strength, stroking and seeking places as if to lay claim to what would be his alone. "I think we ought to lie down together on that couch," he said with a persuasive smile. "Just in case you feel faint."

He slipped his arm beneath her bottom and carried her the short distance, kissing her again before lowering her to the chaise. She landed in a delicate disarray of silver gauze and blush-rose silk. Her full breasts rose and fell in rhythm with her increasing breathlessness. Her blue eyes clung to him, innocence giving way to invitation.

"What a lovely sight," he said, sinking into the space beside her.

She turned and found herself trapped between his hard torso and the arm of the chaise.

"Look up at me."

Her heart fluttered at the unmasked intent in his eyes. Slowly he lowered his head. The taunting brush of his mouth against hers brought her bliss. She sighed and placed her hand upon his lean torso. There was something about this man in evening wear that made her head swim.

His fingers caressed her cheek, lulling her into acquiescence. But his lips seduced her soul, promising devotion and deeds. A surge of overpowering desire coursed through her veins.

He stared at her half-recumbent form, her skirts drawn up to one thigh. "I think you need more than a few kisses tonight."

She stared up into his eyes. "Do you indeed?"

"I can give you everything you need."

"I don't doubt it."

"And I need you," he said.

Why hadn't he realized it right away? She was delightful company during the day. In bed she would be a sensual challenge that demanded skill and perception. He could not have found a better candidate for a wife. Charlotte deserved a slow introduction to the pleasures no one had shown her before.

He settled one arm under her shoulder. She was captured in his hold, close enough now that he could ease his hand under her gown and over her thigh to stroke the drenched warmth between her legs. His belly tightened in anticipation.

He heard her sharp draw of breath as he played her. "Now this," he whispered, staring down at her in fascination, "is what I call a treasure hunt." His fingers slid inside and pushed as high as he could reach. She closed her eyes, trembling, drenched in her own desire, drowning, adrift.

"That's what you need," he whispered, his thumb flicking upward and faster. "Just let me show you. Part your legs a little more so I can enjoy your release."

His shoulders tightened. He wanted her. He could have taken her without either of them undressing.

But he didn't want her to feel any shame the first time he made love to her. This wasn't the time or the place. When their moment came, he would unravel her and kiss and lick every delectable spot on her body. He would heighten her arousal until she begged for him. Until the ache he denied would grow and torment and tempt him beyond endurance. He was so hard right now he might explode.

"Gideon," she moaned, throwing her arm over her face. "My heart is going to burst."

"Mine, too," he whispered, quickening his fingers. "Give yourself to me." He laid his head against her upraised knee and gazed down into the hollow of her thighs.

Her response excited him. Her passionate displays grew wilder every time he stole a moment with her. She undulated her hips like a siren. She moved as her instincts guided her, her response so enticing that his throat tightened and he was only a blessed instant away from burying himself in her beautiful body.

He reached up his other hand and unfastened her bodice, bending to her unbound breasts to suck at their distended tips. She whimpered and twisted at the waist. "Gideon. I can't—"

He sat up and drew a harsh breath as she shattered, her body swept by helpless spasms. Her nipples darkened. Her eyes were glazed and dilated. She shivered and curled in against his arm, whispering, "*Gideon.* That was . . . Oh."

He threw himself back against the couch, reluctantly drawing his hand from her warm flesh. "It certainly was."

She darted him an inquisitive glance. "But I didn't pleasure you."

"Oh, you did." He inhaled, rousing himself to move. "You've no idea how much. I expect that in a short while you will learn."

She looked down at his hands as he relaced her gown. "Is it an art that I should study?"

"Study? You have a natural talent for bed sport."

"There are wives in the ton who pay a fortune to study under Mrs. Watson," she said after a hesitation.

He gave her a rueful smile. She looked tousled and delectable. "You're tempting enough without professional tutelage. I prefer that I have the advantage. Now we are going back downstairs before a search party is sent to find us."

"I'm sorry, Gideon," she whispered with a laugh as he pulled her to her feet.

"For what?"

"For dragging you to the altar."

"Do you see a ball and chain attached to my body? Do you see a man who has no mettle nor the means to express it? I am not entering this union against my will, my dear."

She stared up at him in consideration, then lifted her hand to stroke the cleft of his chin. "I see a man who has his heart hidden away."

"There's far more to you than meets the eye, too." He smiled. "Remind me that I am never to trust a first impression again."

# Chapter 25

$\mathcal{M}$illie hunched down in front of the broken looking glass in the corner, struggling to button the
back of her dress.

"I'm late again," she muttered. "There's nothing
worse than choosing the gents the other girls refused. I
didn't mind it when there was a bully to watch over me,"
she said to the mirror. "But now I could lose me life for
a half sovereign's toss. Do you 'ear me, Nick? Are you
listening to me, you with your thumb up your bum?"

He looked up from the bare pallet on which he'd
fallen, belly first, the diary opened to a random page.
"'Comb your fingers through my silken locks.'"

"Why?" Millie asked idly, hiking up the cotton stock-
ing that sagged below her knee. "Don't tell me you've
caught lice again."

"God," he said, grunting. "It's meant to be romantic."

"Pickin' nits ain't my idea of a lovely time. You and
your palaver with a lady who'd faint if you touched 'er.

You said that book would make us rich. All it's done is make you stupid."

He had never read words put together like this. How'd she do it? How did a lady make lust sound like it wasn't a disgusting secret? That was how Nick thought those fancy folk regarded it.

He hadn't guessed that a woman could think like this. Maybe she was cracked. He didn't mind if she was. He'd never met a completely sane woman in his life, starting with his mother.

He'd never learned pretty language, either. Still, he could patter slang in his crib with a few pals or to an enrapt audience on a street corner, passing a bottle 'round and 'round.

There wasn't any other way to survive the streets where he'd been born unwanted and would die unmourned.

He rolled onto his back and stared at the boarded-up window. "Sapphires. That's the color of 'er eyes."

"The eyes that nearly popped out of 'er skull when she caught you at the window? You've gone daft, Nick. You ain't done more than a few jobs since you stole that bloody book. I never thought to see the day that you'd turn into a sop."

He snorted. "Didn't I steal the stockings that you're wearing tonight?"

"Stockings. My four-year-old nephew pinched a paisley shawl at the market."

"Then stuff it in your mouth," he said as she stomped to the low steps that led up through a stairwell into the street. "Just leave me be for once, would you?"

He set his teeth and closed his eyes, waiting for her to slam the door. She did. Fragments of plaster floated down upon the open diary and his face. He swung upright and blew the debris from the pages. No sooner had he hidden the diary under the loose floorboard than he detected the clatter of heels coming down the cellar stairs.

"What did you forget now?"

"I forgot how rank this place smelled," a tart voice answered from the door as it was unceremoniously flung open. "Don't you ever empty the chamber pot?"

His eyes widened in speculation as the slight figure appeared on the top of the steps. "Well, well, well, if it ain't the duchess stopping by for a spot of tea. What brings you to the slums, dearie? Missin' your old pals?"

His old friend Harriet lifted her lace handkerchief to her nose. "Have you taken to burying your victims under the bed?"

"Careful where you step," he said, propping himself up on his elbow.

"What a disgusting hovel," Harriet said through her handkerchief.

"I'm movin' out soon enough," Nick said. "I got some merchandise to sell and then I expect I'll 'ave fancy lodgings."

Harriet scraped a rickety stool to the bed. "I'm looking for a lost diary," she announced without preamble.

He whistled. "I never knew you kept one. There must be some shocking tales in that. Tales about you and me."

"This is important, Nick. The diary is going to turn up sooner or later. If I find it before anyone can read and release the contents, there will be a reward, and no questions asked."

He studied her face. "What will it bring?"

"Five thousand pounds out of my purse."

"That's all?"

"What do you mean, 'that's all'? As if you come across cash like that every day."

"I used to," he said softly. "You and me. God, what a rum couple we was."

"Do you know where it is?"

"For only five thousand pounds I can't even remember *what* it is. You and I brought in more than that paltry sum on our housebreaking lays together. I miss those times. I'll never forget the night—"

"I'm not here to reminisce," Harriet said, drawing her ankle from the hand he'd reached out to grasp it.

"Who wants it the most?" he asked.

"The person who wrote it," she answered. "It's important only to . . . well, to the owner."

"Why would anyone else keep it then?"

Harriet narrowed her gaze. "I'm not giving you any more information, knowing what a head you have for business and a heart for vice."

He chortled. "I deal in jewels. Silver. Gold. Not in books."

"The reward could go up, Nick."

He grinned. "Then so could the price."

"Keep your eyes open."

He smoothed back his hair. "Who's the author again?"

"A distant relative of mine."

"Time ago you and me was family. Never thought you'd give it all up for a fancy title and a castle in some foreign land."

"It's Wales, Nick. And my husband isn't a foreigner. You know everything that's going on in the streets. If anyone stole it, the news will get out eventually."

"A book. Who'd steal a book?"

"Books are beautiful, Nick."

"Gawd. Pardon the vomitus that is clogging up my throat."

"This is a private journal. It contains thoughts that can cause great embarrassment to individuals I care about."

"Tragic. An invitation to infamy. All those lords at your disposal. Another crisis that poor Nick is called upon to settle. Do you want to walk with me to the pub?"

She frowned. "No."

"Why not?" he said, offended now.

"Because you reek like gin, you've a hole in your shirt, and you're ignorant, that's why."

"I can read, you know."

"Then read the posters that went up this morning advertising a reward for a certain thief. You'll hang if you don't change your ways. You know it as well as I do. Maybe if you did good for once, someone in authority would give you another chance."

He looked her straight in the eye. "You've got a way with words, love. You always did 'ave a gifted tongue. There's a Bible sitting on that table behind you. Go on. Pick it up. Mind you don't knock over the bottle of gin beside it."

She hesitated, then rose to lift the Bible in her hands. "Are you going to swear on it?" she asked, taking a cautious step in his direction.

He stared down at the floor and shook his head. "Nah. Not today. But do me a favor and wedge it in the door crack on your way out. I feel a nap comin' on and don't want another female slamming and yammering about to disturb my dreams."

He looked up and flashed her one of the grins that

made the girls go weak. Harriet slowly lowered her arms and placed the Bible on his bed.

"Something is rotten in the state of Denmark, Nick Rydell, as sure as I'm standing before you. I don't know yet what, but I swear you've stepped in it knee-deep, and if I find out you betrayed my confidence I will hunt you down and skin you until you're grinning out the other side of your arse."

It was almost twilight when Gideon stepped outside his house. He was expecting a visit from Sir Daniel, and while he waited he realized that he hadn't asked the regular street vendors whether they'd recently recovered any articles of interest in the gutter.

The watercress woman shook her head and hurried off, not even trying to sell her wilted produce. Then the butcher rode by on his old horse with a basket of pig trotters. Gideon lifted his hand to slow him but the man pretended not to notice. The street people acted as if they were afraid of him.

Was he rude to others of a different class? He thought back. Perhaps he shouted more than he should have when the gingerbread seller approached him outside his door.

Why should he care what strangers thought? Except that Charlotte was anything but a stranger; he had not realized that his behavior caused offense, and he didn't know how she had done it, but she'd made him value her opinion of him.

"Your Grace! Your Grace!"

He stared at the elderly gentleman gesturing with a cane in the middle of the street. It was old Major Boulton, a widower who lived in the town house that faced Gideon's residence.

"May I have a moment of your time?"

"Yes, but not in the middle of the street. You'll be run over at this hour. I thought you were away."

The cane flew up. "And it's a damn good thing I was or I'd likely have been murdered in bed. I was robbed, you know. I don't suppose you've noticed any strange characters about the place?"

Gideon saw Sir Daniel walking toward them. He motioned him to hurry. "No, Major, I didn't know. But here is someone who might be able to help."

"What is the matter?" Sir Daniel asked as he reached them, leaning back from the man's cane.

"I was robbed last week!" the man fairly shouted in Sir Daniel's ear. "It happened when I was out of town. My butler did not even realize the house had been burglarized until this morning, when the chambermaids aired the upper floors."

"What is missing?" Sir Daniel asked.

"My wife's sapphire necklace. A few banknotes, and my silver snuffbox. Of these items I am sure. The thief may have taken more. But as these were all kept in my dressing closet; I'd venture a guess that he was in a hurry."

"Or merely a professional." Sir Daniel stared across the street. "How did he enter the house?"

"I don't know. The door locks are intact. I assume he scaled the wall to go around the back. The ivy on the side of the house was damaged, but that could have been the duke's tomcat chasing the females again."

"You will need to make a formal report," Sir Daniel said. "And I suggest, if you haven't done so, that you install lever locks."

"The locks look fine," the major insisted. "They are brass and steel."

"Which indicates a skeleton key was used," Sir Daniel said. "As for you, Your Grace, perhaps you were victimized by the same burglar who mistook your darkened house as a sign you were not at home."

Gideon frowned. "Do you believe that?"

"It is logical."

"I'd no idea that you had been robbed, too," the major said, lowering his cane. "Although to be perfectly frank, Your Grace is given to hosting parties for young ladies in the dark. It is difficult to tell whether you are in or out. Or how many people you are entertaining at one time."

Gideon coughed. "My days, or nights, rather, of entertaining in the dark are coming to end. I am shortly to be married, sir." Which did not actually mean that Gideon would not be up to mischief in the dark, only that he would play to a private audience of one.

"I wish I'd been informed that there had been another burglary in the square," Sir Daniel said after a long pause. "I shall make inquiries. And, Major, I suggest you and your staff try to recall any suspicious persons you may have noticed in the neighborhood, perhaps even going back a month or so."

"I shall do that right now. I doubt any of us will sleep well until the bastard is caught."

As soon as the major was gone, Gideon took Sir Daniel into the house. "Have you learned anything?"

"Yes."

"What?"

"That the person who stole the diary was most likely a professional thief."

Gideon looked unimpressed.

"It is not a small discovery, Your Grace. It narrows the number of suspects I have been considering."

"I can understand the theft of a sapphire necklace, but a young lady's diary? And from my carriage?"

"Perhaps the culprit was interrupted and grabbed the diary without knowing what it was. He might have been hiding in your carriage before or after the other theft. The necklace will no doubt end up in a dolly shop before long."

"And the diary?"

"We can hope it was destroyed."

Gideon sighed. "Do you believe that?"

"Not for a minute."

"Damnation, neither do I."

"I wonder . . ." Sir Daniel's voice trailed off.

"You wonder what?" Gideon inquired, gesturing encouragingly with his hand. "Speak your mind, sir. I do not have the patience for innuendo."

Sir Daniel looked embarrassed. "Well, I wonder what was in that diary that a person would go to any lengths to steal it, assuming that this was the case."

Gideon forced himself not to react. Far be it from him to reveal that he was the subject of the scandalous contents. "I can only hope that it is recovered before that question is answered."

*"Hmm."*

"'Hmm' what?"

"I tell you this because the young gentlewoman is your fiancée and it seems that there are no secrets between you, but Miss Boscastle admitted to me . . ."

Gideon gave him a hard stare. "Go on. There's no reason to hem and haw."

Sir Daniel shook his head. "She led me to believe that what she had written could be viewed as controversial. Considering her flawless reputation, I doubt that anything she could pen would cause a stir. Don't you agree?"

Gideon smiled inwardly.

"Your Grace?"

"Yes, yes. I agree. She must have been overwrought to confess such a thing."

"Overwrought." Sir Daniel nodded slowly. "But now I do wonder . . ."

"What?" Gideon said tersely.

"That face at the window. Do you suppose that something in her diary could have attracted an undesirable's attention?"

"Yes," he said after a pause. What else could he say? The few entries that he'd read had enthralled him. Why wouldn't another man, another undesirable, react the same way? He wasn't going to spell it out for Sir Daniel. He would hold out hope that the diary would be returned on the quiet to Charlotte. And if it wasn't he would do everything in his power to protect her from whatever unpleasant consequences she might face.

# Chapter 26

Audrey excused herself from the guests she had been entertaining and escaped to her private suite. She had a full crowd, including a young, virile earl whose eyes had seduced her on sight. His look said he wanted her in his bed tonight. She couldn't remember the last time she had slept with a guest.

She took off her jewelry and went to the window. Her nemesis hadn't appeared this evening, but she swore she felt his lingering presence—or did she hope he would return? That was dangerous. She would put a stop to that desire right now. She knew well that Daniel wanted her to be a woman with no past, without a voice or choice. She would never give up the security she had built for love. She had been trapped in an abusive marriage once, broken by a man who had betrayed both her and his country. It seemed like another life. She had threatened to turn her husband in as a traitor to England. In response, he had her imprisoned in the wine cellar of their London home while in the study above he plotted with other spies.

One night she recognized the voice of the close friend whose capture and torture her husband had once arranged.

It was Colonel Lord Heath Boscastle.

Honorable, intelligent, tested by trials he would never reveal, Heath had rescued Audrey and ended her husband's reign of cruelty and treason. She respected, admired, and adored Heath, but he did not love her, and she wouldn't lose herself to a man she could never have.

She was determined to control her life. She enjoyed variety, a steady flow of friends, money, and an amusing profession that surprisingly brought her respect. There was no emotional turmoil when a woman played with men only for pleasure and profit.

Sir Daniel Mallory was the thorn in her side.

"Madam," her maid said, slipping in through a side door with a pile of warmed towels. "Are you entertaining tonight?"

"No, Fanny. I'm going to read in bed."

"Is he there again on the corner?"

"No," she said, but as she pivoted she noticed a caped figure emerge from the direction of the corner pub. "At least I hope not."

"Sir Daniel is persistent. He'll be back."

"I can't imagine why he lingers. I don't have any information for him. And he hates this house."

"He hates to see you here."

"He thinks that my profession puts me at risk," Audrey mused, reclining on her chaise with a bitter smile. "He has no idea how dangerous it was to be another man's wife."

"Not all men are monsters, madam," Fanny said, coming to the back of the chaise to unpin Audrey's auburn hair.

"Yes, I know. But at my age the ones who aren't are married."

"Sir Daniel is not."

"Is the earl still in the house?"

"Yes. I don't know where, though."

"Ah. He couldn't wait."

Audrey sipped her wine, her eyes closing. This past spring she had turned down Daniel's proposal, insisting she could not serve as a fit mother to the niece and nephew he had taken under his wing. She hadn't even been able to save the child of his that she had carried. And when Daniel suggested she had brought on the miscarriage with her decadent habits, she had ended the affair.

He had been wild with rage, accusing her of infidelity and immorality, not allowing her a chance to explain that she had never been able to carry a child to term. He had never forgiven her for the loss. And she had never forgiven him for not realizing that she was grieving, too. And for not believing her when she swore that she had never been unfaithful to him.

"I'm sure a child is an inconvenience to a woman of your social influence," he had stated.

"We both took precautions, Daniel," she'd said, hiding her own hurt and anger. "I did not ask for the pregnancy. Nor did I seek in any way to end it."

"I have offered you marriage, which you declined," he said, his face shuttered. "I shouldn't be surprised that you would resent being swollen with my child when more influential men seek your bed."

"I knew that this would be a mistake," she said as

coolly as she could. "I am devastated that I lost the baby, but now there is no reason for you to return."

Wounded, they had both retreated, she into the profitable decadence of the demimonde, Daniel back to his campaign to purge the city of crime and punish its prime offenders.

"That diary is only an excuse for him to harass me," she said as Fanny lifted Audrey's hair to place a warm towel around her neck and shoulders. "When they find it, he will have to invent another reason to condemn me."

"I think he still cares for you."

"Cares? It is an act. He has threatened to expose customers whose confidentiality I've guaranteed. He has appointed himself my judge and jury because I made the mistake of taking him to my bed."

Fanny frowned in concern. "What shall I say if he asks to see you again?"

"He shouldn't make it past the guards. If he persists, we shall notify the authorities."

"Nobody would arrest him, madam."

"True," Audrey said, her mouth curving in a thin smile. "But no one will arrest me, either, which doesn't mean he can't cause trouble in spades. I ask you, is that the behavior of a man who cares for me?"

"It might be. Do you wish to change for bed?"

"No. In fact, bring out my dark red dress. I feel invigorated. I can't go to bed this early because a thief taker doesn't approve of my profession."

"The silk or the satin?"

"The silk. And, Fanny, if Sir Daniel does come to the door tonight, have the guards explain to him that in the future he must have an appointment."

# *Chapter 27*

*C*harlotte composed herself to make her farewell before entering the classroom. She refused to fall apart in front of her girls during her last days at the school. She wouldn't confess to them that when all was said and done, she doubted that being proficient in the language of fans would take them far in the marriage mart. But the steps leading to a proposal—she couldn't give them any helpful advice about that either, not given her accidental strategy. She was determined to leave some impression of dignity and encouragement at the academy. Unfortunately she hadn't stood like a pillar of propriety as her proper world dissolved around her.

The girls respected her. And she would miss them. It was a blessing that their innocent minds could not understand the scope of the imbroglio she had created with her wicked chronicles. And that no whiff of scandal had reached their parents yet.

Her pupils looked to her as a model of correctness

and she would protect their tender illusions with her last breath. She prepared herself for emotional outbursts and plaintive voices begging her to stay.

She girded her loins for the good fight and opened the door.

Not a head turned. Not a tear fell in the cluster of whispering girls at the window.

"He's keeping a woman at Mrs. Watson's."

"He's only marrying her because the marquess threatened to kill him if he didn't."

"Why did she go to his house in the first place?"

"Why do you think, pea brain?"

"I don't believe she went there for what you're thinking."

"She went there for something."

"It was her diary, and we're not supposed to know."

"Oh, right. She and the duke just fell in love on the spot and had to get married. She was duke hunting."

"They *were* together at the dance."

"I wish they had carried on here so that we could have watched. How will we ever learn anything about love?"

Charlotte's voice dropped to a pitch used only by demons in the deepest recesses of hell. "*Ladies!* I cannot believe what I'm hearing. Haven't you learned anything from this school?"

The girls scrambled back to their chairs, guilty faces avoiding Charlotte's withering stare. Not that Charlotte's own conscience was unburdened. However, as Grayson had pointed out, it remained a primary rule in the polite world that admitting an indiscretion was worse than committing it at the start.

She waited for the last whisper of silk to subside.

"That is much better. Today, ladies, we continue to learn the subtle language of the fan. As you know, a proper fan is an essential fashion accessory for a lady. To carry an article one does not know how to use is gauche."

She paused, suddenly tempted to confess that a fan would have been a useless weapon against Gideon's powerful allure, but she could not confide to the girls that she had brought his attention on herself. The truth was that *she* had seduced him, however inadvertent it had been, and . . . and . . . she wasn't at all sorry.

"One day," she said in the most even voice she could manage, "I might understand enough about love to explain it to you. Or maybe I'll never know what it is. Maybe one of you will be able to elucidate it for me when you are older. Until then there are feminine arts that can be taught to hasten our progress on the path of matrimony."

She looked into the angelic faces and smiled, and each girl looked back at her in complicit understanding. "Open your fans."

There was a moment of silence followed by the precise clack of eleven fans unfolding before the last snapped like a pistol shot carried across the room. Charlotte winced.

"Verity, you may discharge your fan like that only in an emergency. Can you imagine what effect your action would have upon a suitor's hearing?"

"I keep forgetting, miss."

"No one is liable to forget you if you disrupt an event with such a noise. Now, you will recall that the last five letters of the alphabet are known as the fifth movement. Bring your fan—delicately, ladies—to your forehead."

She surveyed the class with satisfaction. "Very nice. Now signal to me the following message: 'Dance with me,' using the movement of your right hand to the left arm to begin."

"Miss Boscastle, Verity spelled out a vulgarity to me!"

"Verity—"

The girl stood and pointed her fan at the window. "He's back!" she said excitedly. "The man in the window, miss. I just saw him peeking in at us. Let's get him, girls."

"Let's not!" Charlotte said in a horror. "At least, not any of you."

She rushed to the bell cord, motioning to one of the older girls on her way. "Fetch Ogden and the footman." Then: "Are you sure you saw someone, Verity?"

The girl nodded vigorously.

"Line up, ladies, and exit by the side door."

"What about you, miss?"

"I shall be fine." And she knew that she would. A peeper was unlikely to threaten her in broad daylight, when the streets hustled and bustled with witnesses. She wasn't alone. She was prepared this time. She would get a better description.

She hurried out into the hall to intercept Ogden in the act of answering the door. "Stop," she said. "Don't let that fiend into the house."

"The fiend, miss?" the butler said in confusion, staring at the man who stepped into view.

"Phillip," she said in astonishment. "Was that *you* staring at us through the window?"

He swept off his hat, his red hair windblown, his manner grave. "I was hoping to catch your attention."

"You certainly accomplished that," she said, her lips tightening. "You have upset everyone in the house."

"By trying to attract your notice? I thought I was quiet."

She felt the servants gathering in the shadows behind her. "It wasn't *you* who was prowling outside the window the other night, was it?"

"Good God, no. And please refrain from using your fan."

She lowered her voice. "What are you doing here?"

"May we speak alone?"

She glanced around. "It isn't a good time."

"Please." He gave her the insincere smile that used to melt her heart. Now it insulted her intelligence. What had she ever seen in him? How wretched it would have been if he had returned her affection and she had married him, forever believing herself to be a giantess with big teeth, instead of the goddess Gideon could not resist.

"Your brothers told me that I should not come here," he added. "I am risking their friendship to see you."

She sighed. "Very well. Come with me into the drawing room. Rankin." She turned to the young servant who had silently entered the hall, a bat clutched in his hand. "You can put that down," she whispered. "But I'd like you to accompany us. Goodness knows the girls don't need another scandal to set them off."

"I would prefer to talk to you alone," Phillip persisted as she led the way to the formal room.

"That isn't done," she said, dismissing his request with the confidence that had come from . . . Gideon. He might not ever love her, but he had respect for her feelings.

"You've been alone with Wynfield."

She spun around, her fan poised. "Is that what you wanted to talk about?"

He stepped away from the fan.

"Are you going to brain me again?"

"Not unless you give me reason."

"I feel stupid gadding about London with an egg-size lump on my head."

"You should have thought of that before you accosted me in the theater."

"Accosted you?" he said in disbelief. "How can a man who is hoping to save you from your regrettable affair with the duke be accused of anything so dastardly?"

"You're the one who's behaving like a dastard," she said. "Now come with me or go away."

He sighed. Then he followed her, and the footman followed him, positioning himself between them like a garden wall.

"Does he have to stand in the middle like that?" Phillip asked over Rankin's shoulder.

"Yes, I'm afraid he does."

"Charlotte, I am here to offer you a chance to escape your sordid engagement."

"My what?"

"I know that this match with Wynfield was the result of an innocent indiscretion."

She pursed her lips. "Do you?" She was sure that she had been indiscreet. But her thoughts about Gideon hadn't been innocent at all.

His jaw hardened. "I also know his reputation as a libertine. He took advantage of you. How else could it have happened?"

"Oh, Phillip, Phillip." She leaned to the right of Rankin's shoulder to address the question. "It was the other way around. I trapped him. In fact, I had been laying my trap for months. I wove a web that neither of us could escape."

He smiled uneasily. "You don't have to defend him to

me. I saw what a beast he was at the theater. An arrogant bully. A domineering—"

"—duke?" She sighed. "Why the rush to wed me now, Phillip? Were you waiting for the moment I fell in love so that you could ruin another dream for me?"

"Another dream?" he asked slowly. "*I* was your dream?"

She shook her head. "At one time. Incredible, isn't it?"

"I think you've become far too—" He frowned, breaking off. "Very well, I shall be truthful. My cousin Ardmore has no male heir except me. I am to receive an inheritance upon his death."

"And?"

"And—" His face reddened a shade lighter than his hair. "He will give me half of my legacy now if I marry into an aristocratic family."

"I should have known," she said in chagrin. "Well, there are other families in England to exploit." She gestured to the door. "Happy hunting."

He changed his stance. "You are guileless, Charlotte. He's taking advantage of you."

"I'm as guilty as sin. It's a fact. Accept it."

"Let me marry you. We shall elope this evening."

"Elope? Gideon would tear you into a thousand pieces before we could leave London."

He gave her a pitying look. "No, he won't. He will thank me for rescuing him from a marriage he never sought. You're not the type who attracts men like him."

She turned away.

She knew better than to let Phillip's opinion wound her. It would have been perfect if Gideon *had* chosen her of his own will. If she were honest with herself, she had to admit he intended to be her husband in name only. She knew his tastes ran to sultry trollops who had studied the art of seduction.

But she wasn't about to give him up without a battle. She could still be the most polite lady at the ball and a passionate companion in the bedchamber. If Gabrielle and her ilk thought to steal Gideon from his wife, then Charlotte would take off her elbow-length gloves and do battle with all the fire of her Boscastle forebears. And if Phillip thought he could win her back — well, it wouldn't happen. She didn't want to spend her life with a man she had academically and romantically outgrown. He was yesterday's news. The duke was tomorrow's scandal.

"Charlotte," he said urgently. "You must decide. We've known each other for years. I lost you through my own mistakes. But I have changed."

"So have I," she said. "You have to let me go, because even if he doesn't love me, I do love him."

She would rather grow old with Miss Peppertree than marry Phillip. The two spinsters could dodder around together, meddling in other people's lives. Because if Charlotte didn't marry Gideon, she would never marry at all.

"Listen to reason," Phillip said, his voice rising in anger. "The duke is only going to break your heart."

# Chapter 28

*G*ideon had spent the morning with Devon, attending a fencing exhibition that Kit had performed in Knightsbridge. Ordinarily he would have returned to the salon with Kit for a celebration. But he couldn't stop thinking about Charlotte. He'd like to believe, as she did, that there was no connection between her lost diary and the face she'd seen in the window. But it was too much of a coincidence that her diary had gone missing the same night the major had been burglarized. His mind kept trying to put all the pieces together.

And his inattention was obvious to his friends. "Do you want us to drop you off at Charlotte's academy?" Kit asked slyly, lounging across the carriage with his sword in his lap.

"No. I need to practice today."

Kit pressed his sword to the window. "Aren't we close?"

"Very close," Devon said, serious for once. "Perhaps

we should stop by, Gideon. In case that man is still in the area."

"I don't know," Gideon said, watching Kit slide a soft cloth over his sword. "She's probably in the middle of a lesson."

"I think you're dying now to see her," Kit said. "I think that she means more to you than you want to admit."

Gideon slumped back against the squabs. "Does it really show?"

Kit laughed. "You're trying to convince *us* that you're marrying her only because it's the right thing to do."

Gideon shrugged. "She's lovely; I do admit it, and there's something about her that makes me . . . insane. You must help me. I don't know what happened. I'm dying to bed her— Excuse me, Devon. I was speaking frankly and forgot for a moment that she's your cousin."

"That's perfectly all right," Devon said. "I enjoy bedding my wife, too, and Charlotte will be yours in a few days."

Gideon shook his head. "She makes me laugh when I don't feel like laughing. Take this diary nonsense, the things she wrote about me. I ought to be furious. I *was* furious. But now I don't quite understand what I feel."

She had deemed him deserving of her love. As a result he found himself wanting to live up to her expectations of who she thought he was. Without even realizing when it happened, he had stopped playing a role. And he would marry her with an open heart.

He should have resisted. But it was far too late. She was in his blood, under his skin. He would never be able to live the parallel life to hers that he originally had planned.

"When she looks at me . . . I feel like I've been struck with a strange fever."

Kit glanced at him. "Maybe you have a medical condition. Would you like a surgeon to examine you?"

"No. Have him examine Devon's head."

"He already did," Devon said. "He took some instrument and stuck it right into my ear and looked."

"And?" Gideon said.

Devon shrugged. "He said everything was clear."

Kit lifted his brow. "No. He said that he could see clear through to the other side."

Gideon grinned and subsided into his thoughts as they began insulting each other.

Perhaps he could learn to be content. Perhaps he was content now. He hadn't believed it possible.

Charlotte *needed* him. And in a sense that went beyond the physical.

But perhaps he needed her more, and so did his neglected daughter. He had missed so much of Sarah's life. He could not salvage what they had lost. But he wouldn't repeat that mistake. Not with her or with the siblings he hoped she would soon have. He thought Emily might be pleased.

He couldn't have chosen better than Charlotte if he had spent the rest of his life searching for a woman to replace the mother his daughter had lost. Now there would be someone besides his butler and disgusted housekeeper to care whether he drank himself to death. With his marriage to Charlotte, he was gaining more than a wife. He would have a family.

"Fine," he said, sitting up. "You've talked me into it. Let me off on the corner. I'll walk the rest of the way to the academy. Charlotte probably won't like my coming there, but it's her last day. I'll just stay a few minutes. I'll wait in one of the rooms where I won't be a distraction."

Miss Peppertree virtually dragged him into the house and down the hall to the formal drawing room. "Thank heavens you are here!" she cried, her spectacles sliding down the end of her nose. "Hurry! He has her alone. Well, Rankin is there, but he's not the force that you are. I was listening at the door, for her protection, you understand, and I heard the word 'elopement.' That would be the end of her. The school. Of me."

"Calm yourself, Miss Peppertree," he said, while a haze of fury filled his mind. "You must have misunderstood. Who is with Charlotte? Sir Daniel? Her brother or one of her cousins? They might have said 'engagement.'"

Gideon considered Phillip, but the man would be courting a death wish to force his presence on Charlotte when he'd been warned by Gideon to stay away. It couldn't be the lout.

"There, Your Grace," Miss Peppertree said, pulling open the door. "See for yourself."

He froze, catching the line of what must have been a very disturbing conversation, to judge by the look of relief on Charlotte's face when she saw him.

"This duke of yours will only break your heart."

"No." Gideon banged the door open with the flat of his hand, eliciting a gasp from Miss Peppertree, who had slipped around him and barely escaped being flattened to the wall. "You're wrong. Her duke will only break every bone in your body."

"Not in the academy!" Miss Peppertree exclaimed in horror. "I will not have it!"

Phillip turned, his smile reckless, unconcerned. "You took me off guard at the theater. I am prepared for you now."

"Good." Gideon wrenched off his glove and slapped Phillip as hard as he could across the cheek. Phillip did not flinch. But his eyes went black, and his mouth hardened as he turned his head to stare at Gideon's face.

Charlotte turned pale. "Oh, no. Don't do this."

"He already has," Phillip said, fingering the welt on his cheek.

Gideon flicked her an annoyed glance. "Please leave the room. This is not a matter to be settled in front of gentlewomen."

"I—"

*"Now."*

She hesitated, then lifted her dress and hastened away, sharing a shaken look with Miss Peppertree. Rankin moved to the duke's side, assuming an air of confidence now that Gideon had taken control of the situation.

Gideon glowered at Phillip, who appeared to be shrinking, as if he finally realized what manner of enemy he had crossed. "We will meet tomorrow, sir, to settle this for once and all. Your choice of weapons?"

Phillip swallowed. "I'd be a fool to ask a student of Fenton's for anything except pistols."

"You were a fool to set foot in this house after I gave you the chance to escape with your life." Gideon glanced around, at the sound of footsteps, astonished to see Kit and Devon entering the room. "What are you doing here?"

"Devon recognized Phillip's servant standing outside," Kit said, shaking his head. "He thought there might be trouble. I take it there is."

Gideon nodded. "We are meeting tomorrow to clear the air. I will be in contact with you, sir, about the particulars."

"You fool," Devon said unsympathetically to Phillip. "You deserve whatever he dishes out. I am tempted to settle this myself. She is my cousin."

Phillip did not answer, striding from the room in tight-lipped silence. If he regretted angering Gideon he concealed it. And if he wasn't sorry yet, Gideon thought, he would be tomorrow.

Charlotte came to a halt in the middle of the hall, Miss Peppertree at her heels. "The girls must *not* hear of this. It mustn't happen. I have to stop it."

"I agree," Miss Peppertree said. "If you don't it will be the absolute ruin of us. There will be witnesses and a recounting in the papers. And if the duel ends badly for either man . . . well, I shudder to think of it."

"I *shall* have to stop them," Charlotte said with a growing sense that she would not succeed.

"How?"

"What do you suggest?" Charlotte asked. "I can't think. Why do men act like this? Please, Daphne, give me your advice. What can I do to intervene?"

Miss Peppertree's eyes narrowed behind her glasses. "You could invite the duke to supper and drug his wine."

"Were you reading that book on the Borgias again? Why are you drawn to these morbid subjects?"

"I don't know," Daphne said, wrinkling her brow. "Why are you drawn to dangerous men?"

Charlotte didn't have an answer.

It *had* been dangerous to fall in love with the man she

had made him to be in her diary. A man she could manipulate at will. But the Duke of Wynfield was neither a dream lover nor a complete wastrel. He was something real.

She had dreamed up so many happy endings. She had dreamed that a dark-haired duke would notice her in a crowd and never look at another woman again. She'd had to keep him secret. And now that romance had found her she understood why no one in her family acted with any logic whatsoever once that right person appeared and threw everything off course.

"Perhaps you should reason with His Grace," Daphne suggested.

"That would be my preference, but I'm afraid he is not in a reasonable mood. Did you not sense his wrath? Do you think a man of his nature would appreciate a lecture at this point? He would not forgive me."

And as if to confirm this statement Gideon emerged from the drawing room to stride past the two ladies with only a curt nod to acknowledge their presence. Kit and Devon followed at safe distances moments later.

"I see what you mean," Miss Peppertree murmured. "He is a formidable man when aroused." She pressed her hand to her mouth. "I meant when his passions are . . . Well, not that sort of passion."

"I understand what you meant," Charlotte said. "But I have to try to stop him."

Miss Peppertree blinked like a barn owl. "I know what I would do under the circumstances."

"You . . ." Charlotte studied her with fresh interest. "Would you?"

The woman gave a stiff nod. "A lady must use all means at her disposal to avoid an unpleasant outcome. I daresay a duel to the death qualifies as such."

"To the death." Charlotte bit her lip. "And I am the cause."

"Then you must be the solution."

"Oh, Daphne. I never realized that you understood these affairs."

"Understanding and approving of them are two different matters altogether. You are caught in the middle of this. Perhaps you can prevent the worst."

Charlotte drew in a breath. "I can only try."

# Chapter 29

*I*t was almost midnight. Gideon had settled down in his study with a brandy. A letter had arrived earlier in the day from his daughter's governess. Mrs. Stearns wanted to inform Gideon that she and Lady Sarah had left Wynfield House and did not expect to arrive in London before the wedding due to travel delays; assuming that the weather remained mild, they hoped to be there shortly afterward, though.

> *Lady Sarah is beside herself with excitement, Your Grace. Of course, she wishes to see you again. But more than anything she cannot wait to meet her new mother, whom I presume to be a lady of refinement. . . .*

Gideon sighed. The fusty woman was never going to let him forget that she had caught him in bed with one of his neighbors, a widow whose lust and aversion to remarrying had exceeded his own. Well, he'd have the last laugh once he introduced her to Charlotte. Mrs. Stearns would not believe her eyes. And maybe she would be the one to laugh at him. Maybe she wouldn't even recognize him. He was unknown to himself these days.

Charlotte had changed everything.

He put the letter back on the table.

Charlotte had changed *him*.

Unfortunately she had not changed his possessive nature or his tendency to act on his anger. In fact, Charlotte seemed to bring out the best and worst of him, sometimes at once.

Apparently she had the same effect on other men. Look at the country bumpkin Gideon would have to take down a peg tomorrow. Gideon would give the man credit if he had the ballocks to show up.

"Your Grace?"

"Yes, Shelby," he said moodily, without turning to the door.

"Will there be anything else tonight?"

"Everything is ready for tomorrow?"

"Absolutely," Shelby said with an enthusiasm he rarely showed. "Your dueling pistols have been checked and your boots have been polished to a high sheen. The carriage will collect Sir Christopher on the way. I will accompany Your Grace, I assume?"

Gideon chuckled. "You need not anticipate the event with such relish, Shelby. It hasn't been that long since the last duel."

"I have respect for tradition, Your Grace. We must not allow modern times to make us lose sight of where we began."

Gideon smiled, staring into the fire. "Admit it. You are happy to see me leg-shackled again."

"It will be a relief to see you settled down, Your Grace. And, if I may add, the staff is gratified that you are doing the right thing by Miss Boscastle as well as by Lady Sarah. It is high time, too, I must add."

"Good God, you are impertinent—" Gideon broke off, realizing that Shelby had dropped that last remark like a grenade and then wisely disappeared. What could Gideon say? He, too, was anxious to make amends to Sarah. He removed his jacket and vest. He loosened his neck cloth and started to unbutton his shirt.

He rubbed his face. He had been abrupt with Charlotte today. He had barreled past her in the hall without a word, because the only words that came to him at the time had been obscene. But she could hardly expect him to care about etiquette when he'd caught another man attempting to lure her away. And when he thought about how that man had insulted her and caused her grief before he was in her life to protect her . . .

He had to put her out of his mind until after the duel or he would be tempted to murder his opponent, when his intention was only to wound him as a warning. He needed to relax. But it took effort to keep his thoughts from wandering.

It was as if she had become part of him, as if she were standing behind him, as if she were whispering in his ear—

"Gideon."

"What the hell?"

He surged to his feet, knocking his knee into the table that sat beside his chair. It was a blessing that he'd emptied his glass, as it rolled across the carpet. "Damnation! What in the devil's name are you doing here again at this time of night? Am I dreaming? Am I losing my mind? Are you out of yours?"

He shook his head. Nothing changed. It *was* her, in the flesh and not a figment of his imagination. It was his betrothed, swathed from throat to ankle in her blue evening cloak, her eyes widening in dismay—as if he had startled her out of her wits and not the other way around. He swore again, threw up his hands, and circled her.

"Your Grace, control yourself this instant," she said, virtually imprisoned by his circling. "I will not tolerate such shameful language in my presence."

"In your presence!" he bellowed. He ground his teeth. "Control myself?" He chased her around the chair. "You're the one who needs to be brought under control. I hope you did not come here by yourself. Because if you did I shall seriously have to contemplate building a stone tower in which to protect you when we are apart."

She blinked, her gaze dropping and flying back to his face. "You are half-dressed."

"Am I?" He yanked off his neck cloth and tossed it in the air. "I do not sit about all hours of the night in a top hat and long-tailed coat waiting for the next woman to burst in unannounced."

"Oh? Is that right?"

"Don't 'oh' me. Yes. I'm half-dressed. And when I go to bed, I take off the rest of my clothes. Sometimes I sleep in my raw state. What do you expect when you sneak into a man's castle this late at night?"

She blinked again.

"How did you arrive here?" he demanded, taking a step forward.

"Devon brought me. Harriet is with him, too."

"Where is he? I've had enough of his interference."

"I'm not sure where he is," she said, looking insulted. "I asked him to come back for me in two hours. You can't go outside like that, anyway."

"How did you get in the house?"

"Your—"

He clapped his hand to his head. "Don't tell me. Let me take a wild guess. It was Shelby."

"Yes, but—"

"Two hours, you say. For what? Let me guess again. You think that in two hours you will be able to talk me out of the duel tomorrow."

"If there is any way—"

"Try it. Do your best." He reached out and unfastened her cloak. "Convince me. But bear in mind that my butler will be upset if there isn't a duel tomorrow."

Her eyes clung to his. "I don't want blood to be spilled over me. Is that unreasonable?"

He lowered his head to hers. "Dearest, would you feel better if I promise to shoot him in a part of his body where the wound will not show?"

"I . . ." She threw her arms around his neck and drew his head to hers.

Despite his anger at her motives, he found himself aroused by her inexpert attempt at seduction. He felt his cock thicken uncomfortably in his trousers. The blood in his veins came to a boil and surged. The dominant male in him would take anything she offered, delaying conscience for another day. The pleasures of the night reigned for now.

"Gideon, please," she whispered against his mouth. "For the sake of decency—"

"Decency is the last thing on my mind. And on yours, it appears."

"It's dangerous for you to duel."

"Not as dangerous as it is for you to be in the position you are right now."

"Then I—"

"No. You're here now."

His mouth absorbed her involuntary cry as he drew her down against him on the carpet. He harbored the softer curves of her breasts and belly against his body. For a moment he simply reveled in her captivity, in the sultry heat that rose from her skin. She gave a tentative push of her shoulder against his. He gripped her buttocks, and his body went hard. He shifted, raising his knee to nudge her to his thickening shaft.

"Gideon?" she whispered, her mouth slipping from his.

She hadn't even lifted her head when he turned her onto her back and with indolent deliberation unhooked her cloak and then the front of her gown. He swiftly stayed the hand she raised to shield her breasts from his scrutiny. He lowered his head and drew one tender nipple at a time between his teeth. She made a sound in her throat that destroyed his control and set his fiercer instincts loose.

"You came here to make a case, Charlotte." He reached down to raise the ruffled hem of her dress. "I think I should hear your pleas before I decide what I'll do next. If I can still think in a few moments, that is."

She smiled the dreamy smile that unfailingly disarmed him. "You've been drinking brandy," she murmured as his hand climbed from her ankle and past her knee. "I can taste it on your lips."

"I'm dying to devour you," he said, lifting her dress up past her rounded belly to expose her silky triangle of hair. His fingers slid up her thigh and parted her plump flesh. Her moisture glistened upon his hand as he played her with shameless enjoyment.

"Oh." She caught her lower lip between her teeth, a sob escaping her. He smiled. She turned her head and closed her eyes, her back arching in a pose that made his heart race.

"Raise your knees," he said quietly. "And open your legs for me. What did you want to tell me?"

"I . . . can't remember."

His body clenched, every muscle wound tight, as she obeyed, the fire's glow highlighting the warm hollow that drew his fascinated gaze.

"You ought to be ashamed of yourself," she whispered, her hips slowly rotating in a sensuality that sent his pulse soaring.

"But I'm not," he said, positioning himself at a perfect angle between her upraised legs. From here he could study her slightest response. He eased one finger at a time into her soaked heat, his blood flaring, a river of fire racing through his veins.

Her belly tensed. She pressed her knees together to fight his invasion, then slowly yielded to his demand. "Delicious," he said, his eyes heavy-lidded with unconcealed encouragement as he savored her, concentrated his every sense on forcing her complete surrender.

"Decadent," she whispered, twisting at the waist in a bid to interrupt his play.

He shook his head, and her grasp loosened; her eyes locked with his in a small war he would not let her win. He drew in a slow breath. The perfume of her desire intoxicated him. He raked his thumb through her wispy curls to tease her where she was most sensitive and responsive to his touch.

He watched her intently. The pressure built inside her. He saw her hips twist, her belly contract. The pink tips of her breasts darkened to deep rose, tempting him beyond what he could resist. He lifted his other hand to tug and twist each nipple, deliberately heightening the havoc he inflicted on her.

She shuddered, spreading her legs even farther apart to ride his hand, gasping as he flicked his thumb faster. "I can't," she whispered brokenly. "It's too much, Gideon."

"I know," he soothed her. But it wasn't enough for him.

"I want . . . I want . . ." she said, moving her hips now in time with the relentless caress of his thumb.

"I know," he murmured again. "I know what you want." His rod strained and pulsed in rampant demand. He summoned his will and focused his skill on unleashing her senses. She was so close he could feel her muscles tensing in the silent torment that heralded release.

God help him. Her sobs punctuated her broken exhalations of breath. She lifted her hips and a powerful lust blanketed his awareness. Soon. Soon. *Now*. His thumb moved faster. She wasn't in control; he was. His fingers penetrated her folds, drove so deeply into her warmth that he felt the cresting pleasure of her climax as if it were his own.

He closed his eyes, lowering his forehead to her knee. The part of his mind capable of thought took note that she was wearing plain cotton stockings, a testament to the fact that she needed no adornments to reduce him to a primitive state.

He stood, breathing hard, willing his body to settle down. He was afraid to touch her again. He was hesitant to even look at her. He stared into the fire. The thought of taking her maidenhood would keep him awake for the rest of the night. He might as well not even try to sleep. Whatever she had hoped to accomplish by coming here hadn't worked.

She sat up. He glanced back instinctively and realized that she hadn't drawn her chemise over her plump breasts or rehooked her bodice. She looked tousled and . . . just like the unrestrained temptress of a few moments before.

"What are you thinking?" she whispered, her eyes climbing from his boots to his face.

"That I need to sit in a cold bath until my b— my body turns blue."

"You'll stimulate your blood by cold bathing this time of night," she said.

His gaze dropped to her breasts. "I doubt a bath could be more stimulating than you."

"Have you reconsidered the duel?" she asked, and he'd be damned if she wasn't deliberately planning to provoke him by not even pretending to shield herself from his scrutiny.

He laughed. "No. All you've done is convince me that I don't want another man anywhere near you."

She looked chagrined. "Well, I will have to try another tactic. A more persuasive one."

"I am persuaded more than ever that you need protection against men like Phillip, if not like me."

"You mean you let me act like one of your trollops and had no intention of changing your mind?"

"Basically."

"That is unconscionable."

"Probably."

"You led me to believe that if I distracted you I could influence your decision."

"I never said any such thing, darling. That was your intention, not mine."

"Well, you certainly led *me* to believe you were enjoying yourself."

"I was. Immensely. I could have enjoyed myself that way for the rest of the night. But you see, despite your charm, I will fight a duel in the morning, and if I feel like a ravenous beast right now, I doubt my mood will improve before dawn."

"Sit down on the couch, Gideon."

He stared at her, his brow furrowing at her deep tone of voice. He remained motionless. He watched her hand drift down to her breasts, her tapered fingers touching the tip of her nipple.

"Please," she said with a siren's smile.

"Why?" he asked, almost dropping to the floor to beg for mercy.

She shrugged. If she had decided to lecture him, he would retaliate by pretending to fall asleep.

"Fine," he said tersely. "I'll sit. But I'm not of an attitude to pay attention."

That was what he had thought.

Charlotte had set her mind on seduction. But after what he had just done to her, she was more than a woman on an unselfish mission. She was a woman giving herself to her desires.

It was daring to perform an act that she had seen only

in a picture on a man of Gideon's expertise. He might mock her unskilled efforts.

And hopefully she would change his mind about the duel.

But if he liked it, she was one step closer to proving that he was not marrying the reserved maiden she had been when they met. She would come to this marriage fully prepared to satisfy his needs. And hers.

She slid to the floor, balancing on her knees, her hands lifting to slide down his chest to his stomach. His head jerked back. She was unsure how to go about unfastening his trousers, but at her hesitant try, his face darkened in disbelieving comprehension and he took over the task himself.

She watched avidly as he eased his pants down over his narrow hips to the tops of his boots. He was hard and well sculpted and beautiful.

His phallus rose thick and straight from the dark hair that grew beneath his flat belly. "Go on," he said, his breath a rasp that sent shivers through her. "Touch me."

She lifted her hands to wrap her fingers around the base of his organ. He sat forward, staring down at her, his face incredulous, dark with elemental desire.

"Are you going to take me in your mouth?" he asked in a raw voice.

"Hmm." She sighed, and very gently leaned closer to lick the entire length of him from the base of his engorged shaft to its head.

"Jesus God," he said, his hips bucking at the exquisite sensations that inundated him. He had never felt or seen anything as erotic as her soft pink mouth closing around the crest of his cock and sucking him for all she was worth. He slid to the very edge of the couch, jerking involuntarily when she took him even deeper into her mouth. He closed his eyes; then he opened them. He wanted to see her sucking and circling back to the knobby tip of his erection.

She was beautiful. He stared at her down-bent head, her hair flowing to her rounded breasts and her swollen nipples.

"You'd better stop now," he warned her, tempted to thrust and let her swallow him whole. Where had she learned this? Was she a natural wanton at heart? He hoped so. What more could he want than a wife who was as sensually adventurous as she was caring and un-tainted and . . . sweet?

"Am I doing this the way you like it?" she whispered, and gave him no chance to reply before resuming her welcome assault and bringing him to the brink.

"I like it so much I am going to come in your mouth if you don't stop," he said, his belly drawing tight.

But she didn't. And he allowed her to continue, losing all sense of time.

She kept up the blissful agony, and the tension inside him kept building, intensifying. She must have sensed it. Her lips closed tightly, her tongue flicking, and she drew at him harder, faster. And then he knew it was too late to stop.

He spread his thighs and closed his eyes, climaxing in spasms of helpless release that he was afraid would never end.

But they did. The act had drained him. It had also in-vigorated him. It filled his body and soul with a satisfac-tion, a rightness, that he had not known he could feel.

And it was more than gratitude for a sexual act. It was a sign that she would go to any lengths to please him.

"Thank you," he said, putting his head back and breathing out a sigh. "I will sleep well tonight." He fumbled back with his hand and found a clean handkerchief in his vest pocket. He unfolded it and slowly forced himself to move.

She quietly made herself presentable and smoothed back her hair. "I'm glad," she said. "You can sleep through the morning. I'll have Devon—"

He leaned toward her. He gently wiped the side of her mouth and chin, staring into her eyes. "You will do nothing of the sort. I'm fighting that duel, and nothing is going to stop me."

"The pair of you should sit down over coffee and hammer your differences out like—"

"Charlotte, sweetheart, do I tell you how to conduct your etiquette classes? Do I suggest that you teach the language of the fan in a manner that gentlemen, aside from Sir Godfrey, can understand it?"

"True gentlemen *do* understand it."

"Maybe I'm not refined at heart."

"Refinement is an art that requires practice."

"Teach me at a later time," he said quietly, unable to stop looking at her.

"Then my visit tonight was a mockery of your respect for me."

"I assure you, nothing I did was to mock you."

"My female charms have failed to persuade you."

"On the contrary, your female charms are the reason I am fighting this duel."

"And there is nothing I can do to stop you?"

"Not—" He cut himself off, turning his head. "Hush a moment. Did you hear anything at the window?"

She listened for a few moments. "It's probably only

rain. The window looks a little steamy, from what I can see of it."

"Well, I don't wonder why." He pulled on his trousers and strode to the window to look through the curtains. "I swear it wasn't rain I heard. But I do see Devon's carriage waiting down the street. I shall hand you back to the meddlesome rogue and warn him that if he brings you out again at this hour, he will regret it."

They quickly dressed. Charlotte walked with him to the door, hazarding a resigned look at his profile. "Well, at least you might sleep through the night. I won't catch a wink. I should have realized it wasn't your body that demands satisfaction. It's your dangerous pride. Will you promise to be careful?"

"Only if you will promise the same, Charlotte. It seems that if you are not visiting a rogue, you're being pursued by one."

"You have no need to worry. Someone has already caught me."

"That doesn't seem to discourage other men from chasing after you."

"No one chased me before you brought me to notice," she said wistfully.

He shook his head. "I doubt that. Knowing you as I do now, it seems more likely that you were pursued and never noticed."

She caressed his cheek with the back of her hand. "I don't care. It's only you I want. Please."

He grasped her hand. "I'll walk you to the carriage. And tomorrow we will confront whatever other crisis comes our way."

# Chapter 30

*N*ick stared up at the cracks in the ceiling, listening to the drunken laughter that came from the room above. The candle had burned out, and the smell of cheap tallow combined with the stench of the over-flowing gutters that drifted in through the half-closed door. He'd grown up with that reek. So had Millie, even though she'd been retching when she got up to work. He almost felt sorry for her except that she'd bungled a chance to help him break into that duke's house earlier that night. God, women made such noise.

No point in getting up to close the door. She would come home soon to stuff it shut with rags, whining that some customer had played too rough, and why hadn't he protected her like he'd promised when she moved in? Well, he'd taken care of one before daybreak. He couldn't kill every man she'd slept with, or he'd halve the populace.

"Hey, Nick, are you dead in there?" a youthful voice

shouted through the passageway to the street above his cellar abode.

"Who wants to know?"

"Your mother. She said she's dying and you need to bring 'er some spirits to ease 'er pain."

"She's always dyin'," he muttered.

"Surgeon swore it's true this time." The owner of the voice materialized in the stagnant gloom, a young street thug in a cap and patched-up trousers. His name was Barney and he was a right pest. "Are you sick, too? You oughta drink some gin yourself."

"Where's Millie?" he asked without any inflection.

"She climbed in a coach with a customer and ain't been back. She was cursin' you up and down for 'er condition." He bumped into the chest that served as a dinner table and nightstand. "A book? Are you using it for kindling?"

Nick jumped up and swatted the grimy hand that reached down for the diary. "That's not suitable for youngsters. Anyway, you can't read."

"I didn't think you could either," Barney said with a brashness that he'd learned from Nick. He could open up an academy himself. "Are you coming to Piccadilly with us or not, Nick?"

"Later. Bugger off for now."

"What about your ma?"

"What about 'er?"

"Nothing, Nick. I'll wait for you at the pub in case you change your mind."

He scratched his ribs. "Wait. What condition was Millie complaining about? If she got caught—"

"The lullaby cheat," Barney answered on his way out.

"A baby?"

"Yeah."

Nick kicked the door shut and swore as it creaked back open. He thought of his mother for a moment; he thought of Millie and how different she and his ma were from the lady who'd written those fancy words in her diary. He could imagine Millie telling every Tom, Dick, and Harry that Nick had put a bun in her oven. That was rich. She was a walking mattress. It probably wasn't his seed. Odds were against it. What the hell would he do with her?

He hit his fist against the wall and the cracked looking glass in the corner reflected a face so contorted with anger that he reared away.

He remembered the horror on the lady's face when she'd seen him in the window, and he laughed and shook his head; no one could deny he'd made an impact. She wouldn't forget him in a hurry. Should he go to her and tell her about the other lady who had it in for her? Would she give him a reward?

He buttoned his shirt and picked up his jacket from the clothes strewn about the place. Then he lifted up one of the loose floorboards and wrapped the diary up in one of Millie's smocks and hid it from prying hands. He wouldn't risk taking it out in the damp. "Barney!" he shouted as he opened the door and saw three figures loitering about the stairs. "Go find Millie's little sister. I'm gonna further her education tonight."

It was misting lightly by the time Gideon escorted Charlotte to the carriage parked in the street. She was still overwarm from their encounter, and the cool air felt wonderful against her face.

So did Gideon's hand around her backside as he

stood, frowning at Devon and Harriet, and hoisted Charlotte into the carriage.

"Good night, Gideon," she whispered over her shoulder. "I wish you the best tomorrow. I—"

"I shall see you afterward," he said with confidence, and turned on his heel to let the footman fold up the steps and close the door.

"Well?" Devon asked as the carriage set off into the dripping night. "Did you convince him?"

"He is convinced that I am brazen and that you are reprehensible. And I can't disagree."

Harriet tossed her head. "I knew it wouldn't work. Men like him thrive on taking risks."

Devon folded his arms behind his head. "He isn't taking any risk. It's Moreland who'll end up dead."

"Don't say that," Charlotte whispered. "I don't want anyone's death on my hands."

"Perhaps it'll be raining in the morning," Harriet said. "They won't face off unless it's clear."

"Do you think it's possible?" she asked hopefully.

"It won't matter if it snows," Devon said with mordant certitude. "They'll only put it off another day. Phillip asked for this, you know. Gideon has no choice but to carry through with the challenge he was dealt."


Gideon did not return immediately to the house. He knew that it wasn't rain he had heard at the window. Still, he hadn't wanted to alarm Charlotte. Nor stop her from trying out her charms. He walked across the street and stood against the wall of Major Boulton's house, earning nothing for his trouble except a damp shirt from the mist.

Suddenly a light flickered behind the fanlight above the front door and a figure appeared on the steps. It was a man wearing a cap and nightshirt, an old flintlock musket raised at Gideon's chest.

"Halt there, you blackguard, or I shall blow you to kingdom come!"

"Please don't, Major. It's only me, Wynfield."

"Wynfield?" The major lowered his firearm. "What are you doing out this time of night? And in a drizzle without a coat?"

Gideon ran up the short flight of steps to the door. Both men then retreated into the candlelit vestibule, where a butler stood brandishing a poker.

"I thought I heard someone prowling about my window less than an hour ago," Gideon said. "Have you noticed anything out of the ordinary?"

The major chortled. "No disrespect intended, but it's difficult to assess what is unusual with the traffic to and from your house during the night."

Gideon suppressed a grin. "I apologize for that."

"Why? I wouldn't if I were your age." Major Boulton looked back at the butler. "It is only the duke. Reassure the staff it is safe to go back to bed."

A round-faced woman in a robe came into the hall with a lantern. "Father, what were you doing outside in your nightshirt? Really. You talk about the morals of the neighbors, but you are just as bad."

"Leave me alone," the major snapped.

"I will not," she said. "Look at the both of you. You in a nightshirt. Him without a coat on. People breaking in and stealing the family jewels. If this is life in London, then I'll stay in the country with the cows."

"Good idea," the major muttered.

"I heard that," she said, shining her lantern in his face. "You're too old to understand what's good for you. Next thing I know you'll be killed in the street, and think of how that would look if you're not properly dressed."

Gideon cleared his throat, reminding himself that he had an appointment in the morning that he could not miss. "I'm sorry to have disturbed you, Major. And your daughter. I didn't realize she was still here."

"It's quite all right. I am fortunate to have a neighbor who concerns himself with my welfare."

"Think nothing of it," Gideon said, bracing himself for a sprint across the wet street. And as he hit the sidewalk he heard Major Boulton call down at him before he closed the door, "Two in one night! You keep it up for them, and keep 'em apart if you don't want to start a war!"

# Chapter 31

The adversaries met at daybreak in Hyde Park. Gideon wore a top hat, a new white neck cloth, and a gray morning coat for the occasion, so that he looked suitable to attend breakfast afterward. The wet grass brushed his boots as he walked toward the group of— Dear God, the marquess and his towering footman, Sir Daniel, Drake, as well Devon and Kit, who would serve as his seconds and had been invited. A line of fashionable carriages had already parked for a bird's-eye view of the duel.

He lifted his brow at Grayson. "I don't suppose you thought to bring along an orchestra?"

"I didn't," Grayson replied. "I will next time."

Sir Daniel gave Gideon a reproachful look. "I would like to remind you that dueling is illegal."

"Noted. Remind me, sir, that I would like to talk to you after the match."

Gideon did not look at Phillip. He did, however,

glimpse Gabrielle standing behind Charlotte's brother. Apparently his almost-mistress hoped to witness his death. It was a shame he would disappoint her yet again. He had no intention of losing.

The seconds were checking the firearms for the last time. The surgeons stood at the ready with their instrument cases. Gideon smothered a yawn behind his fist.

"Here," Devon said, handing him his pistol. "It was nice knowing you."

"Well, I can't say the same."

It was time for the combatants to walk their twelve paces and await the signal. Gideon finally glanced at Phillip and thought the man looked a bit green around the gills.

"Fire!"

Gideon lifted his arm, took aim, and— A shot rang out. To his disbelief he realized that Phillip had discharged his pistol before he even raised his hand. Gideon blinked, firing his own gun into the air as his rival released a bone-chilling howl of pain and reeled full circle before collapsing to the ground.

"Good God," Grayson said in disgust. "The nitwit has not only broken protocol. He's shot himself in the foot."

Devon winced. "It must hurt like the devil. I go mad when I step on a thorn."

The surgeons ran to the spot where Moreland had fallen. Gideon sighed, handed his pistol back to Devon, and walked forward to take stock of the situation. Moreland noticed him and struggled into a sitting position, throwing Gideon a look of pain-laced resentment.

"I hope this makes you—" He clapped his hand to his mouth. "I'm going to be sick."

"Not on my boots, please," Gideon said with a grimace, beating a quick retreat. "My butler takes great pride in their polish." He glanced at the group of men gathering around him. "Somebody give the wretch a dose of laudanum, tend to his foot, and then load him in a country-bound stagecoach."

"I told him he should have stopped drinking after midnight," Caleb said rather unsympathetically.

"The duel is over!" a witness called from the crowd. "Honor has been met!"

Gideon shook his head. "That's a matter of opinion."

Caleb stepped over Phillip's top hat and approached Gideon with a sheepish look. It was unfortunate that his blue eyes reminded Gideon of Charlotte and therefore predisposed him to liking the young man in spite of the company he kept.

"I had to stand as his second, Your Grace. I hope you understand. The hothead has no other friends in London."

"I can't say I'm surprised." Gideon thought again of Charlotte, and some of his irritation melted away. "I do understand. It's an admirable trait to stand beside a friend even when one knows that the friend is wrong."

"I trust it will not taint our association in any way, Your Grace?"

"Not in the least. I've a feeling I will need all the male support I can muster after I wed your sister."

Caleb nodded in gratitude. "It's a comfort to know that Charlotte has found such a staunch protector. She has always been rather timid in the company of gentlemen."

She hadn't been timid last night. In fact, Gideon was beginning to question whether the entire world had misread her character. It was true that he'd underestimated her—at his peril, not to mention his pleasure. To think he'd avoided the quiet type all his life.

But this was not a subject to discuss with his future brother-in-law.

"The family has been afraid that she might be vulnerable to a rogue's pursuit," Caleb added.

"Dear, dear. That would have been tragic." He glanced at the men carrying a stretcher through the park. Then he turned to find Sir Daniel, but the agent had already disappeared from sight before Gideon could talk to him at length about his investigation.

Charlotte had fretted and paced through Jane's bedchamber until light streaked the sky and the city's steeples assumed their familiar hodgepodge on the horizon. But finally the weight of fatigue and worry were too much to fight. So she pulled a chair to the window and waited. She had wanted to be with her family in case anything happened to Gideon.

Chloe stretched her arms across the pillows, slowly opening her eyes to stare around the bright room. She looked at Jane slumbering in the bed beside her and sat up to stare at the figure sitting desolately at the window. "Is it raining?" she asked, combing her hand through her black curls.

Charlotte sighed. "There isn't a cloud in the sky. Nothing but sea-coal smoke."

Chloe swung her feet to the floor, the bed creaking slightly. "It will be over soon."

"What's over?" Jane murmured drowsily.

"The duel." Charlotte sprang off her stool. "It's

Weed," she said. "It must be over. He's waving up at me from the back of the carriage."

"Is it a wave of relief or one of distress?" Jane asked, looking anxiously at Charlotte.

"How can you tell?" Charlotte was putting on her slippers. They weren't hers and she had to force them onto her feet.

Jane crawled around Chloe and sprang from the bed to the window, her honey-colored hair streaming down her back. "It's relief. Gideon must have won the duel. Which isn't a surprise."

"Oh, thank . . ." Charlotte straightened. "I don't suppose you can tell from Weed's wave whether Phillip survived or not."

"No. But Grayson is getting out of the carriage." Jane opened the window. "Grayson! What happened? We are dying to know!"

"The idiot shot himself in the foot!"

Jane bit her lip, drawing back against Charlotte. "I think it's safe to assume that he isn't talking about the duke."

Gideon had asked Grayson to reassure Charlotte that both parties had survived the duel. He would have called on her himself, but on the drive back from the park it suddenly occurred to him that the major's parting words to him last night were rather odd.

*Two in one night! You keep it up for them. . . .*

Two . . . ladies? What was Boulton talking about? Yes, obviously he had spotted Charlotte, who was an eye-catching lady and would stir curiosity by sneaking into

Gideon's house. There had been someone at the window last night. Could it have been a lady?

Had Major Boulton seen the person Gideon had missed? It hadn't been Harriet, had it?

It was conceivable that she had peered inside the window to make sure that Charlotte was perfectly safe. Alarming but conceivable. The most disturbing thought was that someone had been trailing her—the same person who had frightened her at the academy. Coincidence? He should have asked Devon whether he'd seen anyone while he waited outside.

It was also possible that the thief had been hoping to strike the square again. If Gideon had not been so distracted by Charlotte's visit, this might have occurred to him at the time. But how well could the major see across the street? The spry rascal must be in the habit of watching Gideon's house for his nightly entertainment.

As soon as his carriage stopped, he jumped out and crossed the street to knock again at the major's door. A maidservant answered, gazing up at him with an awestruck expression. "Your Grace," she said, stuffing a stray lock of hair into her cap. "To what do we owe this honor?"

He gave her a terse smile. "Excuse me for the interruption, but if you don't mind I would like to speak with the major for a moment."

"Oh, I don't mind." She wrapped her chapped hands around her mop handle and sighed. "You can interrupt my chores anytime you like. This is my mopping day."

"I shall remember that. Is he indisposed?"

"Who?"

"The major. The gentleman you mop for."

"Oh." She and the mop straightened at the same time. "He isn't here. He and his daughter left for the country after breakfast this morning. Is there anything I can do for Your Grace?"

Another maid appeared behind her with a bucket. *Damnation,* Gideon thought. He could hardly track down Boulton on a country road to ask him a simple question.

"My domestic needs are being met at this time," he said, pivoting on the step.

"Ooh, I'll bet they are," she cooed, erupting into a storm of giggles that followed Gideon into the street.

*Chapter 32*

$\mathcal{G}$ideon had decided that he might indeed commit murder before his accelerated courtship had been played out. Not fifteen hours after that sorry excuse of a duel, he was reminded that a protector, even one supposedly in name only, could not afford to lower his guard.

In fact, he had sensed a week ago, when Shelby brought him the invitation to this evening's masquerade supper at the Opera House, that to accept would be a mistake. But Charlotte hinted that several members of her family would attend and that she loved fancy-dress balls. He agreed to take her. However, he felt like a fool for letting Kit convince him that the fencing pupils of the academy should costume themselves like a crew of buccaneers. When he asked why, Kit had replied, "It's one of the few chances that will come your way to wear a genuine cutlass and be admired in public for your blade."

Protesting inwardly, Gideon put on a pair of snug black leather breeches and a flowing white Holland shirt beneath a quilted scarlet waistcoat. Then he donned a long brass-buttoned coat and a plumed hat. He buckled on a sword belt and strapped on his cutlass.

He refused to blacken his teeth or to wear the gold earring that Kit had sent along.

The odd thing was that Jane, Harriet, and Charlotte all stared at him in obvious approval as he climbed into the carriage. Grayson grunted in amusement.

"Would you like us to drop you off at the Thames?" he asked in a snide voice.

Jane was disguised as her namesake, Jane Seymour, in a blue velvet dress with a ruffled collar. She lowered her mask and gave her husband a stern look. "Grayson, a man who is dressed as Robinson Crusoe has no right to talk. That beard is disgusting. It looks like something in which a pair of mice might reside. I have to wonder what you and our valet were drinking. It's a good thing Weed didn't see you."

"Maybe he didn't feel like shaving," Harriet said, adjusting her laced bodice. She looked fetching as a tavern wench, with her gamine face and red-gold hair.

"Thank you, Harriet," Grayson said, nodding at her.

Finally Gideon glanced at Charlotte, intending only a courteous exchange. But her costume rendered him wordless. He had never seen a fair-haired Cleopatra in a crown, arm circlets, and diaphanous robes. He thought she looked more like an Ophelia, and altogether too alluring for the other men to resist.

He was annoyed with her display of sensuality and struggled to hide it. "That is an original costume," he said after enough time had elapsed for everyone in the carriage to sense his disapproval.

But Charlotte's cool smile gave him the impression

that she knew why he disliked her costume. "Thank you, Your Grace. In Renaissance paintings Cleopatra was portrayed with light hair even though her ancestry was actually Greek."

"Fascinating," he said, and turned his head the same instant another smile lit a fire in her eyes.

"Your Grace?" Jane said, leaning forward.

He glanced at her in reluctance. "Yes?"

She was holding a . . . a basket under his chin. "Would you care for a fig? They're good for unstopping one's system."

Harriet burst into laughter, Grayson made another rude noise, and when Gideon met Charlotte's gaze, something in his heart broke free.

It hurt. It felt like a shovel digging into stone. He fought it, the rawness of emotion, the withering of darkness under light.

"I don't care for figs," he said, frowning sternly to prevent himself from giggling like one of the girls. Then, to his relief, the carriage rolled to a stop behind the procession of vehicles that had already arrived at the party.

Quite unexpectedly, as he climbed out of the carriage to take Charlotte's hand, he found that he was looking forward to the night.

He felt something beyond desire for her, presumably the start of affection. It seemed she was full of surprises for him. No one would have guessed the depths of her sensuality on the basis of a casual acquaintance. Or how much of an effect she could have on him.

Perhaps he would dance with her this evening. He didn't like dancing much—still, it would provide an excuse to be near her. And it was something he could do to please her.

If only he could have managed to keep her in his sight. Hardly a quarter hour passed before they were separated in the flow of costumed guests that poured into the ballroom.

"Don't you look like a wicked buccaneer?" a playful female voice remarked, and Gideon glared down at a face half masked in black velvet. The lady was, he thought distractedly, Charlotte's cousin Chloe. He recognized her by her smile.

"I feel like a proper moron," he said darkly.

"Shall we dance?"

He stared over her head, half listening. "Where did she go?"

"She's probably somewhere in the ballroom," she answered.

She clasped his arm. He hadn't a notion what her costume was meant to be. She was wearing knee breeches and a tight frock coat that made him think of his butler, Shelby. "What does she look like, pirate?"

He turned to study her more closely. It sounded like a peculiar question, but then Charlotte and Chloe had arrived separately and might not have known what the other planned to wear. Women held strange notions about their apparel. "She's Cleopatra," he said.

"How intriguing," she whispered with another teasing smile. "There are only twenty of them here tonight."

She was right. There were. Some flaunted dark lush curls and monstrous headdresses. One wore leopard skins. An older lady looked mummified in white silk and pearl bindings.

But there was only one dreamy-eyed Cleopatra who stood taller than the others and appeared . . . Her eyes met his. She lifted her feathered fan to hail him. He looked past her, irritated at the attention she was drawing. He didn't think she realized that a young gallant in a cape was staring at her as if she were his next meal. It wasn't her old love. The blockhead could hardly hobble his way through this crush, let alone dance.

"You'll have to pardon me, Chloe," he said to his forgotten companion. "The wolves are about to pounce again."

She refused to release his arm. "My name isn't Chloe," she said, her face lifted in flirtation. "It's Florence. And I'm available."

"Good Lord. Let me go."

He shouldered, elbowed, asked to be excused, and forged a path across the room. Wearing a cutlass on his hip and a plumed hat that obscured his vision didn't make this an easy task. It wasn't particularly helpful either that three of his fencing cohorts, sensing trouble, decided to follow in his wake.

The young gallant had positioned himself at Charlotte's side, but she appeared too engrossed in waving to Gideon to notice.

The man in the cape did notice his approach.

He took one look at Gideon's face, glanced at the three buccaneers behind him, and quickly melted into the crowd.

"Charlotte." Gideon heaved a sigh of frustration. "Why did you wander off?"

"I didn't do it on purpose. I was talking to Miss Martout's mother and the next thing I knew she and I were pushed apart."

He glared at a gentleman who turned his head to stare Charlotte up and down. "What are you looking at?" he said contemptuously.

"I— Nothing, sir. I— Good evening. Enjoy the party."

Charlotte was jostled against Gideon. "Do not start again, please," she whispered.

"Your Grace," one of the fencing pupils asked, "do you need our services? Would you like us to escort him outside?"

"No. I need . . ." He swallowed.

He needed Charlotte.

"Go on," he answered without turning around. "Thank you for offering." He glanced down slowly at the gold necklace that glistened above Charlotte's bodice. Until now he hadn't noticed the bloodred rubies fastened between the links. "Are those gemstones real?"

"Yes."

He lifted the necklace from her throat with his forefinger. "They are," he said in surprise.

"Gideon, there are hundreds of people here tonight. And they're watching us."

"That I noticed. Who gave you this?"

"I borrowed it from Jane. Didn't you see it in the carriage?"

"No," he said. "I was trying not to stare at you." He raised his gaze to hers as he released the necklace. "Do you like jewels?"

"I've never had much occasion to wear them at the academy."

His gaze traveled down her throat to the hem of her robes in flagrant disregard of who might be watching. He forced his gaze back to hers. "What inspired you to dress as Cleopatra?"

Her self-conscious smile was more seductive than she could know. "It was one of the costumes we used for plays at school."

"I like to play."

"Gideon."

"You do, too. I read it with my own eyes."

"Your eyes are reflecting your inner demons at this moment," she said, turning her head aside and exposing the tempting curve of her nape.

"Darling, my eyes could not possibly reveal the diabolical things I intend to do to you."

"Well, not here. And not dressed like this."

"Then let's get undressed." He caught her hand, drawing her from the floor. "That's better."

"The dance is starting," she said.

"Yes. I know."

"Why are we leaving?"

"Because I don't want to take you on a dance floor."

He wanted her on the dais, a woman of wicked legend who invited powerful men to master her.

"Gideon," she said, resisting. "You're behaving like a—"

"—buccaneer?"

"Now that you mention it," she said breathlessly, and caught her crown before it slid off. "Yes. That was one of your friends you almost bowled over."

"If he's a friend then he'll understand."

She muttered an apology over her shoulder. "You won't have friends for long if you charge at them like a frigate."

"I have plenty of friends," he snapped, nodding to Kit and his wife, Violet, who stepped back simultaneously to let him pass.

"Where are we going?" she demanded, waving to Harriet and an older lady he didn't know but who appeared to recognize him.

"Wherever I don't need to build a fortress around you."

Charlotte would have followed *him* anywhere. Even though she'd be horrified if he got in another duel, she had felt a secret thrill when he'd chased off the impudent gentleman whose leering attention she had ignored. She was immensely relieved that Gideon hadn't resorted to brute force.

Her conscience could not have borne two duels fought over her in the same day. Or any day. He was exceeding her dreams at a dizzying rate. And did she attempt to discourage him? He was unpredictable, protective, and ... hers. The bond between them was growing stronger. She wanted to keep him away from other women with a passion as intense as, if better contained than, his.

He led her from the stuffy, brightly lit ballroom and down a dark corridor that was occupied by another couple engaged in ... Charlotte looked away.

"Excuse us," Gideon said loudly.

"Excuse yourself," the man murmured, flicking his fingers dismissively over his partner's bare shoulder. "Busy here. Pillage another passageway, mate."

Charlotte gasped as Gideon released her hand and drew his cutlass with efficiency and without hesitation.

The man, a mask looped over his wrist, looked up in disbelief. "You wouldn't dare use that."

"Yes, he would," Charlotte said. "Please believe me."

"It's the Duke of Wynfield," the man's partner cried in delight.

"Wynfield," the man said slowly.

"I think so," she said, grinning at Gideon.

Within moments the couple had disappeared, leaving Cleopatra and an arrogant buccaneer alone in the dark.

He drew her to a recess in the wall and lowered his head. She sighed, unresisting. He lifted one arm over her shoulder and braced his palm against the wall, not only discouraging her escape but shielding her from view. His mouth covered hers in a deep kiss that dominated, devastated, and lit dangerous impulses in her blood.

He was like a bolt of lightning, and he made her come *alive*. His mouth ate at hers. His hands wandered up her sides to softly mold her breasts. Her neck arched. How could she want and ache and need like this? What had happened to her?

"Let me go," she whispered, insensible, incoherent.

"Why should I?" he said with his lips against hers. "We aren't ourselves tonight. You are a legendary queen who lived to torment her male lovers."

"But it's you who are tormenting me."

He smiled, the brim of his hat overshadowing his face. "I'm a buccaneer, and it's my turn to treasure-hunt." His hand traveled between her breasts to her throat.

"Take my necklace. Just remember that it belongs to Jane, and she isn't one to ignore an offense."

His smile deepened. He traced his fingers across the hollow of her throat. "For one thing, I don't want the necklace. I want you, and you're promised to me."

She shivered at the elemental sensuality in his eyes. "But—"

"A promise is a promise. The longer I wait, the deeper I want you."

She closed her eyes. "I feel peculiar."

"If you faint I'll have to throw you over my shoulder and carry you to the coach. People will talk."

"I—"

His hard mouth captured hers again. She felt male heat and the steel of his cutlass as he pushed his body into hers. His strength kept her from a slide to the floor. He kissed her like sin on the prowl. He kissed her until she didn't care whether they were caught and confronted.

It didn't matter anymore which one of them had instigated this burning attraction. Maybe she had poured all her passion into her diary. But he had unleashed it and transformed it from the page to the physical.

"That will have to do for now," he said, breaking away, the imprint of his body on hers so powerful she would be aware of it for the rest of the night.

Her eyes slowly opened; she saw the desire etched in the stark lines of his face. "We should go back inside," she whispered.

He tipped back his hat. "Yes, but I'd rather not."

"I'm sorry that I made you accept the invitation."

Warmth kindled in his eyes. "It was worth it. Although I'll only take you back into the ballroom if you swear you won't let other men stare at you."

"I request the same favor. I saw you dancing with that lady in knee breeches."

"Believe it or not," he said, taking her by the hand, "I thought it was your cousin Chloe."

He didn't leave her side for the rest of the night. He followed her as if he were one of Cleopatra's handmaidens. He thought about what she had said. She might not be experienced in worldly matters, but . . .

It was true. He had plenty of friends. But for too long he had lived without a family—no brothers to offend or sisters to defend. There was no one he could rely on in a crisis except Kit, who had started a family of his own.

Later that night, when Gideon returned to his house, he realized that the servants were the only ones left of the past with whom he could share memories.

He could rely on them.

And he realized that his single living relative, Sarah, the young daughter he rarely saw, should have been able to rely on him, and he had failed her.

He had sought refuge in a black mist when his father and wife died. He had been one of the walking dead himself. One drunken day had blurred into the next.

He had agreed when Sarah's dying grandmother had insisted it would be an abuse on his part to expose a little girl to his hedonistic lifestyle. It hadn't occurred to him to change the way he lived. He couldn't pull himself together long enough to care whether he lived at all. He had been so immersed in self-misery that if he could have obliterated the past and prevented the future all at once it would have been a relief. And yet there was only so much a man could blame on grief.

Did his daughter miss him? How could she when he had never played a prominent role in her life?

He wanted her back.

He wanted to make amends to her for the past.

He wanted his daughter to have a real family again.

And more than anything he wanted as his wife the woman he hadn't even had the wisdom to choose.

# Chapter 33

The well-sprung carriage flew along the Windsor Road. One of its passengers, the Duchess of Scarfield, had been spurring on the belabored coachman with promises of high promotion if he made it to London in time for the wedding. Indeed, in her husband's estimation, the weather was afraid to disobey his wife.

"Calm down, Emma," Adrian said, his head comfortably settled on her lap, above which his heir had taken residence and was growing by the minute. "The family wouldn't dare hold a wedding without you."

"Do not placate me with such nonsense, Wolf. There is nothing my family will not dare. This is what happens when I am not there to offer them guidance."

"We'll be there soon enough, love."

"No, we won't. It is already too late. How many times did I warn Charlotte not to put secrets on paper? Why do I hope for better? My family is destined for disgrace."

He smiled to himself. As Emma increased with this

pregnancy, she reminded Adrian of a delicate bone-china teapot whose function was to release frequent bursts of steam.

"You're worrying for nothing, Emma," he said to soothe her. "I doubt that Charlotte has any secrets to tell."

"I don't want to arrive a minute before the wedding."

"Of course not."

"I want to be there for the preparations."

"That's understandable."

"Are you trying to placate me?" she asked.

"Well, no —"

"If I know Jane and Chloe, they will have Charlotte wearing a dress from that scandalous Madame Devine. I don't suppose you remember her. She makes provocative attire for mistresses and West End Wives."

He looked up as innocently as he could.

She frowned down at him as if he hadn't deceived her for a second. "Don't answer. I have enough on my mind. And what about the academy?" She fidgeted, leaning over to lift up the curtain. "Can't you make this coach go any faster?"

"We wouldn't want to harm our little heir, would we?" he asked, sitting up in resignation. "The academy will survive. Do not worry."

"Of course I will worry. No one else is willing to take the burden from me."

"Well, what good does it do?"

"Men simply don't understand."

The former Emma Boscastle, the widowed Viscountess Lyons or, as she was known in the family, the Dainty Dictator and Mrs. Killjoy, was considered to be the anomaly in the London line. Militant in her quest to reform the unrefined or scandal-prone, she had considered it her calling to open an academy for young ladies as an example to her own family members, who continued to embarrass her with their incessant love intrigues. "I thought I'd found a kindred soul in Charlotte," she mused. "She was almost as levelheaded as—"

"—you."

She nodded. "She thrived under my tutelage. She admired me, you know. But perhaps I set a bad example. I was a hypocrite."

"Emma, if you had not set a bad example we would not be married and expecting our child."

"True enough."

And a moment later she was tapping her toe against the door, her aggrieved face framed in a wreath of apricot-gold curls. "This is exactly what Lady Clipstone is waiting for—the final fall. I have to be there to prevent it."

"What fall? If I read the situation correctly, Charlotte was caught in a trifling affair with a man who is marrying her. A wedding, Emma, end of story."

"A missing diary, Adrian. Beginning of the end. She may as well have published an encyclopedia of embarrassment."

"Well, you'll be there soon enough to sort it all out."

She subsided with a deep sigh into his arms. He nestled his face in her hair. "Stop," she said halfheartedly, laying her head back on his chest.

"No." He locked his hands beneath her breasts. "You can't make me."

"I could, you know."

"Then try it."

"Perhaps I don't want to," she said, conceding to him with a smile.

"Four years of marriage," he mused. "Don't forget that we were a scandal at the time. I've always wondered, and perhaps I'm better off not knowing, but what turned you and Lady Clipstone into such bitter rivals? Weren't you once friends?"

"We were going to open an etiquette school together," she mused.

"And?"

"And I have to keep some secrets, Adrian, unless Charlotte has spilled them all with her indiscreet pen."

At length they stopped at a coaching inn outside Camberly. Once a mercenary and soldier of fortune, Adrian rarely had to use his rank to secure a decent room in the taverns he visited. He was as rough to the observant eye as Emma was dainty.

But he was especially protective of her during this first pregnancy. He walked up the stairs behind her, ready to catch his little teapot if she should slip, which she almost did when a small girl on the escape from her governess came flying down like a fury.

"Honestly!" Emma exclaimed to the harried governess, who squeezed past her on the stairs in pursuit of her fleeing charge. "Aren't children taught any manners these days? That little girl needs a firm hand."

"She needs a pair of prison guards, madam," the governess tossed back at her. "And as soon as she is delivered to her parents, I shall be delighted to retire my hand."

Emma glanced at her husband, shaking her head. "A girl that boisterous is destined to cause trouble; mark my words. I know an undisciplined child when I see one."

"Shocking," he said, thinking of the tortures he had carried out at that age. "What is the world coming to?"

She picked up her skirt and huffed out a breath. "I see that grin on your handsome face. You do not fool me for a moment. *Our* child will not be allowed to run willy-nilly in public places. Nor in private ones, either."

"As you say, my little teapot."

"What did you call me?"

He laughed. "Nothing, dear heart. Don't upset yourself or the baby."

Grayson rarely let a fortnight pass without giving a party for one reason or another. To receive a gold-edged invitation to one of his lavish affairs was an honor in the aristocracy indeed. His Park Lane mansion never went to sleep. Sentries and servants patrolled the grounds around the clock, fortified by steaming mugs of hot cocoa made from the fresh milk the dairymaids delivered every day. Bakers brought trays of hot bread, pastries, and savory meat pies to the tradesmen's door in the basement kitchen.

But now there was to be a wedding. The house buzzed like a beehive. The kitchen staff ordered the other servants around, and the other servants obeyed. The best cutlery must be brought out of storage. The table linens had to be pressed with hot irons. There had to be room cleared for guests and for the great piles of gifts sent from well-wishers. The menu for the wedding breakfast needed the approval of the marchioness. The footmen needed new soft-soled shoes so that they could glide about as quietly as ghosts. It took effort to make a Mayfair wedding look like a scene from a fairy tale.

*Chapter 34*

$\mathcal{S}$ir Daniel had an unpleasant day ahead of him. His first task was to visit the duke and Miss Boscastle at the Park Lane mansion where she was residing until the wedding. Harriet was present, which did not surprise Daniel. Still, he could not look at her so elegantly dressed without remembering the tangle-haired guttersnipe she had been when he first arrested her, and how she fought him when he had entrusted her to Emma Boscastle's care. Her life had been transformed from that moment. How he wished he could sweep every vulnerable young boy or girl in London off the streets.

"Your Grace," he said with a deferential smile, bowing over her hand.

"Don't," she whispered. "Just tell me that you have found the diary."

He shook his head and straightened. "I wish I could. If anyone knows where it has gone, it is a guarded secret.

I have interrogated all of my sources, with nary a clue overturned as to the diary's whereabouts."

"Oh, dear," Charlotte said faintly. "I think I shall need something stronger than tea."

Sir Daniel glanced away, but not before noticing the concerned look that the duke sent his demure fiancée. Was it possible that this arrangement was deepening into genuine affection? Perhaps this diary affair had brought some good, after all. Daniel believed in love and marriage, even if both had eluded him.

Gideon stirred. "And the sapphire necklace has not passed hands?"

"Not in the obvious shops," Sir Daniel said. "Which is in itself unusual. It might be that the thieves have escaped the city."

Charlotte gave a soft sigh. "I so wanted this to be cleared up before the wedding."

"There are still four days left," Gideon said, his gaze turning introspective.

Harriet lifted her chin. "He's right."

"I have a horrible feeling," Charlotte said softly, "that it has indeed fallen into wicked hands."


Gideon walked slowly across the street, holding up his hand to interrupt the flow of midday traffic. It stung his pride that he would not be able to keep his promise to Charlotte's family. He had failed to recover the lost diary before the wedding.

"Damn," he said as a small carriage hurtled toward him, forcing him to jump onto the sidewalk. "Who the blazes drives like he owns the street?"

"Wynfield!" Devon shouted from the seat of his phaeton. "Would you like to go to the arcade for an hour? I am in need of a new hat."

Gideon was about to refuse but then he shrugged. "Why not?" he muttered as he climbed up beside his future cousin-in-law. Devon had already done his worst—unless he ended up causing an accident with his reckless driving.

"I should buy Charlotte a wedding present, anyway," he said to himself.

"Don't buy her another blasted diary."

"I have something else in mind."

He and Devon parted company as soon as they entered the emporium. Sir Godfrey noticed Gideon right away and abandoned another customer in the middle of a sale to attend him.

"Your Grace! Your Grace!" he cried, in the event that no one had noticed a peer of the realm in their midst. "How good it is to see you again this soon! What can I do to be of service?"

He stared down in embarrassment into the man's expectant face. No wonder Kit had stolen Sir Godfrey's intended for his own. The blundering fellow didn't have a clue except when it came to business.

"Would Your Grace like to examine the hunting horn more closely? I have a knife that complements it."

"I'm looking for a wedding present, sir. The weaponry will have to wait until our anniversary."

Sir Godfrey's eyes widened. "Oh, good one, Your Grace."

Gideon nodded at a group of young ladies who had stopped to stare at him. "I would like a fan—"

"Ivory, gilt, or feather?"

"Is there a difference?"

"A difference?" Sir Godfrey shuddered. "I should say. We also carry tortoiseshell or mother-of-pearl—"

"It—"

"Silk or chicken skin?"

"Chicken skin? Definitely not."

"A fan with a peephole to convey mood, or a mounting for the more modest?"

"I'll be damned if I know. One of each, I suppose. I would like to surprise my betrothed before the wedding."

Sir Godfrey flagged his assistant down with the fan he had removed from a counter display. "Please bring out every fan we have in the shop for His Grace."

The assistant shook his head in apology. "You're holding it."

"What?" Sir Godfrey said, snapping the fan shut. "We had three dozen in here the day before yesterday."

"Yes, sir. But yesterday a lady came in and bought up the whole lot."

"Who was she?" Sir Godfrey asked.

"The head of that academy, sir. She had it put on her account."

Sir Godfrey handed the fan to Gideon. "Bring me the account book."

Gideon crossed his arms, tapping the fan in irritation. He caught Devon's eye across the store, and before he knew it Devon was standing at his side.

"What do you want me to do?" Devon asked, turning his head to the side.

"What are you talking about?"

"Your distress signal." Devon glanced down at Gideon's hand. "You summoned me over with your fan."

"I did no such thing—do you mean to tell me that *you* know how to converse with a fan?"

"For God's sake, Gideon, there isn't a gentleman in London who doesn't know at least the rudimentary language of the flutter. It isn't only a matter of seduction. It is about survival."

The assistant reappeared with the heavy account book opened in his hands. Sir Godfrey stared at the names listed in the previous day's column of sales.

"Lady Alice Clipstone," he said, his lip curling in recollection. "That would be the owner of an academy that struggles to attain the reputation enjoyed by Your Grace's fiancée. She has bought on credit again, I see."

"Are you suggesting there is a rivalry between the two academies?" Gideon asked, motioning at the account with the fan.

"Oh, indeed. I would say, in fact, that you would not find more intense competition between the various fencing schools in town."

Gideon considered this. He would mention it to Charlotte and to Sir Daniel.

"Thank you, Sir Godfrey. This has been an elucidating conversation. I would like to purchase the diary and silver inkstand that Miss Boscastle admired."

"Yes, Your Grace. They will be delivered to—"

"The Marquess of Sedgecroft's residence."

"And a magnificent place it is, Your Grace."

# Chapter 35

*T*he duel was behind Gideon. The energetic schoolmistress whom Charlotte had hired as her replacement was ensconced at the academy. At last Charlotte
felt free to indulge in joyful anticipation. It was impossible, actually, to feel anything but joy, with Jane and her
female entourage celebrating this marriage as if it had
not come about by unconventional circumstances.

Still, from a Boscastle perspective, all was well that
ended in a walk to the altar. Everyone in the family
knew that a genuine romance followed no proper rules
at all. But somehow all the ingredients—a dose of passion, a sprinkling of secrets, a measure of honor, and two
hearts drawn together by an intangible force—combined
to make a union that would not only survive but thrive
over the course of time.

Charlotte had given up hope that her diary would be
returned. The only consolation was that none of her
writings had shown up in the scandal sheets. Gideon had

mentioned Sir Godfrey's remark about Lady Clipstone's rivalry. Charlotte explained that it had something to do with her cousin Emma, but she didn't know what, and besides, she had more urgent matters on her mind.

Her wedding dress had finally been finished by a dedicated corps of seamstresses whose needles had flown and stitched morning and night to create magic. Now all that she needed were her corset, chemise, and a few traveling essentials. Jane's Italian shoemaker had fashioned the most perfect wedding shoes in the world—burgundy leather adorned with diamond-studded buckles that glittered like stars.

Jane was also taking her to the controversial dressmaker this afternoon. Madame Devine had a talent for designing attire that drove men so wild they willingly drained their pockets.

Charlotte was amazed at the bystanders milling about the Georgian-style brown-brick shop. "What are all those gentlemen waiting for?" she asked Jane.

"They're hoping for a glimpse of the customers, many of whom are Cyprians and courtesans."

"Then what are we doing here?"

Jane stepped out of the carriage, lifting her head at the low whistles that followed her to the door.

When Charlotte hurried to join her and a chorus of cheers went up, Jane laughed and pulled her into the care of the two footmen who escorted customers into the shop.

"I was mortified the first time Grayson brought me here," Jane whispered as they climbed the stairs to the fitting rooms. "Really, Madame creates her fashions for one purpose only—for the pleasure of a gentleman to remove."

To Charlotte's surprise Madame Devine already had

a corset selected, ivory silk with steel underpinnings that pushed up Charlotte's breasts, nipped in her waist, and emphasized the flare of her hips. Charlotte felt as if she were fitted up more for a medieval joust than a marriage, but the result was so provocative it seemed certain Gideon would liberate her from the contraption before long. Miss Peppertree would approve.

"The duke will be delighted," Madame Devine announced when the fitting, exhausting for everyone, finally came to an end.

An auburn-haired woman in a leghorn bonnet and a striped scarlet-and-gold silk dress stepped forth from a dressing screen.

"Audrey," Jane said warmly. "Have you met Miss Boscastle?"

"I haven't had the honor." She lowered her voice. "But I'm happy to admit that I have not seen His Grace since the news of your engagement broke."

Charlotte smiled, knowing that her family considered Mrs. Watson a friend. "I hope you never see him at your house again," she said honestly.

Audrey took in Charlotte's face and figure. "I've a feeling he will not return."

Charlotte would make him sorry if he did, especially since she was ordering evening dresses and gauze night rails that only a courtesan would wear. She might not have convinced him not to forgo the duel. But she was determined to keep practicing her ways of persuasion. After all, she studied for years to be a lady. She didn't expect to put less effort into becoming a wife.

"Mrs. Watson," she said, glancing around to make sure no one could hear them, "I am grateful for the information that Jane passed to me from you."

"Oh, good. I hope you'll put it to use."

Charlotte smiled. "I already have."


Millie woke up screaming the moment that Nick put his hands to her throat. He leaned back, clapping his hands over his ears, and muttered, "Oh, my God, not you, too," and fell back onto the pallet.

She stared down into the bodice of the dress she hadn't bothered to remove for bed. "What are you trying to do to me, Nick Rydell? I 'ad a bad enough time of it last night. Don't you see these bruises—"

"Look at it." He sat up and fished the ornate sapphire necklace out of her cleavage. "I was trying to clasp it on you. I saw the bruises. Gimme his name and I'll take care of the sod tonight. Can't you find a better class of clientele?"

She stared at him suspiciously. "'Ow much gin did you drink?"

"None."

"What are we gonna do for money if I keep this thing?"

He reached behind him for his trousers. "I didn't say you could keep it. I only wanted to see what it looked like on you."

"You woke me up for that?" She thumped back onto her pillow, her arm covering her face.

He pulled her arm down from her face. "Don't let no one else see it. I'll be back."

She studied him in curiosity. "You're gettin' rid of that book?"

"Yeah."

"Thank God. It was unnatural to see you readin' every night."

"Well, it's over." He went to the door. "Don't go to work tonight. I'm taking you to Vauxhall."

"I don't 'ave a clean frock."

"I'll find one." His gaze strayed to the bruises on her neck. "Go to sleep. You look . . . I don't know."

"Hey." She sat up again, grasping the necklace in her hand. "I forgot to tell you. Your old friend Sir Daniel was lookin' for you last night. I told 'im you was dead."

"Good girl."

"Threatened to 'ave me carted off if 'e saw me on the corner again."

"Time to rest up then."

"Rest?" She sank down again. "You shouldn't read, Nick. I think that book made you go off upstairs."

He hesitated. He almost asked her whether what Barney had said was true. Maybe he didn't want to know yet. But he did know that he couldn't afford to sit about another day losing himself in a damn diary. Millie was right. It was unnatural. Ever since he'd started to read the thing, he'd slipped from his game. He wanted to be rid of it. He wanted his wrath back because without it someone harder would take his place on the streets.

# Chapter 36

*C*harlotte looked at the bridal gown that hung from the wardrobe door. It was so beautifully made that she had fallen asleep last night staring at it. She could not wait to wear it for Gideon tomorrow at the wedding. And then, later that evening, to let him release her from the layers of figured silk and frothy lace.

She touched the skirt like a talisman as she passed the wardrobe to enter the dressing closet. She had just heard one of the maids come in through the adjoining door, presumably to tidy the chaos that Chloe and Jane had created, bringing various shades of stockings to match the vibrant pink of the gown.

She pushed open the door, a smile on her lips that vanished as soon as she saw a strange man sifting through the jewels on the chest of drawers. He spun around to face her.

She gasped in recognition. "You. You're the one I saw at the window."

He clasped his hands together. "Please don't scream again. I'm not gonna 'urt a hair on your lovely 'ead. Just listen. I'm beggin' you. Do you understand?"

She nodded, her heart beating erratically in her throat. "What do you want?"

"I brought you back your diary. Look. On the desk behind you. There it is. Not a page missing."

Her eyes lifted in disbelief. "*You* took my diary? You were the face in the window. But why? I don't know you. Who are you? What could have possessed you?"

"You 'ave a rival. She paid me to do a job, but I don't like 'er. I like you."

Charlotte closed her eyes for a moment, gathering her wits. "You shouldn't like me. I have caused more trouble than you can believe."

He laughed. "Me, too. I never knew a lady had thoughts like you. I never looked at love like you do, if you know what I mean. All these things men and women do together, well, you made 'em sound pretty."

"No." She felt a lightness spreading through her. "Yes, I do know, actually. And you're not going to do anything horrible to me? I'm about to be married to the duke of my dreams, and even though he doesn't love me, I have loved him since the day I first saw him."

"The duke's a fortunate man."

"He won't be if he finds me dead."

"Dead? Oh, love, you don't understand. All I want is a dress and a token of your esteem given without a fuss."

"A token? What sort of token? Wait, don't answer that. Did you just say that a *lady* paid you to steal the diary?"

"That's right. I can't give you 'er name. But I started to read it, and I was moved by your passionate confessions."

Charlotte sensed he was omitting a crucial part of this story, but as long as he gave her the diary and didn't hurt her, she would play along and make sense of it later. "You . . . were *moved?*" She lowered the fan she had covertly pulled from a half-closed drawer to protect herself if he laid a hand on her. "You mean someone paid you to steal my diary and you're returning it because —"

"Yeah. I'm losin' money on this transaction. If anybody on the street 'ears what I've done, I'll be laughed out of St. Giles."

She forced herself to look deeper than his scarred face and long hair and mouse gray coat. If he washed up, combed his hair, and put on a suit that fit, he could be presentable. He— Her thoughts froze. In the doorway that led into another bedroom was the new chambermaid who had passed Weed's inspection. Their eyes met. She willed the girl to keep hidden.

"You did the right thing," she said, looking away from the door. He hadn't seen the maid. Charlotte was afraid to upset him. Who knew how he might react? He made her so nervous that her mouth went dry. Perhaps if she was nice to him, he would go away. "I am proud that you listened to the voice of your conscience."

"Yeah, whatever that is. But I gotta go. All I want is a dress for my girl. Something pretty and frilly and light to wear out."

"I don't know what would fit her," Charlotte said, lowering the fan she had poised to attack. "Come with me to the wardrobe and pick, but please don't touch my wedding dress."

So they went into the other room together to the French gilt armoire, and Charlotte managed to talk him into choosing a turquoise silk with beribboned sleeves and an embroidered hem. "I haven't worn it. There's room if she needs it. Just help her adjust the laces, and, of course, a good corset helps. Does she have anything to support her?"

He frowned. "She goes to the Female Penitentiary Society from time to time and they give 'er some grub once in a while. But other than that, I pay for what she needs."

"No. I mean does she have a good corset? A garment designed to shape her unmentionable parts into— Oh, never mind. Is that all you want?"

"I'll take that ruby necklace on your dressing table as recompense for my time."

"It isn't—" She nodded. It was worth a fortune. And yet Jane would have to understand.

"So even young ladies like yourself want a man to whisper rude words while they're making the two-backed beast?" Nick asked Charlotte, grinning at her.

"I highly disapprove of this conversation."

"You're the one who wrote about it."

"And look at all the trouble I have drawn upon myself and those I care about. Besides, writing about a private matters is not the same as discussing it. Don't you understand the difference?"

"Yeah." He chuckled. "Ain't the same as doin' it, either. But you know all about that."

"I don't, actually."

He winked, looking her over. "I'll keep it secret."

"I would appreciate it." She drew in a slow breath. "Do you have a name?"

"It's Nick. She'll look nice in this," he said, holding the dress Charlotte had chosen to his chest. "Not as nice as you, though."

Charlotte nodded. She would have pulled out every dress she owned and offered to make alterations if it kept him from hurting her. "She'll look like a lady."

"Nah. It would take more than that, but maybe she'll feel like a lady."

Charlotte lifted her gaze. The chambermaid hadn't moved from the door. It was clear she realized Nick had broken in and didn't belong. She looked petrified. Charlotte prayed she would stay calm and not do or say anything to set the thief off.

It was all she could manage to encourage this alarming character to leave without making it obvious that he was deplorable company. Only then could she release her breath and take time to examine her diary and check for missing pages. "How are you leaving?" she asked, trying to keep her anxiety from her voice.

"Out the window, closest to the tree," he said.

"Well, good luck," she said, swallowing hard.

"Yeah. Same to you. That duke had better do right by you."

"Yes. He'd better."

"Send Nick after 'im if he don't."

How Charlotte managed to nod graciously at this disconcerting offer she did not know. She hadn't the smallest doubt that Gideon would have challenged him on the spot.

"Where is Charlotte?" Jane asked Weed, who had arrived before she had released the bell cord. "We were supposed to review the guest list together so she could help me to remember the correct titles."

Chloe breezed into the room, stunning in ice blue satin. "I just saw a footman go up to her room. Or he could have been on his way to Emma's. She was supposed to be looking over the list with Charlotte, too."

Gideon turned from the window where he stood with Grayson watching Sir Christopher in the garden instructing Lord Rowan how to lunge.

"I don't mind going up to fetch her," he said, hoping to take advantage of the fact that no one was paying more than token attention to anyone else. "No one objects?"

"I do," said Jane slyly. "And I've got my eye on you. This is the one time that we must exercise restraint and follow the rules."

Weed frowned. "There is no footman in her room. I have just finished a last-minute inspection of the livery of each servant for the wedding. The footmen have each been instructed to repowder their periwigs and brush off their coats."

Chloe's forehead creased. "This footman was wearing street clothes, now that you mention it. He carried something in his hand. He seemed to be in a great hurry. I assumed someone had instructed him to go upstairs."

Gideon stared across the room. "Then who is he?"

"Didn't you have a present sent to her?" Chloe asked.

"Yes. But Weed had it put away. I'm giving it to Charlotte on our wedding night."

"Thank you for bringing back the diary," Charlotte whispered, her nerves frayed.

"Thank you for writing it—and for the dress." He doffed his cap.

And at last he hurried to the window, the turquoise dress billowing like a parasol as he leaped onto the tree branch that grew under the window.

"My stars!" Charlotte exclaimed, swinging around to face the maid. "Did he have to escape in full view of the drawing room windows?"

"I'll warn them," the maid offered, and eagerly took off before Charlotte could explain that warning anyone in this house might do more harm than good.

"Tell them to let him go! Oh, bother. I might as well go down and tell them myself."

The maid had already run to the top of the stairs and grabbed the valet, who was on his way up to lay out a change of clothes in Master Rowan's room. "Hurry!" she said. "There was a strange man in Miss Boscastle's room and he's taken one of her dresses with him out the window!"

"My God!"

The valet ran downstairs and narrowly escaped colliding with the butler, who was carrying a tea tray to the drawing room. "Hurry! Get help! A thief broke into Miss Boscastle's room. He's stolen the dress she was wearing and escaped out the window!"

The butler's mouth dropped. "The dirty bugger! I'll put Weed on it this minute."

And the butler bustled into the drawing room, where everyone was waiting for tea, and shouted at Weed, "Sir! Sir! A thief has broken into Miss Boscastle's bedroom and jumped out the window wearing her wedding dress!"

"What?" Gideon said, moving to the door. "Which window? Where is he going?"

Jane grabbed his arm. "Go out into the garden to catch him."

"What about Charlotte? I ought to check on her."

"I'll do it," Jane said. "Grayson, put down that biscuit and go with Gideon."

But by the time Gideon and Grayson ran out into the garden with Weed and three other footmen, the thief had dropped from the tree to the wall and taken off pell-mell for the secret route to the stews. From the garden gate all one could make out of him was a billowing skirt in a lovely shade of turquoise blue.

"I'm going to hunt him down," Gideon said, unbuttoning his coat. "I want to strangle him."

Grayson shook his head. "You'll have to wait until after the wedding, unless you wish to upset every woman in this house. You might not even have a wedding if you get into a brawl with a gang of thugs. We can hunt them down another time."

"But he's wearing her bridal gown. How's the wedding going to take place without it?"

"He is not wearing her wedding dress," Grayson said. "That's a promenade dress, which he is holding under his arm, by the way."

"You're right," Gideon said, impressed by Grayson's knowledge of female costume. "Look, I don't care about protocol. I need to see Charlotte with my own eyes. If only for a few moments, and I swear I'll be good."

A firm but gentle voice entered the conversation. "You cannot see her now," Emma said. "However, I have just intercepted her in the hall. She is preparing for a bath to calm her nerves. She is shaken but otherwise perfectly fine and in good spirits."

He frowned. "Then I should have followed my instincts and chased after him. What did he want with her to begin with?"

"He returned the diary," Emma said with a sigh of relief. "Now it is onward to the wedding, and may it please heaven that nothing else threatens that event."

Gideon stared at the garden wall. "The diary was brought back by the man who escaped with a dress? There has to be more to this story. I wonder—it probably has nothing to do with this—but what do you know of a Lady Clipstone?"

Emma's brow lifted. "She has sworn to ruin the academy. Why do you mention her?"

"Do you think she is capable of theft?"

"I doubt—"

"Or of hiring a thief?"

"Yes," she said slowly. "She has held a grudge against me for years, but it never occurred to me that she would act upon it." She shook her head as realization dawned. "*She* had the diary stolen. What a spiteful witch. Oh—I could shout at her."

"Shout at her? Grayson said. "That's an ominous form of revenge if I've ever heard one. That woman has brought us inexcusable woe. I don't think a mere shout is suitable punishment."

Emma's hand slipped to her rounded stomach. "A lady does not seek revenge. She rises above it, and, if she is a person of strong character, she forgives."

"Forgives?" Grayson shook his head. "Why?"

"Her scheme might have brought us a bit of woe,"

Emma replied, her calm demeanor restored once again.
"But it has brought our family together for another wedding. Consider that the primary objective of the academy
is for our pupils to marry well. We might suffer the lam-
entable scandal now and then. But in the end we are still
considered a cut above the rest. Despite Lady Clipstone's
nefarious efforts, she has ruined neither Charlotte's reputation nor the academy's."

*Chapter 37*

Charlotte had dreamed of her wedding day for years. She had described it in her old diary to the last detail. And the next time she had a moment to herself she would record the actual events of the day in the new one Gideon had given her, along with the silver inkstand and a heavy sapphire-and-diamond ring that he said had reminded him of her blue eyes and the starlight in their depths. The first page of her diary would be marked with one of the red roses he had sent to her right before she met him at the chapel.

The dream had become real; the vows had been spoken by a husband and wife who were too overcome to do anything but smile at the mayhem that erupted from the pews filled with Boscastle family members. She felt herself torn from his side, embraced and congratulated by friends and family. She cast a look for Gideon in the crowd, and their eyes connected. Neither of them had to say a word.

That evening a small article in the broadsheets mentioned that a mysterious intruder had broken into the Marquess of Sedgecroft's mansion. There were no witnesses to the crime, although a bystander who had been standing outside the mansion's gates had seen a suspicious-looking young man earlier with a package in his hands. Speculation over its contents swirled about London.

Still, details of the wedding, the discreet selection of guests, the gifts received, soon eclipsed the lesser gossip. It was a seed that had been cast to the wind and had failed to sprout.

The house was quiet when Gideon carried Charlotte to his room and unbound her from the ties and tapes of her wedding dress. The provocative corset she wore beneath surprised him. "That is a wicked garment," he murmured in approval. "It pushes your pretty breasts up quite indecently. I can even see your nipples."

Charlotte flushed, staring past him. "I knew I shouldn't have worn it."

"Oh, but you should," he said quickly, bending his head to lick the rosy tips that peeked out over the confining garment. "Except that it does give you the advantage, and I can't allow that to continue."

He spent hours kissing and caressing her, unlocking the secrets of her body as easily as he had her heart. She let him reduce her to breathless urgency in the shadows of his bed. She could not have broken free from him if the house had caught on fire. Damp heat gathered between her thighs. A craving pulsed from deep inside her.

He hadn't touched her there, and she knew this ploy

was a deliberate act of seduction on his part . . . one that accomplished its goal before she could retaliate.

"Your time will come," she said, staring up into his hard, unyielding face.

He smiled, the sensual knowledge in his eyes beckoning her to make good her threat. "But in the meanwhile, I wield the upper hand."

She reached up and locked her arms around his neck. "Do you?"

She kissed him before he could reply. Her tongue grazed his in flirtation and invitation. She arched upward, offering herself, and he took, needed, and claimed.

His breath came faster. He kissed her shoulder, her breasts, sliding his hands around her back to draw her from the bed and to her feet, where they stood facing each other, bound by an oath, bound together for an eternity of moments and secrets of the heart.

"I want you on the floor."

Her lips parted, swollen and enticing. He pulled her unresisting body down against his. "And I want you on your knees."

He drew back slowly, her hair falling over her breasts, hiding her from his burning stare. "Now, Charlotte."

He waited, enrapt as she obeyed, her lips lifting into a smile. He dropped behind her, his hands kneading the firm cheeks of her bottom, raising her to a tempting angle. He flexed his back.

His fingertips followed the line of her nape to the base of her spine. Her skin felt like watered silk. "I can see us in the looking glass," he said. "Lift your head. Look at yourself."

She raised her gaze, meeting his eyes in the mirror, the lamplight enhancing the decadent image captured in the glass. Her hair hung in coils down her arms and around her face.

He pressed his jutting erection against her. A soft exhalation escaped her. She stared, mesmerized, at the man and woman in the mirror.

"What a wanton duchess you are," he said. "Does anyone else know that you can be so wicked?"

"It's supposed to be a secret."

"Then I won't tell."

He felt her body tighten as he guided the crown of his shaft between her thighs to penetrate her cleft.

Not all at once. Not her first time. He set a measured rhythm, sank into her a little deeper each time, then withdrew. Too late, he realized he was caught in a trap of his own invention. The teasing stabs of pleasure brought him to the edge so many times he began to rely on instinct alone, to surrender to sheer feeling. He rubbed his belly against her backside and heard the low moan that caught in her throat. No need for French letter. This was his wife.

"Charlotte, forgive me. . . ."

The cords in his neck knotted with the control he exerted to keep from embedding himself completely in her warmth. Deeper. Slowly. His hands clasped her hips, stilling her as her body accepted, absorbed the length of him.

"Gideon," she whispered, and he glanced again at their reflection in the oval glass, transfixed by the raw beauty of her submission. "Be fire to fire."

He drew his fascinated gaze from the looking glass. "And flesh to flesh. I'll remember this moment forever," he said. "Let me make it unforgettable for you." He went still so that she couldn't breathe before he drove back inside her with a force that breached her last defense and filled her to overflowing and made her his own at last.

Audrey had entertained the earl from the previous evening to the present one, a privilege granted only one of her former lovers. She had awakened before him that afternoon and noted in relief the patch of cloudless blue sky she could see through the curtains.

Even the weather had bowed to a Boscastle wedding, she thought as she drifted back to sleep. She could have wangled an invitation if she had wanted to attend. She hadn't. She was too closely associated with the woman the duke had almost made his mistress.

His bride did not need to be reminded of his sins. Which reminded Audrey that her nemesis hadn't visited in three days. Perhaps she was free of him once again.

What was the point in plotting revenge when the other party refused to participate? As evening fell she eased from the bed, her eyes avoiding the naked earl who was sprawled across the sheets in all his blatant nude splendor.

She put on her moss green silk robe and stared at her reflection in the mirror. She saw a strange woman gazing back at her.

The earl rolled onto his stomach. She glanced at him and quickly escaped through the door to her receiving chamber. Sir Daniel was studying the painting of Venus on the mantel above the pink marble fireplace in which a small clump of sea coals smoldered.

"Mrs. Watson," he said cordially, turning toward her arrested figure. "I hope my visit is not inconvenient."

She resisted the urge to tighten her robe, wishing

she'd at least brushed her hair. "How did you get in here? I left instructions that no one was to be admitted."

"I have an excellent memory." A smile creased his close-shaven cheeks. "Don't you recall leading me through the secret passages of the house?"

"No. I don't."

He glanced around the room as if he hadn't had plenty of time to nose around. His gaze went from the Chinese vase on the sideboard to the brandy decanter on top of the black cabinet. Then his eyes lit on the hat that sat on a corner chair.

He lifted his gaze to hers.

She wanted to scratch his eyes out, to pummel his face and chest and feel his arms enfold her. But she had made the mistake of showing that she cared for him once.

"Forgive me," he said. "I didn't realize you had company."

Her lips firmed. "Did you have a reason to come here?"

He smiled. "Yes. I have received word that Miss Boscastle's diary has been returned to her."

"The Duchess of Wynfield," she said. "She was married this morning, wasn't she?"

The clink of a pitcher against a washbowl came from the adjoining room. Sir Daniel stared at the closed door in unconcealed contempt.

"Good evening to you then, ma'am," he said, turning before she could obey the impulse to stop him. "Do give the earl my regards, won't you?"

Millie twirled around the room in her new dress. "You really didn't steal it, Nick?"

"No," he said flatly, one of his frequent black moods coming over him. "Don't spin like that. My 'ead's splittin' open."

"It's all that gin. I really don't have to work alone on the corner?"

"Do I 'ave to repeat myself again? I will approve of your client first and insist you take along one of the boys to stand guard in case things turn rough."

He heard a banging through the passageway and he glanced up. It was only a friend, an oaf named Hollis who didn't know his head from his behind.

"What do you mean barging in 'ere like the cavalry, I'd like to know?"

"Millie." Hollis whistled through the gap in his front teeth. "I'd like some of that, please."

"Say that to me again and I'll poke your eyes out with this"—she fumbled and raised her hand—"comb."

Hollis leaned against the wall, waiting. "All right. I'd like some of that, please."

"Go eff yourself," Nick said, his hand slipping under his pillow for his gun.

The man snorted. "There's a shipment just been unloaded at the wharves."

Nick sat up. "Yeah?"

Millie turned, in a temper, and tears filled her eyes. "You promised we was going to Vauxhall tonight." She threw the comb on the bed.

"I'm sorry, Millie," Hollis said. "It's business."

She shrugged. "Don't stand there lookin' all Friday-faced. 'Elp me out of this silly dress. It feels like a shroud."

He swallowed, and she turned her back to him. His huge paw fumbled a bit before he said, "I'll take you to Vauxhall, Millie. And we'll eat there, too."

"Who'd you rob?" she said sourly.

"No one. I got a job at the wharves. That's 'ow the boys know about the shipment."

She turned slowly. "You're a nitwit. You think that they'll keep you on at the wharves once they realize you're behind a lay?"

"It's all right. There's other jobs that need a man with brawn."

"Stuff it, the pair of you," Nick said, pulling on a pair of trousers over his bare rump.

"Will you come out with me or not?" Hollis asked Millie.

Nick jammed his gun in his waistband and a knife into his boot. "Let's go."

Nick was back.

He wouldn't change.

He'd fancied a glimpse into another world, but now he needed a fresh infusion of danger. He ruled the rookeries. There wasn't a dark alley, a back wynd, a path to the illegal gambling hells that Nick didn't know. God help the sod who crossed him. Or the female who hoped to leg-shackle him for life with a child that couldn't be his.

He was back. And it was only a matter of hours before he began to forget what Charlotte Boscastle had even looked like.

# Chapter 38

*C*harlotte woke up in stages the morning after the wedding. Her body resisted. She felt warmth, a stinging ache in unfamiliar places. Memories flooded her mind. Gideon making love to her until neither of them could move. His dark silhouette overshadowing her. His weight and heat stealing her sanity, unleashing needs that he satisfied almost before she was aware of them herself.

She shifted closer to his body and listened to the even cadence of his breathing. The tips of her bare breasts pressed against his shoulder blades. Would he awaken if she touched him?

He'd wanted her to last night, and she had loved him with abandon, the wanton Charlotte who had confessed her passion for him not long ago in words. She wasn't sorry she had written them now. She wasn't sorry that Harriet had played a role in making Charlotte's wicked dreams come true.

The door opened. A little girl's head looked into the room.

"Wake up," she said. "I'm here."

Charlotte gasped. "Wake up, Gideon," she whispered.

"I've been waiting forever to meet you," the voice added. "Our coach wheel broke. Then the driver took the wrong road. We got lost and missed the wedding. Please wake up or I'm going to pull all the covers off the bed and then you'll be very cross and embarrassed."

Gideon grunted and lifted his head. "Who in the dickens do you think— *Sarah?*"

"Sarah?" Charlotte said, studying the serious face that stared at her from the doorway. "Is this her?"

"I don't know," Gideon said with a glint of fondness in his eye. "I can't tell if she's a girl or a performer in a traveling circus. What are you wearing?"

"Those are my clothes," Charlotte said with a laugh, pulling the sheet up to her and Gideon's shoulder. "And my wedding slippers. And my grandmother's pearls."

"She's wearing your hair band too," Gideon pointed out.

"Don't you want to go for a walk with your governess in the garden?" Gideon asked his daughter softly. "I know you arrived very late last night. We have a cat that you might like to meet."

She averted her head. "I want to go to Madame Devine's and see the dresses that Cook says the tarts wear."

"Cook is an old busybody," Gideon said. "She ought to concern herself with tarts that are to be eaten."

"Do you want to go shopping with me today?" Charlotte asked her, examining the girl's odd mode of dress. "We'll buy you a new gown."

"I already have enough dresses. I need slippers and a bridal fan."

Charlotte looked impressed. "Can you speak the language of the fan?"

"Oh, yes. And I can hit someone with it, too."

"Oh, that's lovely," Gideon said. "That and spitting on people will make you very popular in the world."

"I don't spit anymore," she said. "You said you would teach me how to swordfight."

"Did I? Well, maybe I will, but I don't think this is the right time, darling. How tall you've grown."

Charlotte studied the girl in wonder. She had Gideon's dark hair and strong chin.

"I have a diary," Sarah said. "And I've already written about your marriage, and the mistresses our father had before, and what the maid saw them doing in his bedroom."

"I'm sure she means playing cards," Gideon said, frowning at his daughter.

"Oh, of course," Charlotte said with a touch of sarcasm. "Why do you refer to him as 'our father'?"

"Mrs. Stearns calls him that because he thinks he's God."

"Oh. I see," Charlotte said, biting her lip. "Look, what do you say the three of us spend the day alone together? Maybe we can buy you the slippers you want. Or go to the fencing salon. Gideon?"

"It will be an honor to entertain the two most important ladies in my life. But, Sarah, you must wait outside."

Sarah clapped her hands in delight. "Will you tell me about how you shot Charlotte's lover in the foot?"

"That isn't at all what happened," Gideon said quickly. "He shot himself in the foot. And he was never her lover." He gave her another frown. "Furthermore, she is now your mother and should be addressed as such."

"Are you her lover now?"

"She is my wife," he said, rubbing his unshaven cheek. "How old are you?"

"Five." Sarah was quiet for some time. "Are both of you naked?"

"Absolutely not," Gideon and Charlotte answered at the same time.

"Then why was she holding that sheet up to her neck?"

Gideon made a choking sound at the back of his throat. "Because it's . . . it's cold in this room, that's why. And you were not supposed to come in without knocking."

"I did knock. You didn't answer."

"Sarah," Charlotte said, her lips twitching, "wait for us belowstairs. Your father and I will come down to have breakfast with you."

"I've already had breakfast. And luncheon."

Gideon and Sarah looked inquiringly at Charlotte, challenging her to address the issue. "Then we shall have a tea party together," she said in an unflustered voice.

"May I dress up?"

"Of course you can," Charlotte said, her tone softening. "That is the proper approach to a party. Would you like me to come and help you?"

Sarah shook her head, backing toward the door. "Not unless you put your clothes on first. I've never seen a naked person in my life. Mrs. Stearns said that I would turn to stone if I did."

"Mrs. Stearns is quite right," Gideon said, assuming a moral tone that might have been effective if he weren't cowering stark-ballocks under the covers. "Now go and find her."

"She's standing in the door," Sarah said. "She's been there the whole time."

"Great God in all His mercy!" Gideon exclaimed. "Can a man not have privacy in his own bedchamber?"

The door was immediately pulled shut.

"Oh, Gideon," Charlotte said with a sigh. "You did not handle that well at all."

"I know, I know. But I couldn't let the child see me in my natal suit. But you, on the other hand—"

She slipped out of his grasp, rewarding him with a flash of creamy skin and streaming blond hair before she escaped behind the screen. "Don't look at me, Gideon."

"Why the blazes not?"

"I heard the warning that you gave our daughter. You will turn to stone if you gaze upon my nakedness."

He stared at her reflection in the cheval glass standing beside the dressing screen. "I know what she means, madam. I am turning to stone as I look upon you now."

Twenty minutes later Charlotte and Gideon were in the drawing room with Sarah. At first she appeared to be uncomfortable in her father's company. And he looked as if he felt the same way about her. Then the next thing Charlotte knew Sarah flung herself into his arms and he caught her, lifting her up by the waist as she playfully pummeled his head.

"Sarah, stop that. I have missed you."

She hit him again, giggling as he scowled and tried to dodge her attack. He glanced at Charlotte. "I told you she had a wicked side."

Charlotte shook her head. "Then I shall have to improve her behavior . . .as well as yours."

*Chapter 39*

$\mathscr{G}$ ideon dropped off Charlotte and Sarah at the crowded emporium the next afternoon. He asked two of his youngest footmen to accompany them and carry whatever furbelows and fripperies the ladies chanced to purchase. He chose to wait in the coffee shop across the street.

Inside the busy arcade Charlotte took Sarah by the hand and did her best to politely squeeze a place for them at each counter. But one customer refused to budge as Sarah pressed impatiently between her and the maid standing at her side.

"Do you mind?" the woman said to Sarah, half turning to reprimand her. "Children should not be brought on—"

She looked up at Charlotte's face; for a moment her eyes flashed in open hostility, and Charlotte would have delivered a few choice words, but she would not condescend to low behavior with her daughter present.

"Your Grace!" Lady Clipstone cried in faux surprise. "How wonderful to see you, and, oh, is this the little lady?" she asked, reaching to pat Sarah on the head.

Sarah drew back against Charlotte with the arrogant scowl she had obviously inherited from her father along with his wicked nature.

"Yes, it is," Charlotte said with a smile so forced it could have cracked her face. "Isn't she a cherub?" She poked Sarah in the arm. "This is Lady Clipstone, dear. She's one of my cousin's *oldest* friends. Give her a smile, Sarah."

Sarah glanced up at Lady Clipstone. Then she glanced back to Charlotte. "I do not want to smile at her. You cannot make me."

"No, sweet, I can't. But I can tighten the purse strings if you persist."

Sarah folded her arms across her chest.

"It's fine," Lady Clipstone said quickly. "She is so *young* to be shopping, and after all the *excitement* in your lives. How exhausting the past weeks have been for your family. Oh—did I forget to offer my congratulations?"

Sarah stuck her tongue out at Alice. Charlotte gasped in dismay. Lady Clipstone stepped back into her maid. "What an *amusing* child."

"Isn't she? I might have to resort to blackmail to influence her behavior."

"Blackmail?" Sarah said, interest kindling in her eyes.

Lady Clipstone's face turned pallid. Charlotte felt tempted to ask at the counter for a restorative before the other woman fainted. But Sir Godfrey had taken note of the two ladies; he summoned the clerk to clear the other customers to another display so that he could personally attend Charlotte's silent call for assistance.

"Your Grace," he said with a bow, "how may I be of service?"

"I would like to look at your diaries," Sarah piped in, granting him a gracious smile.

"Indeed, my lady." He looked up at Charlotte and, almost as an afterthought, at Alice. "What a privilege, I must say, that my humble wares will become part of another legacy."

Lady Clipstone had recovered her color and, it appeared, also her resentment. "You will excuse me," she said in a disgruntled voice. "I have other matters to attend to."

Charlotte drew Sarah back to open a path. "Oh, before I forget—have you heard that Emma is here in London? Perhaps you can meet her for tea and revisit your friendship."

*Chapter 40*

$\mathscr{H}$arriet had gone to St. Giles to visit Nick's mother, who, as she expected, looked ill but not ready to give up the ghost. She informed Harriet that Millie was pregnant, and Harriet had paid her a visit, too, encouraging her to stay off the streets now that she soon would have the responsibility of a child. And after she left, she found herself pondering whether to allow her husband to leave off the French letters so that they could start a family.

Which might never happen if she didn't escape this traffic to prepare for his homecoming at the end of the week. The carriage had broken away from the fetid stews where Harriet had once lived when it came to a complete halt. She tapped her toe and waited. After spending the day in dank surroundings, she wanted to go home, have a wash, and change her gown.

She toyed with a strand of her unruly red hair. She closed her eyes and began to count to a thousand. At three hundred and thirteen she opened the window and leaned outside to ask the coachman or one of the footmen to investigate the cause of the obstruction.

But the coachman didn't respond. He had apparently dozed off, his chin against his chest, his arms folded across his stomach like a shelf. For all practical purposes he was dead to the world.

Harriet sighed in exasperation, staring at the sheep passing by without a shepherd in sight.

And what had happened to the footmen?

Ah, there they were—standing like a pair of bookends against a silversmith's shop front. Several pedestrians and street vendors had squeezed between them for a look-see at the commotion that appeared to have broken out at the corner.

Perhaps there had been an accident. Perhaps a gig had collided with a coal wagon. Or a hackney coachman refused to budge until his passenger had paid his fare.

Harriet would have called the footmen back to their posts, but she doubted she could make herself heard over the laughing, the bleating, the shouting—

The shouting.

She stretched up from her seat to the window again and craned her neck to see above the crowd.

That shouting had a familiar ring.

It sounded like . . . No, that was impossible.

It couldn't be.

It sounded as if it were *her* voice, before two years of Emma Boscastle's intensive elocution lessons. It sounded as if the former unladylike Harriet were making that ungodly racket on the corner and practically inciting a small riot in the street.

She opened the door and descended into the chaos without benefit of folding steps or footmen.

"Hey, madam. Watch the toes, would you kindly?"

"Do you mind not shoving, missus?"

"Take yer turn, lady. Stand in line like the rest of us common folk."

"Common folk," she muttered under her breath, giving him a good poke in the ribs. "Move your carcass, would you?"

The man swung around and stared at her, too stunned to protest. Harriet took advantage of his surprise and weaved through the bystanders. In the past Harriet had bemoaned her disgraceful upbringing. But over time, she had come to realize that being a duchess with gutter instincts was more a help than a hindrance.

"What's the ruckus at the corner?" she asked a flower vendor wearing a fringed red shawl.

The seller looked her over. "I know you."

"No. You don't."

"Yeah. Right. You gotta few pence?"

Harriet reached up and pulled several pearl-headed pins from her hair, which promptly flew about in all directions. Harriet's willful curls had always been a sore point. Even Charlotte, who rarely spoke an unkind word, had made a comparison between the snakes of Medusa's head and Harriet's hair.

She dropped the pins into the basket of flowers. "What's the to-do?"

"There's a girl on the corner makin' a fortune offa some guidebook she got printed on Grub Street."

A girl.

A guidebook.

Harriet wished she could ignore the tingle of recognition that stole down her nape. "A guidebook for what? Riches? Eternal life? What has intrigued so many people?"

The vendor dropped her basket and bent, interlacing her fingers to give Harriet a boost. "Might as well see. Good thing you're light. I think she's sellin'—"

Harriet gasped, swaying in the unsteady cradle of the flower vendor's hands.

"What is it?" the vendor asked, nearly pitching Harriet headfirst into the crowd.

"Oh, my God." Harriet glanced down distractedly at the unreliable footbridge. "I'm going to throttle her. Do you mind holding me a little more securely?"

"Tell me what's she about," the vendor said.

Harriet succeeded in snagging one of the broadsheets from another bystander's hand before she lost her balance. The flower vendor peered over Harriet's shoulder.

"What's it say?"

Harriet pushed back the unruly red hair that matched her unruly temperament. "'The Scarfield Academy's Guidebook for Young Girls Whose Ambition Is to Marry a Duke.'"

"A duke?" the flower vendor said, staring harder at the sheet in Harriet's hand. "Really? She don't look like she could write 'er own name."

"'Results guaranteed,'" Harriet said wryly, and strained her eyes to read the cheap print. "How edifying."

"Well, what's it say?"

"I can't read the whole thing."

"Just the good parts. The 'elpful ones. The parts that'll make a duke marry *me*."

Harriet scowled at her and began to read aloud. "'How did it happen? How did a reserved young schoolmistress wangle a proposal from the dedicated bachelor the Duke of Wynfield?'"

"How?"

"'Was it by design or by destiny?'" Harriet snorted, skimming the outrageous piece. "'How did not one, not two, but *three* schoolmistresses from the Scarfield Academy manage to each marry a devilishly handsome duke? And how can you, dear reader, make your dreams for a similar fate come true? Here are a few snippets to set you on the road to matrimony:

1) Be born into the aristocracy. However, landing a duke is not an impossible achievement for even a street urchin if she is sponsored by a noble family and properly trained.

2) Confess your love for the duke of your dreams in a diary that falls into his hands so that he is made aware of your desire. Risk your reputation to win his love.

3) Be caught in a compromising position in the right place (the duke's arms) at the wrong time. It is crucial to your plan to make sure that this indiscretion is witnessed by friends, family, and foes, so that the only remedy for your ruination is a wedding.

"'For verification of these claims, please contact the staff at the Scarfield Academy.'" Harriet took a breath. "Oh, Verity Cresswell, I'll verify you when I get you alone, you little traitor." Still, part of her felt a reluctant admiration for the girl's penny-press enterprise. It was something Harriet might have attempted herself in the old days. In fact, she decided she would keep Verity's endeavor from Charlotte and Miss Peppertree, or the pair of them would go off like grenades.

"Is there any truth to it?" the flower vendor inquired, her voice hesitant with a wistfulness that Harriet knew would not survive many more years before skepticism set in. Yes. There *was* truth to it. Verity had obviously listened to the other girls gossiping and had turned their talk into a profitable venture. Well, it was better than picking pockets. Indeed, one could even claim that the Scarfield Academy had wielded a positive influence in comparison to the sins of Verity's past.

Besides, who was she to douse the feeble light of hope in anyone's heart? Harriet had married her own duke. She folded the broadsheet into a compact rectangle and tucked it into the flower basket between the fresh buds and the wilted blooms. "I think there might be."

The flower seller gasped in recognition. "I do know who you are."

Harriet wavered. Why was it that every time she tried to put her past behind her, it jumped into her path like Goliath? "Yes," she said, nodding her head. "You do know me. I'm Harriet Gardner from St. Giles."

"What'd you say?" The vendor stumbled back into a cart of secondhand clothes. "And I thought you was the Duchess of Glenmorgan. What right do you 'ave dressing up in that fancy dress and accosting innocent folk like me who're only tryin' to do an honest day's work? I shoulda known a true duchess wouldn't walk up and strike up a conversation with a workingwoman."

"But—"

The flower vendor scuttled behind the old-clothes cart. The barrel-chested owner, who'd been ignoring Harriet so far, lifted his fist to her in menace. "You ought to be ashamed of yourself," he said with the protective indignation that only a street dweller could rally for another when he was in the mood. "Go peddle your wares elsewhere, madam," he added, as Harriet turned away, stifling a horrible urge to laugh, if not lament the insult that she had apparently dealt her identity.

*Chapter 41*

"Oh, Daphne." Charlotte embraced Miss Peppertree's slight figure, whispering the words that she'd never expected to say in her life. "I shall miss you."

"Don't cry," Daphne reminded her, sniffing as she disengaged herself. "It isn't dignified for a duchess to show emotion."

"I'm not quite a duchess in my heart yet."

"But I am a gentlewoman upon whose slight shoulders will fall the duty of upholding the standards set when this academy was started."

"I wish I could have convinced you to take my position. We might have disagreed here and there, but I have the highest regard for your character."

Miss Peppertree shook her head. She didn't appear to be persuaded by Charlotte's attempt at flattery. "Rest assured I'll do everything in my power to maintain the school—everything, that is, except to take the reins."

"But, Daphne, think of the esteem."

"Think of the exasperation. Think of the endless months of teaching a girl to value her virtue, only to have it flung out the kitchen window like old tea leaves the minute a handsome duke presents himself at the door."

"Really. No one in this house has flung her virtue or tea leaves out the window."

"No? Review the academy's history. Remember what happened to our foundress, a lady I would have sworn would walk through the flames of the tempter and emerge untouched."

"But you do recall the unexpected effect of their affair, don't you?"

"Yes. I had dyspepsia and hives for a month."

"I meant the effect on the academy."

"Oh."

"Enrollment soared afterward. And the same thing happened when the Duke of Glenmorgan brought his niece here to study, and he met Harriet. She left to become his aunt's companion."

"I remember," Miss Peppertree said sourly. "More tea leaves tossed out along with virtue."

"But you helped me to entice my duke!"

"I helped you to *encourage* him. What choice did I have?"

"Emma has often confessed how perfect you are for the position."

"You have a formidable young lady anxious to step into your shoes. Besides, the position seems to carry a curse, and calamities come in threes. Our candidate had best be warned that she could be the opening chapter in another trilogy."

"Listen to you. I thought *I* was the one prone to waxing fanciful. What if there isn't a . . . curse? What if it's really a blessing in disguise?"

"I've no desire to marry a duke."

"You were the one who said I mustn't hide my light under a bushel. What about yours?"

Miss Peppertree shrugged. "Perhaps I'm waiting for the right man to light my wick."

Charlotte laughed in surrender. "Then all the best to you. I love him, Daphne."

"Yes." Daphne removed her spectacles to dab a knuckle at the edge of her eyes. "That has been obvious from the start. Better yet, he loves you."

"Do you think so?"

"I have from the night you went into hysterics over that face in the window. He couldn't hide his feelings for you then, and now that you're his wife, he doesn't have any reason to try."

*Epilogue*

$\mathscr{T}$he newlywed couple and their daughter traveled at a comfortable pace by carriage to Gideon's country villa in northwest Kent. A lone horseman might take the winding roads at a greater speed, especially if he had no desire to resurrect memories of earlier times. But in traveling with his family, he heard Charlotte's exclamations of delight as they passed orchards and lanes, smothered in blackberry brambles, that led to villages tucked into green hillside hollows.

The hum and thrum of London receded. A peace he hadn't known in years stole over him, and he was amused to hear himself echo the warning his father had once given him.

"Remember that you shouldn't pick any blackberries after Michaelmas Eve, Sarah. The Devil spits on them after that date to show his displeasure at being evicted from heaven."

Sarah frowned. "I'd spit in his face if I ever see him."

"You will do no such thing," Charlotte said, smiling at her with fondness. "Gideon, I'll thank you not to encourage misbehavior. Nor to engage in it if at all possible."

It wasn't possible, of course.

On their first night back in the country, Gideon decided he would do what he had always done—ride to the village public house and drink with a few old friends. Charlotte and Sarah had gone riding through the woods, and since it was twilight, the groom was old, and she didn't know the paths, he decided to shadow them on a higher bridle trail behind the trees.

He could visit the pub tomorrow.

But then tomorrow came, and as he was about to leave the house, he heard laughter drifting from the drawing room. So he went to the drawing room and caught Charlotte dancing with a young fop in a towering head of false hair. Sarah was curled up watching from the window seat.

"Why is Charlotte taking lessons from a dancing master?" he asked Sarah, squeezing down beside her.

"They're showing me how it's done. Did you know, our father, that 'mind your Ps and Qs' comes from the French?"

"Fancy that," he said, thinking that the fop had put his hands on Charlotte one time too many.

"Yes," Sarah went on. "Ps means *pieds,* which is French for feet, and Qs come from the word for wig, *perruque.*' In the old days, you weren't supposed to dip your head too low when you danced or your wig would fall off."

He raised his voice. "What can anyone teach my wife that she doesn't know?"

"Not much, Your Grace," the dancing master answered. "Perhaps you can bring Lady Sarah here, and Your Grace can partner her to demonstrate good form."

Gideon frowned. He wasn't keen on dancing. "Do you want to dance with me, Sarah?"

"No. I'd like to dance with Mr. Pugh, but he likes dancing with my mother."

"Yes. I see that. Get up. Give me your hand. What are we dancing?"

"A Gypsy reel," the dancing master said, lifting his chin.

"Isn't that a little risqué for ladies?"

"Not if it is danced with decent company," was the lofty reply. "Your Grace, please dance with the duchess. I will take Lady Sarah."

Gideon was in a better mood after that. He always was content when he was holding Charlotte, even though he did not give a damn about counting hops and skips. He did, however, give a damn that the dancing master kept stealing glances at her. In fact, Gideon wasted the rest of the afternoon refreshing his ballroom skills, and he didn't know where the time flew, because it was almost dark when he remembered that he was *not* spending another day at home like a country squire.

But he *was* attending a hiring fair tomorrow with a neighbor, and when he woke up, he noticed that Charlotte must have risen earlier, because her tea tray was on the table, and Sarah wasn't in her room either when he checked.

"They've gone fishing, Your Grace," the governess informed him with a disapproving face.

"Alone?"

"No. They've taken the gamekeeper with them."

"People have drowned in the lake, you know," he said

irritably. Of course, that had been a century ago, during a vile winter storm, but that wasn't the point. Sarah's boat had capsized the last time she was here, and he'd had to swim out to save her. He rode to the water's edge and, with a pair of field glasses, spotted the boat anchored in the middle of the sunlit lake.

"Oh, look," Sarah said, tugging Charlotte's arm. "There's my father."

"I thought he was going to the hiring fair." Charlotte peered into the water, her fishing pole still. "I don't think there are any fish in this lake."

"I don't, either."

"Then why are we here?" Charlotte asked. "Fishing is not the most feminine pastime. Why don't we give a tea party for your friends?"

"I don't have enough friends for a tea party."

Charlotte looked at her sadly. "Well, your father and I are here now to keep you from being lonely."

"Oh! Oh! Look! I've hooked a fish!"

The gamekeeper reached for the bucket. Charlotte leaned over to watch the catch.

"Help me!" Sarah shouted, fighting the pull of her pole. "It's a lake monster! He's pulling me out of the rowboat!"

Charlotte gasped and rose gingerly to grab the girl. But as she stretched out her arm, she pitched forward and toppled right over the side of the rowboat into the lake.

She gasped in shock from the cold.

And as she foundered she felt the hook on Sarah's line snag her sleeve. There wasn't a fish on it at all.

"Help! Help!" Sarah screamed to the shore. "Duchess overboard! Help, Papa!"

The gamekeeper pulled off his boots to dive into the lake. "Stay with Lady Sarah!" Charlotte cried, releasing the hook and paddling to the other side of the boat.

"Don't panic, Charlotte!" Gideon roared from the shore, stripping down to his trousers. "Let the water carry you! Whatever you do, do not fight me when I take hold of you."

Gideon flung off his coat and shirt to take a running leap into the lake, and hit the water bare chested. It was cold enough to turn his private parts blue. Where was Charlotte? Had she gone under?

"Grimes—hand the oar to my wife and tell her to hang on!"

Grimes picked up the oar and threw it in the water at Charlotte. She gasped, ducking her head, and watched the oar drift away.

"That's helpful," Gideon muttered, his powerful strokes propelling him toward Charlotte. "I wanted you to give it to her while *you* were holding the other end. The idea was to keep her afloat, not to knock her block off. I'm coming, Charlotte!"

Sarah hung over the side of the boat, tears welling in her eyes. "I'm so sorry, Mother. I thought you said last night that you knew how to swim."

"I do," Charlotte replied, dunking her head so that her long golden hair rippled out behind her like a skein of wet silk. "But I'm wearing boots and a boned corset that are making it difficult to move."

"Please don't drown," the gamekeeper said, rocking

the boat as he clamped one arm around Sarah's midriff and cast the other out to Charlotte.

"I've got her!" Gideon gurgled, bobbing up and down in the lake like a serpent.

Clever woman that she was, Charlotte appeared to be treading water and waiting for him. Actually, she looked as if she could swim to shore herself, but he wanted to rescue her, and perhaps he wanted to show off a little in front of his daughter, who had never had reason to view him in a flattering light before.

Sarah's father had wrapped his coat around Charlotte's shoulders and was carrying her to his horse. Sarah folded her arms and watched them with a frown as the prow of the rowboat bumped through the cattails that lined the shore.

"Come, Lady Sarah," the grizzle-bearded game-keeper said, giving her his hand. "I'll not be responsible for another accident. You'd best run along with His Grace and tell Mrs. Stearns you're home."

"I am *not* running alongside them when they're acting like that."

"What?" he said, pulling the boat up to the small dock. "Acting like what? The duchess is fond of you; I can tell. Why are you pouting? This is the family you have wanted."

She gave him her hand. "I know. I know. But they do not have time to play with me."

He blinked, glancing up to watch the duke hoist his wife onto his saddled gray. "Well, then, let them be. You'll have a little brother or sister to play with soon enough."

*     *     *

Charlotte leaned against Gideon's shoulder, determined to finish buttoning his shirt before they reached the drive. At length he caught her hand in his. "Stop touching me like that, my love, or I'll be forced to take a detour through the woods."

"I'm soaking wet and cold." She huddled against his back. "And so are you. Thank you for your valiant rescue." She didn't point out that she had been in no danger whatsoever. "I thought you were gone for the day."

He angled his head to look back at her. "So did I. It's a good thing I came back when I did."

The dark emotion in his eyes generated a heat inside her that made her forget the breeze blowing against her dress. "I thought . . . Well, I didn't think I'd see this much of you once we arrived here."

"Neither did I. But then, that is love."

He turned to guide the gray onto another path. Charlotte let the horse's gait jostle her against Gideon's back. "Did you say love?" she asked, sliding her free hand around his waist.

He closed his hand over hers. "Yes. I said it. I'll say it again. I'll say it every day. I love you. I suspect I love you more than you love me. I know I need you more. Now please do not keep giving me cause to worry. I can't spend the rest of my life dancing with men in wigs and jumping into lakes to prove how I feel."

She smiled, her chin pressed to his shoulder.

Hours later, after supper, they were sitting in the great hall in front of a fire, Sarah playing with the two lithe greyhounds she had introduced to Charlotte as Romulus and Remus.

"Did your governess give them their Roman names?" Charlotte asked, kneeling on the floor between her daughter and the rambunctious dogs.

"No. I did." Sarah clambered onto Gideon's chair and settled in his lap. "How long will you be staying here?"

"Forever. Do you mind?"

"You always left me before for a long, long time."

He closed his eyes for a moment. "Oh, Sarah."

"I used to cry but Mrs. Stearns said I shouldn't."

Gideon put his head to hers and brushed his hand over her hair. "I'll send her away for reprimanding you like that."

"Please don't," Sarah whispered, reaching into his vest pocket. "She loves me and I love her."

The governess appeared in the passageway behind them as if she had been summoned. "Come, Lady Sarah. It's time for you to go to bed." One of the puppies growled at her. Mrs. Stearns ignored it.

She started to make a fuss until Charlotte rose from the floor. "Give me and your father a kiss. And do what you are told."

Gideon shooed his daughter along and told her, "Sarah, we have many days to share ahead of us. I'll never leave you for a long time again."

Then Charlotte and Gideon were alone. He stood up slowly. "Come, madam. It's time for you to go to bed."

"Give me a kiss first. And— "

He drew her against him and kissed her in an unhurried taunt that swept her into oblivion.

"Am I still the man of your dreams?" he asked as she arched her neck and felt his hand steal slowly down her shoulder to sift through her hair.

"The dreams that I have when I'm awake or asleep?"

"Both," he said, his eyes searching hers. "Because if you ever banish me from your dreams, I will cease to exist. I adore you, Charlotte. You are more to me than anything I dreamed or deserved."

Charlotte let him lead her to the stairs. It didn't matter how she had won him. The scandalmongers would believe what they would. But just in case Gideon and Charlotte's children were curious, she would keep her diaries to explain how she and their father had fallen in love, and to prove that even the wickedest dreams had a way of coming true.

Read on for a peek at the first captivating
romance in Jillian Hunter's
Bridal Pleasures Series,

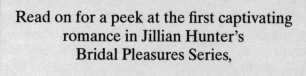

Available now from Signet Select.

*D* on't let any rakes steal you while I'm gone.
      Who would want to steal her?

She wasn't the sort to excite that much passion, even in a rake.

Lily blinked. What had come over her? She would not drink another glass of champagne. At least not until after she ate. And she would not sneak another glance at the man whose stare had practically singed her skin.

She lifted her gaze. Her last look, she promised herself. It wouldn't hurt. No one else would ever know. One. Final. Look.

Relieved and a little disappointed, she realized that he was no longer looking at her. She assured herself it was for the best. Heartbreak might as well have been emblazoned on his forehead. She wasn't surprised that females made up the innermost group of guests that he'd attracted.

Still, how he managed to appear lost and affected

with lethal boredom was a skill that Lily could only admire from a guarded distance. His negligent elegance announced to the room that he accepted his influence and felt no guilt in wielding this gift as he desired.

Lily might not have recognized such inborn arrogance if she had not possessed some weaponry of her own. Nothing of his magnitude. But she adored the thrill of secret flirtations. And—

She wasn't merely looking at him now. She was studying him like a masterpiece in a museum. How on earth did he manage it? He gave the impression of a masked god who had dropped in on the party only to let the world of mortals worship in his shadow.

Was that air of dark indolence part of his disguise? Perhaps he was an actor and that was why he had an audience that basked in his presence. She liked that notion. The longer she appraised him, the more she wondered whether he was holding court as part of a well-rehearsed performance.

Demon, actor, or social darling, she found him captivating, too, judging by her furtive analysis of his person. And then it dawned on her that the weapon at his side was a rusty lance, and he wasn't an ordinary knight-errant. He was Don Quixote de la Mancha, mad and self-appointed protector of the helpless. •

"Lily!"

She turned reluctantly toward the sound of Chloe's voice, her musings interrupted. Then it happened again. Unexpected, breath-catching. Like watching a star tumble from the midnight sky.

He lifted his head and stared at her, as if he'd been waiting to catch her off guard again. What impeccable timing. His lean form straightened. His hard-lipped mouth curled at one corner.

A farewell to their brief flirtation or an invitation to something far more dangerous? Lily couldn't decide.

She started to look away. She knew better than to encourage this sort of nonsense. A man who stared at a lady like that and didn't mind who noticed only offered trouble. But all of a sudden her own instinct for mischief took over. Lily could flirt, too, and the fact that she was wearing a costume gave her a false sense of anonymity.

Just for tonight she wasn't the unsophisticated Miss Lily Boscastle of Tissington, who in a month would become a bride and settle down to a respectable life as Captain Grace's wife.

She would never see this knight-errant again. The unabashed attention he paid her begged for an answer. But what kind? An alluring smile to admit that she was intrigued? A firm shake of her head that meant a definite no? Or perhaps a little shrug to indicate that while he flattered her, she wasn't willing to reciprocate with anything riskier?

Would that be too wicked of her? It wasn't as if he could leap into the air and snatch her up in full view of innumerable witnesses.

She smiled back at him, a playful coquette's smile, over the shoulder, straight in the direction of his handsome face.

*There.*

*Take that.*

And he did, inclining his head in open approval, the devil acknowledging his due. What had she done? She took a breath, transfixed, as he raised his helmet in a tribute that tempted and immobilized her in the same delirious moment.

Several members of his group turned their heads to identify her. He hadn't been subtle at all. She barely felt the person behind her give her another shove. This time she was too distracted to take offense.

In fact, she was so unbalanced that she allowed herself to be propelled directly into an opening in the line, into temptation's path, and heaven only knew how far the shameless man would have carried this scandalous exchange had a firm hand not caught hers and an urgent voice not whispered in her ear, "*Lily.*"

She tumbled back to earth, recognizing the raven-haired enchantress who was rightfully attempting to restore her common sense. "What has come over you?" Chloe demanded under her breath. "What are you doing?"

"I'm not doing anything." Not that she would readily admit.

"I am going to give you a belated warning," Chloe went on in such a breathless voice that Lily was forced to listen. "I assumed that because you flirted so well, you fully understood what a dangerous game it can be."

Lily bit her lip. From the corner of her eye she observed an older, distinguished-looking gentleman entering the room to a chorus of warm cheers. "I've no idea what you're talking about," she lied. "But perhaps you ought to lecture me later. Isn't that our host, Lord Philbert, just making an appearance?"

Chloe was clearly not to be deterred. She pointedly stared at the gorgeous creature standing up against the wall. Lily wasn't positive, but she thought Lord Philbert had broken through the ranks that surrounded the charismatic one, which indicated that while the other man might be a rake, he was, as she suspected, an important one.

At least Lily hadn't smiled at a nobody. There was some consolation in that.

Chloe released her grip on Lily's hand. "Do you have the vaguest idea who that gentleman is?"

"Which gentleman? The room is full of them."

"I saw you smile at only one."

Lily realized it was self-defeating to deceive a lady as observant as her cousin. "I couldn't help it, Chloe. I mean, I couldn't help noticing him. It was wrong."

"Everyone notices him," Chloe continued in a forgiving voice. "There is nothing to be done for that. But the problem is that *he* is making a point to notice you. And that is why it is crucial that I warn you. He is the Duke of Gravenhurst."

Lily knew this announcement should have given her a scare.

"Does the title signify some inherent evil?" she asked cautiously.

Chloe straightened the gold circlet that pressed her fringe of black curls to her forehead. "I don't know all that much about him myself. He is said to have inherited it after some family tragedy when he was a boy. As the story goes, he went a little wild as he reached his maturity. His supporters attribute his rebellious nature to the responsibilities he took on at a young age."

"Supporters?" Lily said, lifting her brow.

"In the House of Lords. He gives persuasive speeches for causes that other people pretend don't exist." Chloe studied her in concern. "He's *very* persuasive, from what I've gathered."

"That isn't a crime, is it?"

"It depends on whom you ask. The opposite party thinks so. As do several parents whose daughters have formed a society to follow him around the capital with telescopes when he visits. His foes consider him a traitor to the peerage."

"Well, I don't plan on joining any admiration societies in the near future, and it's doubtful Jonathan will ever land in the House of Lords. Especially since he cannot even be bothered to finish a book, and his brother is going to inherit the family title."

Chloe calmed down a bit. "At least your captain is a decent person."

"And the duke is not?" Lily asked before she could censor the question.

"A man that handsome, who has only to smile to mesmerize, cannot be unaware of his charm."

"Is it his fault that he is beautiful?"

"He is rumored to run through women like . . . racehorses."

Lily reared back at this appalling image. "That is disgusting. And not beautiful in the least."

Chloe drew a breath, clearly mollified by Lily's reaction. "*If* it is true," she added in an apparent bid to be fair. "I can't honestly say that I've had personal experience with the man. But I seem to recall a bit of gossip— Oh, dear."

" 'Oh dear,' what?"

"I think I read that he wakes up at midnight with one woman and blazes through the streets until dawn in his cabriolet with another. And that he has appeared at three routs in a single hour."

"No wonder he's lean."

"Lily, *listen*. When other gentlemen come home to change into their evening clothes, he is removing his. Do you realize what that means?"

*It could mean anything,* Lily thought. He could be nocturnal by nature. He could be allergic to daylight or city fog. It could mean he preferred the intimacy of the night. Perhaps he was simply one of those men who came alive when the sun went down. Lily knew only that his presence irradiated the room, and that it could be morning or midnight right now and she would not have noticed the difference.

But a man who dressed as Don Quixote at a masquerade *must* harbor a keen sense of humor. A disguise like that mocked beauty rather than enhanced it. Unless, like Lily, he was only wearing the costume that a sharper wit had suggested.

She was afraid that her runaway imagination had gotten the better of her again. It was entirely possible that the duke was no more a misguided knight than Jonathan was a tragic king.

*New York Times* bestselling author

# Jillian Hunter

# A DUKE'S TEMPATION
## *The Bridal Pleasures Series*

The Duke of Gravenhurst, a notorious author
of dark romances, is accused of corrupting the
morals of the public. But among his most
devoted fans is the well-born Lily Boscastle,
who seeks employment as the duke's personal
housekeeper. Only then does she discover
scandalous secrets about the man that she
never could have imagined.

**Available wherever books are sold or at**
**penguin.com**

*New York Times* bestselling author

# Jillian Hunter

# A BRIDE UNVEILED

*The Bridal Pleasures Series*

Violet Knowlton is betrothed to the sensible, if tedious, Sir Godfrey Maitland. When Godfrey escorts her to a fencing demonstration, she looks forward to the adventurous diversion, but everything changes when she realizes the swordsman displaying his skill— and dashing good looks—is none other than her childhood friend Kit.

Soon the flames of their forbidden past ignite into a passion neither can refuse. Although Violet has been promised to another, Kit remains her first and only love. He vows he will possess her, no matter what stands in his way...

**Available wherever books are sold or at penguin.com**